LOVE, GREED and LIE$

A Small Town Mystery

LOVE, GREED *and* LIE$

A Small Town Mystery

D.W. HARPER

HayMarBooks, LLC

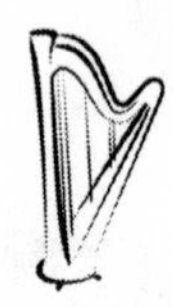

HayMarBooks, LLC

Disclosure:
This novel is semi-autobiographical. While the family at its center is depicted from real life, some of the characters in the story are from the author's imagination. In turn, some of the events are imagined in order to explore certain themes. To maintain creative independence, it was necessary to write this story as a work of fiction; nevertheless, the emotional truth is consistent throughout.

978-0-9848736-1-6 Hardcover
978-0-9848736-0-9 Paperback

Library of Congress Control Number:
2012903390

Published through:
HayMarBooks, LLC
1719 Plantation Oaks Dr., Jacksonville, FL 32223

www.haymarbooks.com
dianeharperbooks@gmail.com
www.lovegreedandlies.com

Cover Design: 1106 Design, LLC
Printed by: Lightning Source

Printed in the United States of America

In Loving Memory of

William "Bill" Wilson

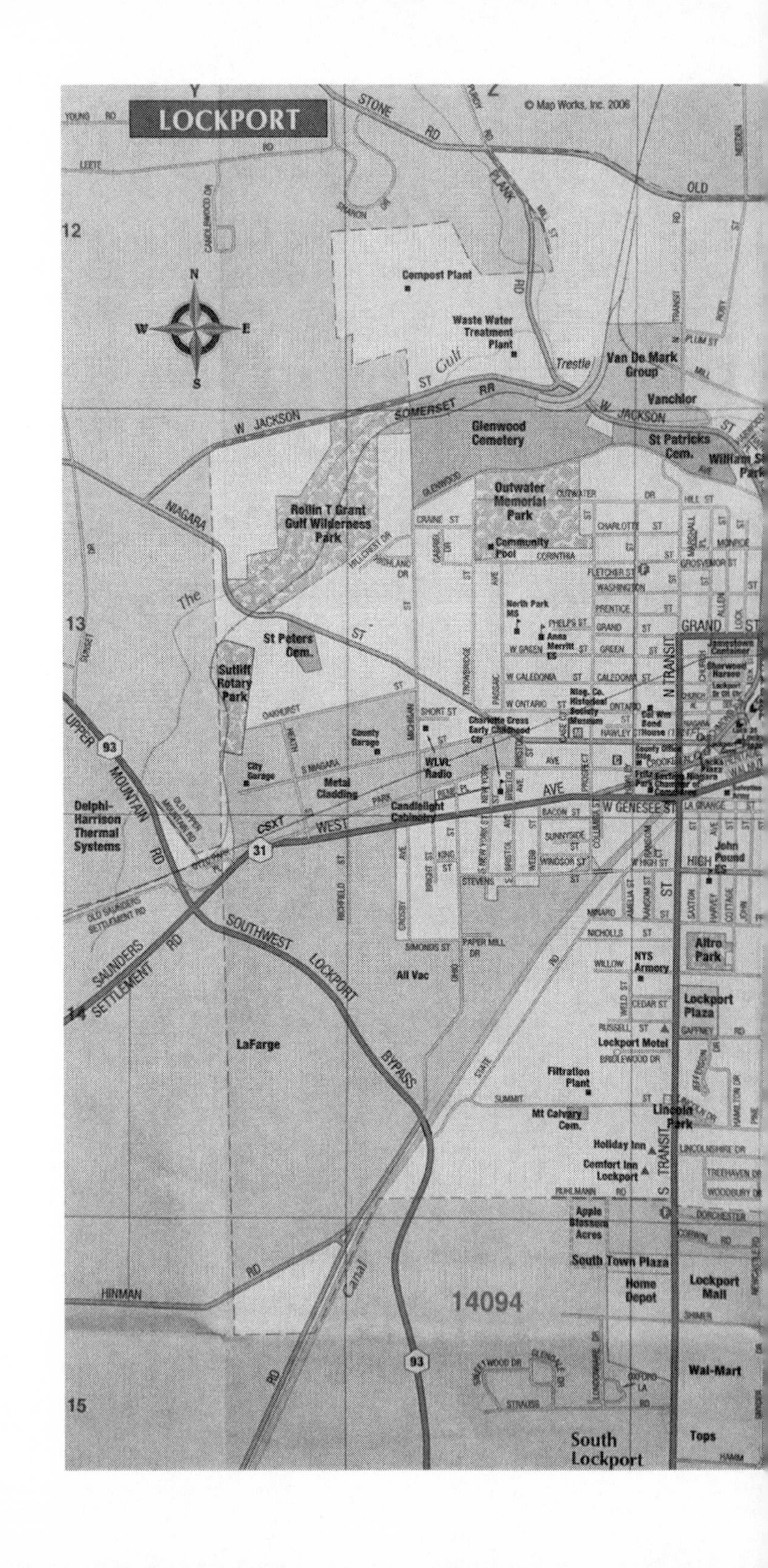

LOCKPORT
© Map Works, Inc. 2006
12
13
14
15
N
S
E
W
STONE RD
PLANK RD
OLD
Compost Plant
Waste Water Treatment Plant
Gulf
Trestle
Van De Mark Group
Vanchlor
W JACKSON
SOMERSET RR
Glenwood Cemetery
St Patricks Cem.
NIAGARA
Outwater Memorial Park
Rollin T Grant Gulf Wilderness Park
Community Pool
North Park MS
The
St Peters Cem.
Sutliff Rotary Park
GRAND
N TRANSIT
County Garage
City Garage
Metal Cladding
WLVL Radio
Candlelight Cabinetry
UPPER MOUNTAIN RD
Delphi-Harrison Thermal Systems
CSXT
WEST AVE
W GENESEE ST
John Pound ES
SAUNDERS SETTLEMENT RD
SOUTHWEST LOCKPORT BYPASS
All Vac
Altro Park
NYS Armory
Lockport Plaza
Lockport Motel
LaFarge
Filtration Plant
Mt Calvary Cem.
Lincoln Park
Holiday Inn
Comfort Inn Lockport
S TRANSIT
Apple Blossom Acres
South Town Plaza
Home Depot
Lockport Mall
HINMAN RD
Canal
14094
Wal-Mart
Tops
South Lockport

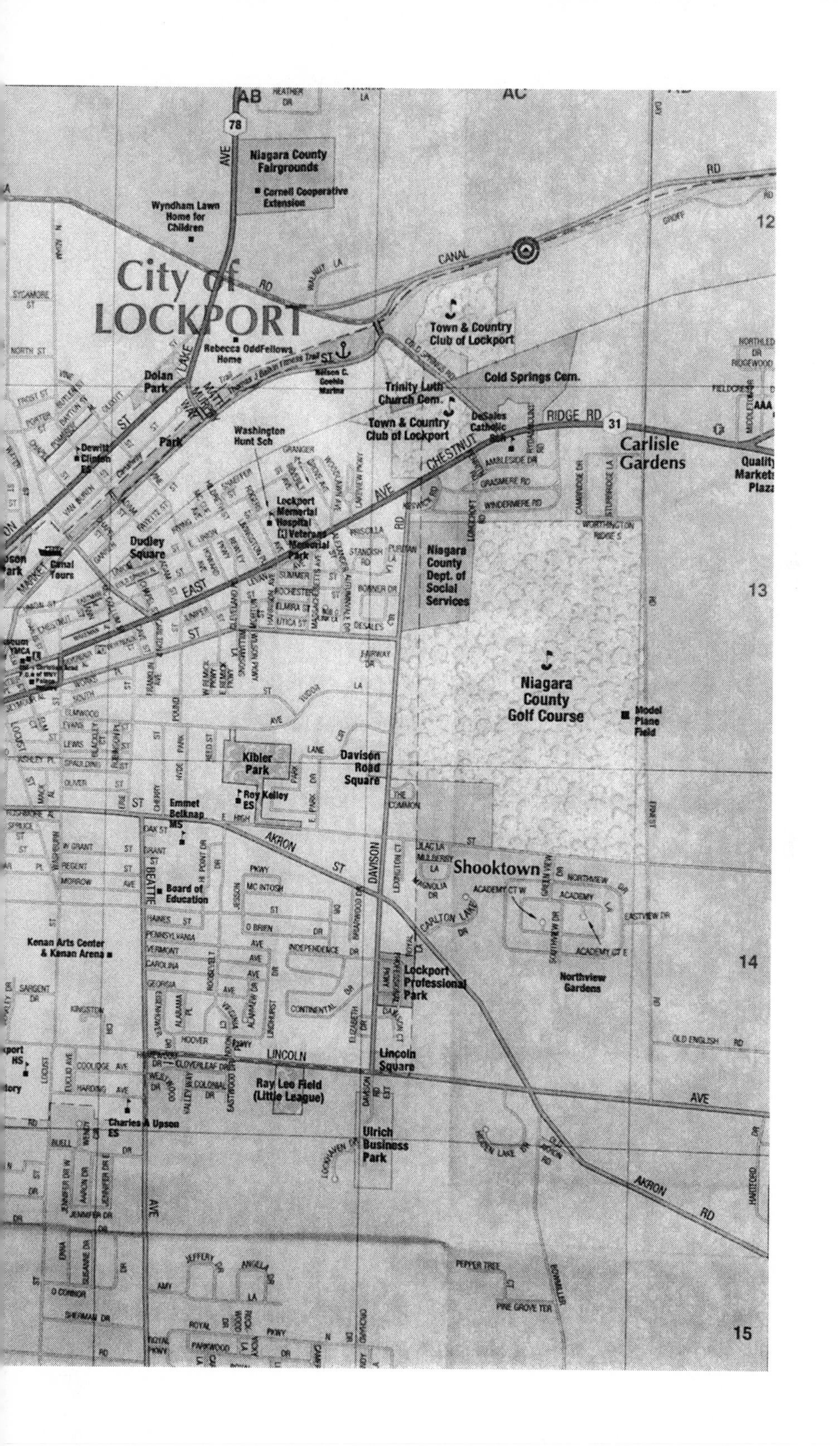
AB
AC
78
Niagara County Fairgrounds
Cornell Cooperative Extension
Wyndham Lawn Home for Children
City of LOCKPORT
Rebecca OddFellows Home
Dolan Park
Town & Country Club of Lockport
Cold Springs Cem.
Trinity Luth Church Cem.
DeSales Catholic Sch
Washington Hunt Sch
Dewitt Clinton ES
Lockport Memorial Hospital
Veterans Memorial Park
Dudley Square
Canal Tours
Carlisle Gardens
Quality Markets Plaza
12
13
14
15
Niagara County Dept. of Social Services
Niagara County Golf Course
Model Plane Field
Kibler Park
Davison Road Square
Roy Kelley ES
Emmet Belknap MS
Shooktown
Board of Education
Kenan Arts Center & Kenan Arena
Lockport Professional Park
Northview Gardens
Lincoln Square
Ray Lee Field (Little League)
Charles A Upson ES
Ulrich Business Park
CANAL RD
RIDGE RD
31
CHESTNUT
EAST AVE
AKRON ST
AKRON RD
DAVISON
LINCOLN AVE
BEATTIE AVE
OLD ENGLISH RD
PEPPER TREE
PINE GROVE TER

Acknowledgments

First and foremost I'd like to acknowledge my sisters Denise Blackley and Daphne Wilson. You truly understand where the motivation and inspiration for this journey originated.

I would like to express my profound gratitude to many people who were helpful to me. Jane R. Wood and Frances Keiser, your recommendations and expert advice helped get this book published. I couldn't have done it without you. I also owe a huge thanks to my fabulous content editor, Emily W. Carmain; you took on this project and gave my story life. Thanks to Maureen Kurowsky for your grammatical assistance and 1106 Design, LLC, for your professional book and cover design support.

I'd like to give a heartfelt thanks to Julie Cornell and Patricia Stritz for proofreading my book, to Dawn Forrest for helping me launch my independent publishing company, and special thanks to Kevin Blackley for his assistance in creating my computer programs—plus much more. To Carol and Bill White, I can't thank you enough for your enthusiasm and encouragement.

Most of all, I want to thank my husband Ron and my children Hayley and Mark; you've given me the space I needed to accomplish this endeavor.

I want to express my appreciation to all the people I didn't list; your invariable interest and support has made this venture obtainable. I'm fortunate to have amazing family and friends in my life, and each one of you have made me who I am today.

"Reflect upon your present blessings of which every man has many — not on your past misfortunes, of which all men have some."

—Charles Dickens

Lockport History

Erie Canal Locks and the "Upside Down" Railroad Bridge

In 1816 the New York State Legislature passed an act that projected the Erie Canal pass through the area now known as Lockport. There was a sixty-foot drop along the banks of the canal and a way had to be designed to raise and lower the packet boats to conclude their journey to Buffalo. Nathan Roberts's idea was a twin flight of locks. In 1821, work began on the locks' construction.

On October 26, 1825, the entire length of the Erie Canal from the Hudson River was opened. Governor DeWitt Clinton came through Lockport aboard the *Seneca Chief* and passed through the twin flight of locks successfully.

The "Upside Down" Railroad Bridge, as it is referred to, is a multi-span bridge built in 1902 by the King Bridge Company of Cleveland, Ohio, for the New York Central Railroad. The main span is a Baltimore deck truss located east of locks #34 and #35 in downtown Lockport. The notion was to build the bridge to limit the size of boats that could use the Erie Canal—tall masts were unable to fit under this bridge. The bridge is currently owned by the Genesee Valley Transportation Company and is used occasionally for freight and scenic excursion trains.

Garlock's Restaurant

In 1821 work on the Erie Canal began that resulted in many buildings being built in the city of Lockport. In 1864 a farmhouse on 35 South Transit Road was purchased by the "Lockport Brewing

Company." Three years later it became a hotel called the "Gerner Hotel" and remained that until 1929. LuLu Dickens bought the building several years later and changed the named to the "Transit Hotel." In 1950 the hotel was sold and became "The Chase Inn."

Garlock's Restaurant was started May 10th, 1946, on Gooding Street. In 1962 Harold "Gig" Garlock purchased the building on Transit Road and opened this location as "Garlock's Fireside Inn." "Gig" was famous for his open steak sandwich. He won the nationally recognized Duncan Hines Award, which was considered a very prestigious award in the 1940s and 1950s. He ran both restaurants until he sold the Gooding Street location in 1969.

The "Fireside Inn" was dropped in 1972 and the name was changed to "Garlock's Restaurant." In 1989 "Gig" Garlock sold the business and building to his long-time manager, Nancy Long and her family. Nancy retired and sold the business to her son Michael and his wife Karen Long. Harold "Gig" Garlock died November of 1994 at the age of 82.

Emmanuel United Methodist Church

Built in 1824, the First Methodist Episcopal Church building was a small frame building constructed on a lot at the edge of a forest located on Genesee Street, between Pine and Cottage Streets. In 1833 the lot and the building were exchanged for property on the northeast corner of Church and Niagara Streets where the congregation built a sufficient brick church. On November 4, 1854, a fire, which had started in a grog shop (a grog shop is a term used for an unlicensed hotel or liquor store), destroyed the church and many Lockport businesses. The congregation was determined to rebuild. On February 22, 1859, worshippers dedicated a new church building.

On December 30, 1928, the congregation bid farewell to their "old" church. The parishioners marched singing and rejoicing up Main Street to their new church, the Emmanuel Methodist Episcopal Church. In 1939, the word Episcopal was removed with the union of several Methodist churches. In 1968, with the union of the Methodist Church and Evangelical United Brethren, the name became Emmanuel United Methodist Church.

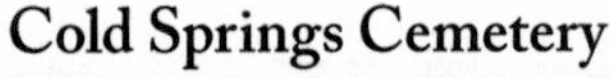

Cold Springs Cemetery

The original burying ground began in 1815 behind a tavern owned by Charles Wilbur. Cold Springs Cemetery is the oldest in the town of Lockport. It was developed with a Victorian rural design and legally established in 1840. The 45 acres is located on a rolling slope facing north beside the Niagara Escarpment; one characteristic is a cold spring that flows through the cemetery. Included in the cemetery are uninscribed headstones to family plots surrounded by cast-iron fences and three mausoleums. Some of the more famous burials in the cemetery include:

Jesse Hawley: (1788–1848), who encouraged the idea of building a canal across New York State as early as 1807.

Lyman Spalding: (1800–1885) one of Lockport's most affluent early entrepreneurs. Spalding purchased land near the Erie Canal when the NY State Legislature approved selling the surplus water rights along the Canal. He was in the process of building a flourmill powered by a tunnel from the canal.

Birdsall Holly: (1820–1894) was the founder of the Holly Manufacturing Company, an inventor who originated several pump designs. In 1863 he invented the fire hydrant. He manufactured pumps and sewing machines and provided a reliable water supply to homes and fire hydrants.

The cemetery was listed in the U.S. National Register of Historic Places in 2004.

Chapter One

Present Day

It was a cold spring day in western New York. Aimee walked up to the door of her mother's house to check on her.

Her sister, Alice, who lived with their mother, was away for a few days, and had asked Aimee to stop by while she was out of town. Alice, with her twin daughters, Kayla and Layla, had left the day before to spend a long weekend at her newly purchased cottage on the lake.

Aimee used her own key as she always did, but it didn't seem to fit; she checked the other keys on her keychain. *It has to be this one*, she thought to herself and tried the key again to no avail. Sighing, she knocked on the door and rang the doorbell several times.

"Mom, are you in there?" she yelled as she looked in the front door, but there was no answer. *She's got to be in there*, Aimee thought.

She walked around the house to the patio and peeked through her mother's sliding glass door. She gasped. Her mother lay on the carpeted floor in the middle of her room; her walker was tipped over beside her.

Aimee ran around to the front door, grabbed one of the planters on the steps and broke the small decorative window pane closest to the lock; she reached in hurriedly and unlocked the door. The minute she walked into the house, she smelt a terrible odor.

Inside her mother's room, there was vomit everywhere, and her mother smelled of urine. Aimee pressed two fingers to her mother's throat; she had a weak pulse and she was barely breathing. Aimee grabbed her cell phone and called 911.

"You have to hurry! My mother is unconscious and barely breathing. The address is 4238 Charles Parkway," she told the woman on the phone frantically.

"Rescue has been dispatched, ma'am; please stay on the phone with me until they arrive. What's your name?" the operator asked in a calming voice.

"My name is Aimee; I'm her daughter. Her name is Emma Jean Wilkinson. I came to check on her while my sister who lives with her is out of town," she said nervously.

"What's the number you're calling from in case we get disconnected?"

Aimee rattled off her cell phone number and, as she was doing so, she heard the sirens in the distance; they got closer with every number she gave the operator.

"How is she doing, Aimee?" the operator asked.

She checked her mom's pulse again.

"She still has a pulse. I'll keep checking it," she said. "I feel so helpless that there's nothing I can do for her."

"It's okay. Is she still unconscious?"

"Yes, I don't know how long she's been like this—she's been unconscious since I got here."

"You said you were her daughter, correct?"

"Yes."

"Okay, let me get some information about your mother." The woman asked her all sorts of questions—Aimee confirmed the full name, how old she was, what medicines she took …

"I don't know what she takes exactly. She takes quite a few—I would have to look," Aimee told her.

"Is she allergic to anything?"

"I don't think so, not that I know of."

By the time Aimee had finished answering questions, the paramedics had arrived, and now they were in the room working on her mother.

Aimee thanked the 911 operator and hung up. She called Alice right away, but her call went straight to voicemail. Then she tried Kayla (the more dominant of her sister's twins), but was also sent to voicemail. Aimee called her husband, Blake, and explained everything that was going on.

"I tried calling Alice and Kayla," she told him, "just before I called you. I can't get a hold of them. They are at her new lake house and they must not have cellular service up there. They are just getting Mom into the ambulance, and I'm going to follow them to the hospital." Aimee was crying.

"I'll be there in a few minutes, calm down and drive carefully. I'll call Lexi and let her know what's going on, and I'll also keep trying Alice," Blake said calmly. "Everything will be all right. I'll see you in a few minutes."

Just before Aimee left the house, she went to her mother's nightstand and gathered her medications. She opened the doors underneath to remove a manila bank envelope where her mother kept a lot of cash. Aimee knew it was there and didn't want to leave that much money unattended. When she pulled out the envelope, it was empty.

"What the hell?" she said aloud.

She looked all around in the nightstand thinking she might have grabbed the wrong envelope—nothing. Aimee walked to the other side of the bed and looked through the other nightstand, thinking her mother might have moved the envelope. The only things she saw were bank receipts and many empty bottles of extra-strength Tylenol. She got into her silver Volvo and headed to the hospital.

Blake had been playing golf at Willowbrook Golf Course. At the time his wife called, he was teeing off on the ninth hole, his favorite hole, a beautiful par four from an elevated tee box. Blake explained to his golf buddies there was a family emergency and he had to leave; he finished that hole and was at once on his way to the hospital.

As he collected his thoughts, he started making phone calls. The first person he called was Aimee's sister Alexandria—Lexi, to her family—in Jacksonville and told her the entire situation.

"We don't have any details as of yet. As soon as we know anything we'll call you. I'm on my way to the hospital right now. Aimee is following the ambulance and we can't get a hold of Alice. She's at her cottage on the lake with her girls."

"Please … let me know as soon as you hear anything," Lexi said. "I can jump on a flight and be there in a few hours."

"We will, I promise."

As soon as Lexi hung up the phone, she dug her suitcase out of the closet and started packing.

The paramedics quickly wheeled Emma Jean into the trauma unit of the emergency department, and Aimee watched as the hospital staff hooked her up to many machines. The doctors and nurses were doing all kinds of tests.

Blake arrived about fifteen minutes later. Quite a bit of time passed before the young doctor came out of the room to update them on Emma Jean's progress.

"First and foremost," he said, "we have to take care of your mother's severe dehydration. We are infusing her with fluids and vitamins intravenously."

"Dehydrated?" Aimee said out loud.

"Yes, we are waiting for more test results on that. However, at this time we think your mother may have tried to commit suicide. It appears she has a massive amount of acetaminophen in her system, which has made her liver fail."

"Acetaminophen? But that's just something for pain, isn't it?" Aimee asked.

"Yes, it's also called 'Ace' and is in medicines such as Benadryl, Sudafed or Tylenol."

The minute the doctor said Tylenol, Aimee turned white.

Blake and Aimee stared at the doctor, speechless. They couldn't believe after all these years her mother would try to end her life.

"We will continue testing," the doctor said. "We have her on life support to keep her liver functioning and we will keep you updated."

"Thank you," Blake said. He was the only one who could speak. The doctor turned and walked down the hall, leaving Aimee stunned as she watched him walk away.

"Hello, I'm Detective Randal," said a voice.

Both Aimee and Blake jumped as they turned and looked at the detective. They saw a stern-looking man with dark hair and dark brown eyes. He was wearing blue jeans, a white collared shirt and a grey sport jacket.

"I'm sorry to startle you. I wanted to let you know that we have an investigation going on at your mother's home. Does she live alone?"

"No," Aimee said, as she wiped tears from her eyes. "My sister, Alice, lives with her."

Detective Randal took a little black notepad from his pocket and started writing. "Where is she right now?"

"May I ask you why the police are involved?" Blake interrupted.

"A police officer was in the area when fire rescue got the call to go to your mother's home. As they worked on your mother, the officer observed the scene in the bedroom and he thought the situation needed investigating."

"My sister is at her lake house for the weekend with her daughters—they left yesterday," Aimee told him. "We've been trying to contact her, but there is limited cell service where they are on Lake Ontario."

"Do you know the address?"

The two of them looked at each other and shrugged.

"We don't. She just bought it—she never gave us the actual address," Aimee said. "All I know is it's near Wilson."

"Who found your mother?"

"I did," Aimee said.

"Your name is?"

"Aimee Matthews."

"Your address?"

Aimee furnished him all the information he needed, her address, cell phone number and the restaurant she and her husband owned. Randal documented the information in his notepad.

"Ms. Mathews, please tell me step by step what you did from the minute you arrived at your mother's house."

"My sister had called me Thursday and asked me if I would look in on our mother, as she was going out of town for the weekend. When I arrived this morning, I tried using the key my mother gave me when she bought the house and it didn't work. I broke a window so I could unlock the door to get in." Aimee told the detective everything that happened after that, as well as the call to the 911 operator who would corroborate most of her story.

"I hung up with the operator after the paramedics arrived. I immediately called my sister and then her daughter Kayla, but both calls went to voicemail. I called my husband, Blake." She reached a hand out to Blake's arm. "I told him everything that was happening."

"You're Blake Matthews?" the detective asked.

"Yes," he responded.

"Same address?"

"Yes." Randal jotted the information in his notepad. "What did you do then, ma'am?" He addressed Aimee again.

"Well, they were putting my mother in the ambulance. I grabbed my purse to follow them, but then I thought I should get my mom's medications so they would know what she takes."

As Aimee said this, she opened her purse and the two men looked at the prescription bottles she had. Randal put his black notepad in his pocket.

"Wait one minute." He took a few steps to the nurses' station and asked for a pair of latex gloves and put them on, then took out a large baggie from his pocket. He took the bottles out of Aimee's purse one by one. He shook them and took a moment to look at each one and put it in the baggie. Most of the bottles were half full.

"Is that all of them?"

Aimee looked through her purse. "Yes, that's all of them."

"Is there anything else you did?" The detective looked as though he was ready to wrap things up at the hospital.

"Well, yes," Aimee said as she looked at Blake. "I opened the bottom door of my mother's nightstand to get her bank envelope—she keeps a lot of money in it. I didn't want to leave it there with the window broken on the front door."

"I can understand that," Randal commented.

Aimee hesitated for a moment. "The envelope was empty."

"WHAT!" Blake exclaimed. "She usually has at least five or six thousand dollars in that envelope!"

"I know, but it was empty," Aimee said again. "My mother has kept money in that envelope for years," she told the detective.

"What did you do next?"

"I looked for the envelope in her other nightstand, thinking she might have moved it. I saw bank receipts and many empty bottles of Tylenol."

"Did you touch them?" he asked as he wrote in his notepad.

"No, I didn't think anything of it at the time."

"Is there anyone else who had access to your mother's house recently?"

"Her cleaning lady, Sarah—she cleans every Friday," Aimee said.

"So she was there yesterday? Do you know what time?"

"I think she cleans in the mornings." Aimee's voice shook as she suddenly felt exhausted from the shock she'd been through today.

"I'm sorry about your mother. I'll be in touch," Randal said as he turned to leave.

"What do we do now?" Aimee asked Blake. As she spoke, Randal turned around.

"The first thing I would do is try to find your sister."

Chapter Two

December 1911

Today was going to be a very special day for Rose; she was now sixteen and this was the first time she had been allowed to go to Lockport's annual Christmas dance. The holiday season was Rose's favorite time of year. She especially liked the calm winter nights when the snow lightly drifted down from the hazy sky, and tonight was one of those nights.

She was going to the dance with a few of her friends from class. The whole town was invited to the festivity and even her parents would be there. A certain boy in the next grade up was also going and she wanted to socialize and dance with him.

Rose wore a striking red floor-length dress with soft white lace trim on the cuffs and neckline. She had made it just for the occasion, and it had taken her several months to design and sew her spectacular dress. Sewing was her passion; she wished she could design and make specialty dresses for all the wealthy women of Lockport.

Her parents agreed that she had a talent. They had told her that if she made a dress for the party, she could purchase the dazzling red hat with white lace that she had found at a thrift store for fifteen cents, matching her dress perfectly.

Rose enjoyed the reaction of her friends when they saw how striking she looked. She was tall, standing nearly five feet, seven inches. She had large, hazel eyes and long, brown, curly hair that she wore pulled back. Glancing in the mirror before leaving home that night, she felt she looked so grown up!

As she and her two closest friends met outside the building where the party was to be held, they were so thrilled to be there that they each gave a shriek of excitement. It was going to be the best night of their lives. Rose had butterflies in her stomach from excitement. The three of them waited in line as they slowly moved toward the building, giggling with anticipation. Rose could not believe she was finally old enough to enjoy the experience that people in town would talk about for weeks afterward.

As Rose slowly crossed the threshold, it was as if she entered a different world, a sophisticated world she had never experienced before, and the butterflies in her stomach disappeared. She had an overwhelming sensation that her life was about to change forever.

She looked all around in amazement. The lights were dim, the music was playing, and she could not take her eyes off the enormous tree in the corner of the room decorated with hundreds of candles that flickered in the dim light. It was adorned with miniature toys, as well as fresh fruit and flowers tucked into its branches. Decorative buckets of water around the tree added to the ambience of the decor, as well as serving a functional need. It was the most exquisite tree that Rose had ever seen.

On the other side of the room, a large table draped with a red and white silk cloth displayed an abundance of food. In the middle of the table stood an enormous ice sculpture of an angel designed by a local artist.

As Rose continued to look around, listening to the festive music, she spotted a stranger standing near the decorated tree; the candlelight shining on his face gave him a spectacular glow. Rose flushed and the butterflies in her stomach returned.

Albert Sterling was handsome and well-dressed, wearing a heavy, dark gray suit, with a high-collared white shirt. Deciding to indulge earlier that day, he had gone to the Men's Store to purchase a red satin bow tie for the event.

Albert, who had turned thirty-six a short time ago, was a quiet man who had recently moved to Lockport. A widower, he did not socialize very much; he focused most of the time on his work as a horologist, a skilled watch-maker.

Several months after his wife's death, Albert had realized that he needed a change. He had to get away from all the memories, all her delicate smells in the apartment, the artistic way she decorated their place when they were first married. He decided to leave Rochester and make a fresh start in an "up and coming" new town located thirty miles west along the Erie Barge Canal. He packed only the things he needed, selling or giving away everything else, and began a new life in the small town of Lockport.

Albert had learned that this dance was an annual holiday celebration held on Christmas Eve. A neighbor had asked if he would meet him at the party and he had agreed. Arriving at the party early, Albert walked around and talked to a few people that he knew.

He had a bite to eat, hardly believing the amount of food there. It was a feast, with all kinds of fruits and vegetables, sliced turkey and ham, pork and veal, several varieties of homemade rolls and a dessert table offering pies, cakes and candy. He had never seen so much food.

He walked over to the superbly decorated tree to get a closer look. People were still arriving; everyone dressed festively for the occasion. He watched the looks of anticipation on the guests' faces as they entered through the decorated archway.

It was starting to get crowded and Albert was getting ready to leave when he looked across the room and spotted a lovely young woman wearing a red dress and a stunning matching hat. Albert saw her at the same time that she looked at him. They smiled at each other, and he decided to stay a while longer.

He could not take his eyes off this tall, dark-haired beauty as she strolled over to the tree. Her friends watched her as she walked away, wondering where she was going.

"Hello," he said as she stood near him, in the soft candlelight from the tree.

"Hello," she responded, blushing.

"My name is Albert Sterling," he said with a smile.

"I'm Rose Neumann." Rose could not believe that she had taken the initiative and walked over to meet this man without her friends tagging along. It was a very adult thing to do, she thought; something had come over her, and she had to go to him.

"Your dress is spectacular, Miss Neumann."

"Thank you," Rose replied. "I made it especially for the occasion. I have been looking forward to this day for a long time." Albert looked at her dress closely, and was truly impressed.

"You are incredibly talented," he told her. "Do you make garments to sell to the town's people?"

"Not yet, but eventually I would very much like to do that." Rose was being evasive with her answers, as she knew Albert thought she was older and she did not want him being apprehensive about her because she was sixteen.

"This is my first time attending this holiday gathering. I am certainly glad I decided to be here." He smiled, looking into Rose's eyes. Albert assumed she was in her mid-twenties; it was improper to ask her age.

Albert talked about making clocks and watches and showed her his impressive pocket watch he had attached to a shiny gold chain.

"You and I should own a small shop one day," Rose said. "I could sell my wonderfully made garments and you could sell your beautiful watches and clocks."

They both laughed at the thought, looking at each other and imagining the possibility. Albert listened attentively as Rose spoke of the people she knew from town. She was respectful and mature and presented herself intriguingly.

Albert's charm and personality swept Rose off her feet. He was very easy to talk to, and they spent the whole evening together. People looked at them strangely, but Rose was not concerned and Albert did not notice. Her friend Grace came up to her and told her that she needed to dance with the boy from school.

"He's getting jealous, Rose," Grace warned her, but Rose did not care. Her parents tried to draw her attention away from Albert as well, to no avail.

The two of them danced, laughed and talked only with each other all evening. It was like a dream to Rose. She was at this grand party, with the most charming man, who was paying attention only to her. He made her feel as if no one else was in the room.

Albert could not believe that the most striking girl in the room wanted to be with him. At the end of the evening, it was late and her friends and parents had already gone. Albert offered her a ride home. It had been the best night of her life. When she walked in the door, her parents were waiting for her.

Her mother's face was red with anger. "Rose, you will *not* see that man again," she declared. "This courting between the two of you is over! There is a twenty-year age difference, for heaven's sake, and, more than that, he has lived a life and previously been married, in front of God. You are a naïve, innocent young woman, and he is taking advantage of you. Can you not see that?"

Rose could understand why she seemed a bit naïve. She knew Albert was older but did not know his age; all she saw was how wonderful and charming he was and how well they got along together. She was sure he was not playing games and he genuinely liked her. They had an attraction that other people could not understand. Neither of them cared about the age difference or wanted to ask.

"How do you know how old he is? Wait …" Rose stopped, confused. "How do you know he was married before?"

"We asked around about him at the dance. What did you expect us to do? You were making a fool of yourself dancing with that older man all night. Your father and I were ashamed," her mother said.

"But Albert is an amazing man, a kind-hearted gentleman. Why will you not try to get to know him, Mama?"

Her father said sharply, "We are not going to discuss this anymore, young lady. You will not see that man again!"

Rose ran to her bedroom and cried.

Despite her parents' forbidding her to see him, Rose and Albert found a way to meet several times in the next few months. They fell in love quickly. Rose could not remember a time when she had not known him. She told him everything—her dreams, things she wanted to accomplish, ideas she had told no one else.

They had to hide their courtship from everyone, her parents, her friends; Rose decided that no one could know. Albert didn't like the idea, but he went along with it for her.

"We will keep it quiet for a while," he told her.

When she encountered her friend Grace, she evaded questions. "You have practically dropped off the face of the earth, Rose. Where have you been? What have you been doing?" Grace asked. Rose never told her the truth.

"I have been making a lot of clothes lately," she lied. Rose's parents kept a close watch on her as well, wanting to know everywhere she went and who was with her. She would tell them she was going to Grace's house to help her sew a dress. She hated having to lie to her parents.

One of their favorite places to meet was under the big bridge along Main Street that crossed over the Erie Barge Canal. Rose told Albert one day that the big bridge was the widest bridge in the world (at the time it was—many years later, it would be the widest bridge in North America).

While waiting for Rose to arrive on this sunny spring day, he carried his fishing pole. He walked down the canal a little way and began fishing, but his thoughts were on Rose. He thought about her all the time, every waking moment. Was he doing the right thing? He only knew that when he was with Rose, he could talk to her easily because she was wiser than her years.

"There you are, my beautiful Rose," Albert smiled, as he helped her down to the canal.

"I don't have a lot of time today—I am supposed to be buying vegetables for tonight's supper," Rose said as she hugged him. She could not be gone long for fear that her father would come looking for her. Her parents would never let her out of the house again if they knew she was meeting Albert.

"Do you want to take home the fish I caught? They are good size and you can tell your mother that a man at the market traded them for some of your beans." He pulled five large fish out of the water, hooked to the end of his rope.

"I am going to do that," she said, surprising herself. "As we sit down for supper to eat the fish, I'll know exactly where they came from and enjoy every bite even more." They looked at each other for an instant and both began to laugh.

Any moment she could find to spend with Albert, she did. They would sit on the side of the canal and talk about everything,

She enjoyed hearing more about the career that supported him—making, fixing and selling clocks and pocket watches. He was an expert at what he did and, in fact, was the only skilled clock-maker in the area who excelled at this trade.

It was intricate, time-consuming work; the clocks he made were beautifully designed. Not many people during these times could afford such a lavish item as a hand-constructed grandfather clock, so he did not sell a lot of them; he focused more on his pocket watches.

Today, beside the sparkling water of the canal, he smiled at Rose. "Fishing is my favorite, most relaxing recreation," he said. "It takes my mind off the involved, time-consuming work I do on my clocks."

They watched the boats go up and down through the canal locks. They also spent time walking across the "upside-down" railroad bridge. This was Rose's favorite thing for them to do together; the excitement and rush of adrenaline walking across the bridge took her mind away from fears of being caught with him … if only for a moment. They enjoyed each other's company; they each listened while the other spoke of their past and dreams for the future.

Albert talked sometimes of his late wife. His voice was solemn when he spoke of their past life on the outskirts of Rochester, near Lake Ontario. They had been married for almost ten years when his wife had come down with a cold and could never quite get rid of her cough. Her health deteriorated rapidly, and she spent most of her last month lying sick in bed as her terrible cough grew worse. The drugs they gave her were not effective; nothing was helping.

Albert had sat by her bedside on the days when she was not able to get up. One night as he watched her, seeing how frail she had become, he wondered what he was going to do without her. Suddenly, he saw that she had become cold; she was shaking with chills, but also perspiring. He covered her with the blanket at the foot of her bed and then got a warm cloth and placed it on her forehead. He also heated up some chicken broth and persuaded her to drink some; she looked up at him with a gentle smile.

Rose had tears in her eyes as he told her the story.

"You are so gentle and caring, I cannot understand why Mama and Daddy are so unwilling to get to know you," she said. "They will not even try to know you, Albert. I hate it and I hate having to lie to them." She placed her head on his shoulder and cried.

"I do understand, Rose," he said softly as he stroked her hair. "Your parents only want what is best for you. I'm twenty years your senior and I have been married before; they think you can do much better than me. I should not be putting you through this, my dear. I am sorry."

"You are what is best for me. I love you, Albert," she said, as she looked up into his eyes.

"I love you, too, my beautiful Rose."

He leaned down and gently placed his lips on hers. It was Rose's first kiss and she knew she would never forget this passionate and magnificent moment.

It had been a year, a year of sneaking around town, hiding their love. Albert asked Rose to meet him in the park at the town Christmas tree, decorated with magnificent red bows draped all around the branches. Snow had fallen that morning and it looked pink as it lay on the colored bows.

They had not gone to the Christmas party this year because they couldn't chance people seeing them together, and they didn't want to have to ignore each other the entire night. It was a calm winter night, with several inches of snow on the ground. They had the park to themselves because everyone else was at the party. He brought a blanket to keep Rose warm; they sat on the bench closest to the tree, and the bright moonlight glistened on their faces. He took her hand in his.

"Rose, you know I have loved before, but never could I have imagined I would love a woman as much as I love you. I want to spend the rest of my life with you. Will you marry me, Rose?" he asked nervously.

He pulled a small box out of his pocket. As he opened it, she watched him and then glanced down. It was a beautiful gold necklace with a single diamond.

"I wanted to get you something you could wear somewhere it would not be seen."

"Yes, of course, I will marry you," she said, glowing with excitement and joy. "I feel the same way about you. I love you very much," She jumped up and embraced him. He took the necklace out of the box and placed it around her neck.

Even after Rose and Albert were officially engaged, they continued just as they had for the previous year. Several months went by and, whenever they saw one another, they would plan their lives together. They decided on three children; they would work hard to be able to afford to give their children what they needed in life. Rose talked about being a caring mother, yet she wanted to design and make clothes to sell at her own store. Albert loved that she wanted to have her independence; he wanted that for her as well.

While time passed and she waited to marry the man of her dreams, Rose made a gorgeous dress of antique white lace dress. She did the sewing at her friends' houses so that her parents wouldn't find out. She finally confided in her best friend, Beth, telling her everything from the past year, and she showed her friend her stunning diamond necklace.

Beth was speechless—she'd had no idea that this was going on. She was also amazed at Rose's talent in designing and making the dress. Rose had even made a delicate lace veil to match.

"It is absolutely spectacular," Beth said, with tears in her eyes. "You are going to look lovely, Rose."

Chapter Three

July 1914

On a summer day in 1914, Rose told her mother that she would be at Beth's house, helping her finish making a dress that she had started. She did go to her friend's home, but it was to get ready for her wedding. Rose was beside herself with excitement.

Albert got up early that morning; he wanted to clean his place, knowing they would be coming back there later that day. He had bought new bedding and made the place look spectacular. He laid a single red rose on the bed by her pillow. It was time for him to get ready and he was a little nervous.

Rose met him downtown at city hall, wearing her lovely lace dress. They were married in a simple ceremony in front of the Justice of the Peace.

During the ceremony, Albert placed an elegant diamond ring on Rose's finger.

"It is incredible, Albert. I cannot believe you did this," she said, crying and smiling at the same time.

"You are the one who is incredible, Rose." He took her in his arms and kissed her.

They couldn't wait to start their lives together—no more sneaking around because now they were married. They knew what they had to do next: break the news to her parents.

They walked hand in hand into the Neumanns' house. Her mother stared at Rose's dress and knew instantly what it meant. She ran out of the room crying. Rose wanted to follow her but saw her father waiting for an explanation. She gave a short version of their romance, getting to know one another, wanting the same things in life and falling in love.

"How could you do this to your mother?" her father said angrily, and then turned to look straight at Albert.

"I love your daughter very much, sir, and I will take good care of her, that I promise you," Albert said quietly.

"You both go sneaking around behind our backs, for over a year, and then run off to wed? She is our only daughter. Did you not think her mother and I would have wanted to see our baby girl get married?" Her father spoke harshly and then he sat down. "I am very disappointed in you, Rose. We have done very well by you, and this is how you repay us."

"I am sorry, Daddy," she said, crying. "You would not give him a chance."

Solemnly, Rose went to her room and packed some of her things, while Albert paced out front. When Rose had packed the things that she needed, she walked over to her father and gave him a kiss on the cheek.

"I love you, Daddy," she said.

Then she turned to her mother, who had walked silently back into the room and taken a seat next to her husband.

"I love Albert very much, Mama, and you will too one day." She bent down and kissed her mother, who stood and hugged Rose hard for several moments.

"I will miss you," she said softly, still holding her only daughter. "You look beautiful, Rose." They all had tears in their eyes.

Rose moved into Albert's tiny apartment, which was located over a garage.

"This is nice," Rose said as she looked around. Now this was going to be *their* place. It was the first time she had ever been away from home and it was forever.

"Let's put your things in the bedroom," he said. At those words, Rose looked away, nervously twisting her wedding ring.

"You're awfully quiet," Albert said as he lifted her hand and kissed it.

"Albert, I have never … and, well, you have … I am not sure what to do."

"Please don't be nervous, darling. We will take it as slow as you wish. We have forever, Rose." He kissed her gently.

"Would you like something to drink?" he asked.

"No, I'm fine."

He picked up her suitcases and headed for the closed door on the other side of the room. When he opened the bedroom door, she tentatively walked through. Her eyes widened in surprise. Albert was a single man living alone; she never anticipated what she saw. There were fresh flowers on the nightstand, with three large candles also flickering on that table and three more on the dresser. The bed was dressed with a soft and elegant handmade quilt and a single rose adorned her pillow.

"You are so thoughtful! What have I done to deserve you?" Rose said. When she saw everything he had done to make her feel comfortable, she turned and hugged him. She softly whispered in his ear, "Thank you."

He put her suitcases near the dresser, walked over to the bed, and sat.

"Come sit," he said gently, tapping a spot on the bed next to him. Rose shyly walked over and sat by his side. Albert softly touched her face, then her lips. They kissed, then stopped for a moment to take a breath, smiling at one another. Rose felt so comfortable; this was her husband and she trusted him with her life.

"I cannot believe you are here and you are my wife." It was as if he knew what she was thinking. He kissed her as he slowly undid the buttons on her dress and tenderly took it off her; his tie and shirt were off before Rose even realized it.

As they lay on the bed, his bare skin touching hers, a rush of excitement went through her body. He placed his fingers in hers and softly kissed her hand, then her neck; he took her hand and placed it around him, and they slowly explored one another.

Albert stopped and looked at Rose's face.

"Are you all right?" he asked.

"I am wonderful."

"Yes, you are." He kissed her passionately. Rose became a woman and a wife to Albert that night.

Rose slept late the next morning. As she woke, she was startled for an instant—she didn't recognize where she was. Then she took a deep breath and smiled, remembering the wonderful night she spent with her husband.

She could smell bacon cooking. As she came out of the bedroom, there was Albert in the very small kitchen cooking bacon and eggs.

"Good morning," he said with a smile. "You slept in."

"That smells so good," she said, feeling comfortable in her new surroundings. "I am quite hungry. Is this how it will always be—I wake up to you cooking *me* breakfast?"

Albert turned and looked at her; they both laughed.

As the weeks went by, Albert enjoyed having time to make furniture for when they had their own house. He continued working on his exquisite clocks, as well. Rose would sit in the shed with him and stitch her garments while they talked.

Rose still loved to sew and made clothes for people she knew, upon request. The newlywed couple was happy and content.

They began having their children right away; Rose didn't want to wait because of Albert's age. Their first child was a little girl. They named her Ruth, and Albert spoiled her with his affection. Two years later their first boy was born—Harold, who quickly became known as Harry—and a short twelve months after that, they had a boy they named Peter. It was the end of World War I. Albert was too old to join the military; however, having children with Rose helped with the disappointment of not being able to serve his country.

The family lived in the small apartment to which Albert had brought Rose on their wedding day. The property owners allowed Albert the use of a shed to work on his clocks and furniture—especially beds. He made sure all the children had a place to sleep.

Their place was very cozy, and Rose had decorated it with charm. But now, she and Albert both knew it was time to get a bigger place.

A few years after they had married, Rose's parents had finally given Albert a chance and gotten to know him; they had to do this if they wanted to spend time with their grandchildren. They could see how blissful Rose was and what a great wife and mother she had become. They also saw how hard Albert worked to provide for his family; he was talented and he was very good with his children. They now understood what their daughter saw in this kind, thoughtful man, and this helped ease their concern over the age difference.

"I understand, Rose, why you love Albert. He is a caring, gentle soul, as well as a wonderful father," her mother said.

"I'm sorry for sneaking around on you and Daddy. I hated it," Rose said. "Albert and I have discussed an idea: what if we have a minister perform a marriage ceremony with you and the kids? Daddy could give me away."

"I love the idea, Rose," her mother said, her eyes shining.

"It will be one of the first things we do when we move into our new home," her daughter told her.

Chapter Four

1920s

Rose was making exquisite dresses, skirts and blouses that she sold at a store in town. Albert marketed his handmade wooden clocks and his attractive pocket watches. It was the "Roaring Twenties" and people were buying. They both worked hard because they wanted their own home.

Among Albert's new products were three grandfather clocks, standing about six feet high. These were all the same concept, but the structural details of each were different. He also made several smaller "jeweler's regulator" clocks, which looked like a small version of a grandfather clock but hung on a wall. Again, each was unique, made by hand and spectacular.

Albert was working on a clock he made especially for Rose as a tenth wedding anniversary gift. A lovely jeweler's regulator, it looked like one of his fine grandfather clocks—a dark tiger oak, approximately seventy-five inches high. The heavy polished brass pendulum swung freely back and forth under the influence of gravity. The Roman numeral face was made of cream-colored ivory—this clock was one of a kind.

One of his favorite clocks, an exquisitely detailed one, was sold to the richest man in Lockport, Mr. Kenan Dean, who owned a lot of property in town. Weeks later, Mr. Dean returned and bought a smaller clock that sat on a fireplace mantel as a gift for his mother. Albert hoped that when people in Mr. Dean's circle of friends saw his magnificent clocks, they would want one as well. This did indeed happen: Albert sold all kinds of clocks and pocket watches to acquaintances of Kenan Dean.

Albert and Rose saved enough money to buy a decent house for their family. When they discussed what kind of house they would buy, they both liked the idea of a boarding house. People were looking for rooms to rent in the downtown area. Rose and Albert found exactly what they were looking for close to downtown. They were going to turn the front portion into six rented rooms. Their family would live in their private residence in the back of the house.

Rose loved their dwelling; it had three small bedrooms, with a newly installed bathroom on the second floor, a little kitchen, a dining area, and a family room with a fireplace. There was also an old outhouse that could be fixed up and used as needed.

Rose did not have the time to make and sell her garments at the family-owned store any longer. Department stores were making and selling mass-produced clothing for less, and fabric was hard to find. Albert was slowing down at building his clocks; he worked on the construction of the six rooms in the front. His father-in-law helped him as much as he could. Times were becoming hard now for everyone, because of the devastating Wall Street Crash in 1929, but Rose and Albert were happy. They had wonderful, well-behaved children who did not want for much, and Rose saw her parents often.

Rose and her mother and daughter started planning the ceremony celebration. Of course, Rose made dresses for her mother and for her daughter, and she was able to fit into her own wedding dress with a few minor alterations. They had the menu prepared and the guest list done. Albert and his father-in-law spent a lot of time in Albert's workshop making furniture for the six boarding-house rooms.

When the day arrived, it was perfect. Ruth was the maid of honor and Harry and Peter stood next to their father. Rose's father walked her down the "aisle"—they walked in the front door, down the hall and into their living area as friends and family looked on. Rose and Albert said their vows after fourteen years of marriage, again, now in front of the minister—and in front of God, which pleased her mother and father.

After their friends had left, Rose's parents were heading home when her mother mentioned she was not feeling well.

"I'm sure it is just because of the long day," she said.

Rose and Albert looked in on the children, all fast asleep, before they went to their room.

"Thank you for doing this for my parents," Rose said, smiling.

"I did it for you as well, my love." He kissed her.

"We get to have a honeymoon all over again," Rose giggled.

"I never really thought our honeymoon ended," he said with a mischievous grin. They talked for hours, made love and held each other until they both finally drifted off to sleep at the same time.

Not long after Rose and Albert's ceremony, both her parents became ill with tuberculosis. The family was devastated.

"I should go and care for them—they have no one else," Rose said. She had no brothers or sisters; her mother had had a difficult time giving birth to Rose and could not have any more children.

"You go, love. Spend all the time you need with them," Albert told her. "Don't worry about us. I will take care of everything here. You need to be very careful, though."

He handed her one of his masks that he used when sanding wood. "Please wear the mask to protect yourself. Your parents will understand. Always wash your hands as well. I don't know what I would do if you got ill," he said as he kissed her.

"I will be careful; I would never want to bring this back to our children, or to you."

The children were supervised, and Albert cooked as best he could. He kept up the house and still had time to work on getting the rooms ready for their boarders. He also found time to take the kids to the park and to the Erie Canal, where he taught them all how to fish.

"Are Grandma and Grandpa going to be okay?" Harry asked his dad.

"I don't know. It is a very bad sickness," his father said.

"Is that why we can't see them?" Peter asked.

"Yes."

"Will Mom get sick?" Ruth asked, scared to hear the answer.

"No, she has taken special precautions."

The family fished for hours and brought home plenty of fish.

"We'll surprise your mother for supper; she loves to eat fish," Albert said with a smile.

After a long day caring for her parents, Rose came home exhausted. Albert had a warm plate of food waiting for her.

"You went fishing—this is delicious!" she said. "What would I do without you?"

At night, in bed, Albert held her in his arms and they took turns talking about each other's day. She felt helpless because there was nothing she could do to save her parents

After three weeks of Rose's caring for her parents every day, her mother died. Three days later her father passed away. It was the worst time of her life.

All six rooms were ready for their boarders. Each room had a double bed, dresser, desk, chair, and a small closet. Four of the rooms were on the main floor; the other two were upstairs. All six were rented the first month, and they even had a waiting list. Five of the tenants shared one large bathroom; the sixth room had its own bathroom.

The boarders were able to purchase a supper for twenty-five cents each night. A couple of the boarders took Rose up on the meals; they found out quickly she was an excellent cook and soon the rest of the tenants also started eating there regularly.

Renting out to the boarders was working out great; the Sterlings finally had that extra income coming in. Rose took one dime each week and put it aside in a can for money to be used for emergencies and for the children's Christmas gifts. Boarders came and went. Rose and the children took care of the upkeep on all the rooms, while Albert worked and sold a few more clocks.

Rose and Albert decided to indulge and take their children out for a special meal. A friend of Albert's allowed him the use of his Ford Model A Roadster for the evening, and the family dressed in their finest. They drove to the restaurant they had heard a great deal about, which was beautiful and the food was spectacular. Rose was impressed with the superb way the entrées were presented. They talked, ate and laughed. The family never forgot the special ride in the Roadster or their wonderful night out.

Although Rose never got the opportunity to open her own store, she was happy with the path her life had taken. She and Albert enjoyed owning the boarding house; Albert had even designed several small clocks and had them mounted on the wall in each of their tenants' rooms.

Chapter Five

1931

Rose and Albert thought their financial struggle was about to get easier. All the children would be out of the house and on their own in the next few years, and soon Rose and Albert would be able to live on the rent from their boarders. Albert was getting old and tired; he was slowing down and rarely made clocks anymore.

Albert was worried about Rose because she hadn't been feeling well for some time. She felt tired and run down and slept during the day, which was very unusual. Finally she went to the doctor to get checked out and discovered she was pregnant.

"I should have known," she told Albert. "I have been pregnant before—why did I not know this? What are we going to do?"

She covered her face with her hands and cried. "I don't know if I can do this again. I am thirty-six years old."

Albert held her close and tried to calm her, but she kept sobbing. "I was looking forward to relaxing with you, not having to stress over our finances. Now we have to start all over again," she wept.

"We will get through this, Rose. We'll take it one day at a time," he told her.

It was a cold winter day in 1932. Rose had been working a job at a tailor shop for several months; she worked there three days a week. One afternoon, she started having terrible pains that came about every hour. She knew exactly what they were, having given birth three times before. She left work early, thinking that if she got off her feet, maybe the cramping would subside. By the doctor's calculation, she still had a month to go before her due date. She had a big stomach with this baby, but thought that was because of her age. The contractions were getting closer; staying off her feet was not helping.

"We have to get you to the hospital," Albert said in concern. They drove to the hospital; the doctor was contacted. The labor pains continued and, after ten hours of labor, they had the biggest surprise of their lives.

"You have a beautiful baby girl, Rose," said the doctor. "Now I need you to push again for me, my dear." The doctor handed the baby to a nurse.

"What? Why? What is going on?" Rose asked between her screams of pain. She was exhausted and in disbelief.

"You are having twins, Rose. Now I need you to push hard."

The doctor saw the crowning of the second baby's head and five minutes later Rose gave birth to a second baby girl. "The babies are small but look healthy enough right now," he said. "We need to keep them for observation to make sure everything is developed. They also need to gain a little weight."

Albert stayed all night by Rose's side. Their other children were old enough to care for themselves, so there was no worry there.

The girls, a month premature, were so small they had to remain in the hospital for over a week, just to make sure everything was functioning satisfactorily. Rose also had a difficult time; she had to remain there for a week as well.

She and Albert had to discuss their options. They barely had any income coming in and knew they were going to have a tough time caring for one new baby, let alone twins. Should they put both babies up for adoption and give them a decent chance at a normal life or should they split them up? A social worker with an adoption agency informed them that the babies would be well taken care of; they would go to different families if they were put up for adoption—families that could give them a good life.

Rose and Albert were torn: they had to come home with a baby because people knew she was pregnant. It was a devastating decision, but they both agreed to give one of the twins a chance at a better life. They were convinced they were doing the right thing. They knew there were wealthy couples out there unable to have children; they could give one of their girls a decent life, more than what they could give her. They just could not give up both children.

Baby "A" was the child Rose and Albert brought home from the hospital in 1932—not for any particular reason, because the twins were identical; she was baby A because she was the firstborn. She weighed two ounces more than her sister did.

The hospital informed them baby "B" was going home with a wonderful couple who were unable to have children. The Sterlings were given no information on the adoptive parents, and they never saw the baby again.

The nurse brought Rose and Albert their baby girl, when they were ready to leave the hospital. They named her Emma Jean. They signed a few papers and took her home. She weighed a little less than five pounds when she arrived at her new home eight days after she was born.

They never told anyone that Emma Jean was a twin—not their friends or family, not even their own children. There were fourteen years between Emma Jean and her brother Peter.

Rose had lost her spark for life. She did not take care of this baby as affectionately as she had her older three children, and even seemed standoffish with this infant. Albert could see she was having a difficult time with their decision. He would reassure her that it was best for all of them, especially the other baby.

Chapter Six

1932—Gloria's Story

It was 1932, in the heart of the Great Depression. Joan and Earl Michaels were among the few who did not have to struggle during these tough times. Joan's parents had died when she was young and left her a large sum of money. They bought stocks in the mid-1920s with some of the money her parents bestowed to her. However, the stock market crash of 1929 hit and devastated the couple's investments, and they lost more than half of their money. But, while most were hungry and out of work, Earl still made a good living, with a respectable job as an engineer on the railroad.

Married for thirteen years, the couple had everything they wanted: a nice house, plenty of food, well-made clothes—everything but a child. They had tried to have children but after four pregnancies and miscarriages, they had given up because Joan could not handle the disappointment. They hired an adoption agency to find them a baby.

The nation was unemployed, and people were struggling to live; having children during these times was tough for families. It was socially unacceptable for single parents to raise their own children; society pressured them to give the children up, and poor woman were also targeted. There were people out there who took advantage of such situations. Joan and Earl had the money and could buy their happiness. They paid quite a lot of money to an adoption agency, and after two years of waiting, the couple was informed a baby was available.

"There was a set of twins at the hospital, born prematurely to a couple that is having financial difficulty—they are older and struggling," the agency director told them. "We have a social worker at the hospital discussing options with the birth parents right now."

Joan and Earl listened. The director continued, "We are hoping they will give up both twins, as we have quite a few clients that are seeking babies." He told them this to scare them, and it worked: they were eager, and this was their opportunity.

"Please do what you can. We have already paid you thousands to find us a baby," Joan said. "Should the twins be split up? Should we not keep them together—I am sure for a minimal fee?"

"You didn't let me finish," the man said sharply. "I have some unsettling news. As is our policy, we have done a background check on the both of you," he told them. "Your husband was convicted of a crime," he said, looking at Joan as if Earl were not in the room. The agency director would work this out so the adoption agency would make a lot of money off this couple, as it did with all its clients who were desperate for a baby.

"What are you talking about?" Joan said in shock and disbelief. "I don't understand."

"I am sorry; your husband has a criminal record," he said again.

"No, he does not! Tell him, Earl." As Joan looked over at her husband, he was staring down, shaking his head.

"Earl? What is he talking about? You have a criminal record?" she asked. "When did this happen? We met when we were in college—was it before then and you never thought to tell me about it?"

Finally, Earl lifted his head and looked at his wife.

"I was arrested at the age of seventeen with several other boys 'riding the rails.' We were hitching rides on freight trains, free," he said. "We would jump on a train and head to Buffalo. The trains were always loaded with hobos; it was a crazy experience. We were caught once, but the laws were not being enforced; we were warned to stay off and sent home. The next time we rode and got caught, a couple of the boys I was with had knives in their pockets, so they threw us all in jail for several months."

"This is not true!" Joan said. "Why would you not tell me?" She started crying.

"It was a stupid thing to do and I was embarrassed," he said. "I didn't think after all these years it would have been a problem—it happened so long ago. I was a stupid kid looking for some thrills. I'm so sorry, Joan," he said, as he comforted his wife.

He turned his attention to the man he despised. "This cannot be a problem. I work for the railroad, for Christ's sake."

"We can work this out," the director said smoothly. "For a price, I can make your criminal record go away. I can also have the birth certificate changed to make it look as if your wife gave birth to the baby." He had the desperate couple right where he wanted them; he was in business to make money.

"I want this done legally," Earl said. "A bit hypocritical of you, isn't it?"

"We will pay you anything," Joan said as she wiped the tears from her eyes.

"Joan, please. How much are we talking about?" Earl asked.

The man pulled a contract from his coat pocket and laid it on the table. He pointed to the extra amount they were to pay, and they both were taken aback.

They paid the man from the agency the rest of what they had left in their savings to have Earl's criminal record disappear and allow them to get one of the children. They were told that the birth mother and father took the other twin home with them. One week later, Joan and Earl Michaels received their newborn baby. They named her Gloria, after Joan's mother.

Gloria had plenty of nice things growing up. Her parents gave her whatever she wanted. However, what they did not give her was the love and affection a child needed. There was never any hugging or kind, reassuring words—no warmth or tenderness. After trying for so many years to have a child and paying a hefty price for what they wanted, neither of them had any familial instincts. They cared for Gloria physically, but not emotionally.

Joan had been very young when her parents died and she had been raised by her aunt and uncle. They had six children of their own, so she never received any affection from them; for them, it was all about the money they received to help raise her. Joan did not have it in her to be a loving mother. She only went through the motions, and sometimes she thought that maybe having this child was not meant to be.

Earl worked long hours at the railroad and would be gone for days at a time. They lived on what he made, because the "cost" of Gloria had taken the rest of their savings. The pressure of the times began taking its toll on him, and he started coming home from work drunk after being gone for days. Gloria started noticing his anger getting worse as she grew older. One night, she saw him slap her mother; she knew it had happened before, but had never witnessed it.

Joan never knew when her husband was coming home, so everything had to be perfect all the time. It never really mattered because he would walk in and start yelling at his wife, for no apparent reason. Gloria would run and hide in her room; she would hear the violence and then hear her mother crying from her bedroom. This went on for most of her childhood.

Gloria grew up a very shy and submissive person. She was never able to express her feelings, and she did not have any friends because of her quiet demeanor. Other kids thought she was a stuck-up rich girl because she lived in a nice house and wore nice clothes.

Whether it was guilt, shame or both, her mother would not let her daughter out of her sight, other than to attend school. She always had things that needed to be done around the house in case Earl came home. Gloria never wanted to upset her dad either; she would do everything she could so that he would not come home and hit her mother. They both made sure everything was exactly the way Earl liked it.

One evening when Gloria was twelve years old, she had just taken her father's work clothes off the clothesline and placed them on the table to fold, when he walked in the door. Earl had been gone for five days and he had come home drunk, as usual. He started yelling when he saw the clothes on the table, first at his wife and then at his daughter. Gloria's mom ran over to the table and started helping her fold the clothes.

"It is okay, Earl. It will just take me a moment and then I'll have your dinner on the table for you," Joan said in a scared tone.

"I am sorry, Daddy. I had just taken them off the clothesline and placed them here to fold them. See? You can feel that they are still warm from the sun." Gloria and her mother folded the clothes neatly, but swiftly.

"Can I not come home to a clean house and maybe have some dinner on the table instead of a pile of clothes?" Earl said to his wife, slurring his words. "I work hard to provide for you and this bastard child of ours."

Joan spoke up quickly. "That's enough, Earl." What he had just said was cruel; thank goodness Gloria did not understand. She didn't want her husband to continue for fear he would say something about the adoption. Earl staggered over to the table and gave Joan a hard slap.

"You do not ever talk to me like that," he said.

Joan fell back, hitting her head on the sink. Then, Earl turned to Gloria and backhanded her; she, too, fell to the floor. Although Joan had been stunned for a moment, she did see him hit Gloria.

"Don't you ever hit that little girl!" Joan screamed. She went after him, scratching and punching him. Gloria got up and ran out the front door to the neighbor's house.

"Please, help my mom!" she cried hysterically as she held the side of her face. "My mom and dad are fighting."

The neighbor held Gloria close while the woman's husband called the police. The neighbors had an idea of what was going on next door. They had heard fighting before, but had never known the extent of what went on. The police came quickly and tried to calm Earl down. He remained irate because he hated people knowing his business.

"How dare you run to the neighbor's house," he growled at Gloria.

The police put handcuffs on Earl, placed him in their car and took him to jail, where he would remain until he was sober or Joan pressed charges for assault. After checking Joan over, they took her to the hospital.

"We will keep Gloria with us for a few days," Joan's neighbor told her, holding onto Gloria the entire time. They were glad they could help this poor abused child. Joan said nothing to her daughter before she was taken away to the hospital.

While Joan was in the hospital, a woman entered the room and introduced herself as a social worker from the state.

"You're Joan Michaels?"

"Yes, I am."

"How are you feeling?" the woman asked.

"I'm fine. Thank you for asking," Joan answered quietly.

"You know why I am here, don't you?"

"Yes," Joan said, and started to cry.

"We have reports of abuse to your daughter and, when we talked to Gloria, she innocently confirmed that you are also abused," the woman said. "I understand you do not want to file an assault charge against your husband."

"My husband has always been hard working. I never thought he could turn so violent. It was the pressure of adopting Gloria twelve years ago; it took all our money and he has turned to alcohol. He was never like this before. It is the times, you know." Joan was sobbing, but she continued to defend him. "No, I cannot do that to him; I cannot have him arrested."

The social worker looked at Joan with a confused look, hesitated a moment as she searched through her paperwork and then said, "You and your husband are not her natural parents? I didn't find any information that she was adopted."

"We went through an adoption agency. They told us they changed the birth records to make it look as if I had given birth to her." The guilt was pouring out of Joan.

She knew she had not been a good mother to Gloria; a child needed love and affection, and she had not had it in her to give. Now, her father was abusing her. Joan knew that there was no question now that the state was taking Gloria from them, and she wanted to let her daughter know how her life had actually begun.

"I am so sorry this has happened. I grew to love that little girl, but I just did not know how to show her," Joan cried. "We had everything at the time but a baby. This agency took all the money we had, and that's why Earl is having a hard time."

"Well, the way I see it, you have a choice to make: you can stay with your husband or you and your daughter can go to a shelter until you get on your feet."

"I cannot leave my husband," Joan said quickly.

"Well, then, you have to tell your daughter what is going on. She's been through a lot and she needs to hear it from you. Today, when she comes to visit, you have to say your goodbyes. I'm sorry."

The social worker was firm, but her eyes showed how she hated her job on days like this.

The Michaels' neighbor gave Gloria a ride to the hospital, and the woman working for the state explained the situation to the neighbor. When Gloria slowly entered her mom's room, she went to the chair and sat.

"Come sit here on the bed," her mom said as she patted a spot next to her. Gloria was afraid to sit on the bed; she didn't want to hurt her mother more. Joan's left arm was in a cast; she had a black eye that was swollen shut and her lip was cut and puffy. Gloria felt responsible for what had happened to her.

"I am so sorry I didn't fold the clothes," she said, with tears in her eyes.

"It's not your fault, so please do not think that. Your daddy is sick and he needs help; his drinking makes him angry. Come sit next to me and give me a hug."

Gloria looked surprised as she walked over to the bed. Joan hugged her daughter for a long time because she knew it would be the last time. Gloria could not remember her mother ever hugging her like this before.

"Why are you crying, Mom? When are we going home?"

"I have to talk to you about that. This is very difficult to explain, but I want you to try to understand," her mother said. Gloria gave her a scared, innocent look.

Joan took a deep breath. "First, I want you to know that I love you very much. You are a wonderful young lady and I am blessed that you came into my life." She felt tears welling up in her eyes. "I'm sorry I didn't give you the love and affection you deserved." Joan stroked Gloria's hair gently.

"We are not going home, not together," she said. Gloria just looked at her in confusion. "Because your dad hit you, you cannot be at the house with him," Joan said, crying.

"But where will we go?" Gloria asked.

"I have to stay with your dad and make sure he gets the help he needs." Joan was choosing her husband over her child.

She knew her husband would not get help and would abuse her again, and she felt as if she deserved it. Joan felt that this whole situation was her fault: she was the one who had to have a baby to feel fulfilled, and that decision had ruined all three of their lives.

"Where will I go?" Gloria cried. "You are my mom and dad—you can't just send me away!"

"I'm not sure where you will go, dear—somewhere you will not be hurt."

Joan hesitated for a moment. "There is something else you need to know about your birth," she began. "Your father and I could not have children. We had someone help us find a baby to adopt, and we adopted you eight days after you were born."

"You are not my real mom?" Gloria gasped.

"I'm so sorry," her mother said again softly. She told Gloria that, although she had been born at Lockport hospital, Joan did not know who her birth parents were.

She did not reveal the sordid details that she and Earl had paid a lot of money for Gloria or that she was a twin. Joan was not positive about that anyway because she had not seen the other child; the man from the agency could have been lying to them.

"Can I just stay with you anyway?" Gloria said frantically. "Please!"

"We lied to people, Gloria, and your father abused you. You deserve better than we have given you, and I am so sorry this had to happen."

The social worker walked into Joan's hospital room and said softly to Gloria, "We have to go now."

Gloria was so confused: they were her mom and dad! Fearfully, she tried to fix the situation. She grabbed her mom's good arm and was not going to let go. She said, "I'm okay. My daddy did not hurt me and he will never do it again. Right, Mom?"

Her mother did not know what to say; she was crying uncontrollably. The nurse came in and gave Joan a sedative, and the last thing she remembered before falling asleep was Gloria yelling, "Mommy! Please!"

Taken from the only life she knew, Gloria was confused and had many questions. Where was she going to live? Where was her "real" mom? Why did her dad have to hit her? The social worker took Gloria to her home for the last time to pack some of her things.

"What should I take?" she asked, as she looked innocently at the woman with tears in her eyes.

"Whatever you want, dear," the woman told her.

Gloria took very little.

Chapter Seven

1930s—Emma Jean's Story

After giving up one of her twin daughters, Rose went into a deep depression for several weeks. Raging hormones and the decision she and Albert had made about the babies took their toll on her emotions. No one understood except Albert. He stepped up and took care of Emma Jean those first few weeks while his wife was melancholy. He got up with their baby girl during the night, changed her diapers, dressed her and bathed her. He took wonderful care of their newborn child while his wife went through a bad time.

Rose cried a lot; in the mornings, she stayed in bed longer than usual. She had nursed her older three children for months after they were born; she enjoyed the bonding, looking into their eyes while she nourished them. Rose did not have those same feelings with Emma Jean; she did not know why, so she blamed it on her depression and age. Rose's breast milk dried up quickly, so Albert fed the baby evaporated milk from a bottle.

Their sons, Harry and Peter, had their own lives, but they helped as much as possible. Her brothers had a gift and they could get their baby sister to smile and laugh whenever they were with her.

Emma Jean ate and slept well and was a very good baby. Albert had always been a hands-on father with all his children, but he was now fifty-six and he didn't have the energy he had had with their first three children. However, he did his best to take care of their infant girl. Emma Jean would not remember the attention and care her father gave her the first several weeks of her life. It would be years later that Albert realized he and Rose should have told her—especially when the tables were turned.

Albert was afraid for Rose because she could not continue along the path she was on and she had to get over her depression.

"Get out of bed, Rose," he told her sternly one morning. "This child needs you. I cannot do everything myself any longer." Albert was pacing. "We both decided to care for this baby as best we could. Remember our motto: take one day at a time."

Rose looked up at him from under the covers. "If you are going to continue like this," he said, "we can give her up for adoption too, and go back to the way our lives used to be. She can get the love and affection she needs from a mother who wants her and cares for her."

Rose heard the harsh words, and she thought long and hard that day. He was right. The next morning Rose was up early; she had to snap out of her despair.

"I'm sorry," she said. "Thank you for being there for Emma Jean when I could not be. Once again, what would I do without you?" She hugged him for several minutes. "I have determination. I *will* get better." She headed to the kitchen to get a bottle of milk so that she could feed Emma Jean.

It was the first of the month, and Rose went door to door collecting the rent from her boarders, as she did every month—only this time she had a baby on her hip. Five of the six rooms had been rented at the time they brought Emma Jean home. An older man in room 5 had just moved out a few days before. He had lost his job, so he was moving in with his youngest daughter; he had given Albert enough notice that he was leaving.

Rose was feeling overwhelmed right now in her life. She always cleaned a room right away after a tenant left; the man who had moved out had occupied that room for several years, and she was moving a bit more slowly these days. She told Albert she would post a "For Rent" sign in a day or two. They asked ten dollars a month for the rooms. Rose went to room 1 and knocked on the door.

"Who is it?" the soft voice asked.

"It's Rose. I'm here to collect the rent." She shifted Emma Jean to the other hip.

"Oh … yes." The boarder undid the chain and opened the door. An older looking woman in her late fifties, she looked like she had had a hard life.

"How are you, Gert?" Rose asked. She liked Gert because she was kind to their children and always complimented Rose on her food. She also paid her rent on time every month.

"I am doing well, health wise. Cannot wait for spring to come, though. I haven't seen you in a while … oh my goodness, Rose, this is your precious new baby? She's a beautiful girl." Gert touched the baby's cheek. "How are you feeling, Rose?"

"I'm fine, just a bit tired. Thank you for asking."

"I have to tell you, that roast you made last night for supper was delicious. I don't know how you do it, with a new baby and all," Gert said, shaking her head.

"One day at a time, Gert. I take it one day at a time. I do have to get going, though, because it's time for Emma Jean's nap." Rose caressed her baby's head. Emma Jean gazed at her silently.

"Let me get the rent for you. You take care of yourself now," Gert said as she reached for the money on the table next to the door and handed it to her.

"Thanks, I will. Dinner will be ready by six as usual," Rose said, with a worn-out smile.

She continued on to the next four rooms, with Emma Jean never making a sound. She made small talk with some of the other boarders. The man in room 2 was in his late sixties and had been a boarder for many years as well. He worked at the main plant downtown at Harrison Radiator Company. Harrison's was the biggest employer for Lockport; they made radiators for General Motor cars. This boarder purchased a meal at the boarding house about three times a week.

The renter in room 3 was a young man in his twenties who worked construction, building roads, and he was handy to have around sometimes when Albert needed help. He came and went quite a lot, but was always on time at six o'clock every night for a plate of Rose's food. He took it to his room to eat. Room 4 was rented by a woman in her late thirties. Rose knocked on the door, but knew she was not there. She was never home during the day because she worked long hours as a server at a local diner. There was never a problem with paying her rent on time. Rose bent down and got the money from under the "welcome" mat, which was where she always left it.

Jimmy and Clair, the young couple occupying room 6, had just gotten married. The room they rented was the largest of all the rooms and had its own bathroom. Albert provided a radio and they asked thirteen dollars rent for the room. The young man also worked in the Harrison's plant. Rose and Albert knew it was just a matter of time before the newlyweds would be in search of an apartment in which to start their lives. Jimmy was a few years older than his wife. The two of them brought back some fond memories for Rose. While Jimmy was at work, Clair would get lonely and come around to talk with Rose, who would bring her back to their main residence so that she could teach her how to cook and sew.

Rose enjoyed teaching this young woman: "Soups are always an inexpensive dinner to make. You can use the bone of a chicken, turkey, or ham from dinner the night before, boil it in a pot of water, add spices and some fresh or leftover vegetables, make some dumplings and you have a hearty meal."

Clair said with admiration, "How do you do it? How do you start all over again with a brand-new baby after you have already raised a family?"

"It's very hard, my dear," Rose replied. "We are both tired and Albert is quite a bit older than I. He was able to help a lot with our older children, but it is hard for him now … hard for both of us. We don't give our daughter the attention she deserves, and I feel guilty about that."

"You do the best you can for her," Clair said.

"I know, but that could have been different." Rose stopped herself from saying any more.

"What does that mean? How could things have been different for her?" Clair asked curiously.

"Oh, don't mind me. I am just rambling."

This pleasant young woman helped Rose with the baby quite often until the newlyweds found a bigger apartment and moved out one year later.

Times were at their worst, especially in the small town of Lockport. The Sterlings had to ration the food they put on the table for their boarders. Their daughter had very few clothes, and her mother used scrap material to sew dresses for her as she grew, although finding thread to sew with was difficult. Emma Jean had few toys. She had one rag doll her mother made from scraps of old clothing that Emma Jean had outgrown, and one coloring book her brothers had used. She would recolor the pages on which they had not colored with bits and pieces of crayons, and she had a few old books that she read repeatedly.

She was full of energy, though, and she ran wild around their big boarding house. For many years growing up, she played hide and seek with her mom or her big brother, Peter.

"Come and find me, Mommy," she would yell.

"Okay, I am counting to ten … here I come." After playing four or five times, Rose was done; she did not want to play anymore. "Okay, that's enough. I have my chores to do."

"Please, Mommy, play with me one more time, *one more time*!" Emma Jean would cross her arms and stamp her foot. Rose did not have the heart to tell her daughter no, so Emma Jean would run and hide one more time. Rose went about her household tasks, not looking for her, and Emma Jean would eventually get bored and come out on her own.

"I could not find you!" her mom would tell her when she saw her. "I hope you weren't bothering the boarders."

"No, Mommy," she said as she looked up at her mother with her bright blue, innocent eyes. She *had* been bothering them. She knocked on their doors and then she ran and hid when they answered. A few of the tenants complained to Albert, because he was the one who disciplined Emma Jean. Bed without dinner was her usual punishment.

"I'm sorry, Daddy. I won't do it again," she said, head down. That night Albert sneaked food up to her room and Emma Jean learned quickly that she could get away with anything. She would take food from their garden without asking and take the tenants' magazines to read and then put them back a few days later. She was disrespectful to the people living in the boarding house, as well as to her parents.

"You have more than most people," her parents told her. "There's food on the table and you have clean clothes to wear and a roof over your head."

Emma Jean did not understand because there were kids at school who had nicer things. She wanted more, of course.

Most of the tenants did not want much to do with Emma Jean. They were pleasant enough to her, but never stopped to talk or tried to get to know her, except for the woman in room 1. Gert felt sorry for the girl and she knew Emma Jean's parents were old and tired.

Gert caught her one day when she opened her door just as Emma Jean turned to run.

"Get back here, young lady," Gert snapped. Emma Jean walked back to Gert's door slowly. They talked about why she would bother people in that manner. "If you are doing it for attention, you are going about it the wrong way. Come into my room and we can talk," Gert said.

After that day, the two were friends. Emma Jean had someone to talk to and Gert would listen. Occasionally, they got together on a Friday night or a Sunday afternoon to talk and listen to Gert's radio.

"Would you like to listen to 'Sherlock Holmes' with me tonight?" Gert asked one day.

"I would like that, and I'll see you a little before seven," Emma Jean said and then went off to read her book. For Christmas that year, Gert had bought her a comic book, *The Shadow*.

Emma Jean came down with a bad case of chickenpox in the beginning of spring one year, and she had to stay home from school for several days. She got a lot of attention from everyone. Rose and Albert had seen death firsthand and it scared them to think their daughter could come down with a terrible sickness. Rose made hot broth especially for her and would sit by her bedside and keep a cold cloth on her forehead

"Are you feeling okay, darling?" Albert asked, as he sat next to his daughter and felt her face to check her temperature.

"Yes, Daddy—Mommy brought me some broth."

"How come I did not get any of that?" he said, joking with her. "How about you read to me while I sit here? I hear you're a good reader."

"Sure, I would love that, Daddy."

Emma Jean hated the itching and the scabs, but she liked the special attention she received. She liked it a little too much. Being sick soon became a habit.

"Why weren't you at school yesterday?" her best friend Marla asked one day.

"Well," Emma Jean said with a smile, "this time I decided I had a stomach ache. I got a lot of attention when I had the chickenpox. My mom brought me food and my dad came to my room and sat with me. He had me read to him and I didn't have to help with chores around the house."

"You shouldn't fake being sick like that, Emma Jean. It's not right. What if you really get sick?"

Emma Jean shrugged her shoulders because she didn't care.

After many years, Rose was having a difficult time keeping up with everything that needed to be done. Emma Jean had chores to do, but she refused to do them, and Albert was getting too old to help his wife around the house. She cooked meals and cared for their boarders, baked pies on the weekend at a local bakery and worked at the tailor shop three days a week. Her daughter was supposed to wash the dirty clothes and hang them out to dry. She was also supposed to help clean the boarders' rooms, but her mother could never find her when the time came to clean.

Peter was not married and he stopped by periodically to look in on his mom and dad to make sure they were doing well and that Emma Jean was not running too wild. When he arrived one day, his sister was nowhere to be found. Peter sat with his dad and talked while they both listened to the news on the radio.

"Remember when we used to go fishing along the canal? Your mom loved to eat the fresh fish we caught," Albert said unexpectedly.

"Yes, she did, Dad." Peter could still see the bond of affection between his parents after so many years together. They had always looked out for one another.

"Peter, please do me a favor and go find your sister. It's supper time," Rose yelled from the kitchen. He got up and went to the kitchen to see his mom.

"This is a big house with too many rooms," he said. "Emma Jean knows what time supper is. Everybody knows it is at six o'clock. For heaven's sake, there are clocks all over the house. She's old enough to show up on her own and maybe she should miss a supper or two so that she knows you won't run around looking for her every night."

Rose knew he was right.

"I'm sorry to be so blunt and I know you do not need this right now," Peter said. "I have to get going. If I see her on the way out, I'll tell her." He kissed his mom.

"Oh, Peter, you don't have to leave yet. Please stay a while longer and have something to eat," she said, hugging him. "You have not seen your sister yet."

"I have to get going, but I'll stop by in a few days." He headed to the living room to say goodbye to his dad, who was still sitting in his favorite chair, listening to the radio.

Peter headed out the front door, shaking his head. "You had the kid, you go find her," he said under his breath as he walked down the front steps. He would never say that to his mom directly.

"Who were you talking to?" Emma Jean asked as she came out from under the steps. Peter jumped and almost missed the last step.

"What are you doing sneaking up on people like that? Is that where you hide?" he asked her angrily.

"Who were you talking to?" Emma Jean asked again.

"I was talking to myself. Mom wants you to go inside for supper."

"I *know* what time supper is and you can't tell *me* what to do," she said in a nasty tone.

"You are a brat and you had better be good to Mom and Dad," he told her as he walked away.

"I do what I want," she said, but he did not hear her.

Chapter Eight

1944—Gloria's Story

Gloria was placed in a transition foster home. The couple she moved in with was caring for many other children. Gloria had her own bed, but she shared a room with three other girls, one older and the other two a few years younger than herself. She was there for several months and saw many kids in the home come and go.

One afternoon, when Gloria arrived home from school, her foster parents were sitting at the kitchen table with a somber man.

"You are Gloria Michaels?" he asked.

"Yes, sir," she said softly.

"Go pack your things. We must be on our way."

Gloria looked over at the couple who had been looking after her. "Do you know where he is taking me?"

"No, we do not, Gloria," the foster mother said. "I'm sorry. Good luck to you, dear."

The man drove through Lockport to the outskirts of town; not a word was said the entire time. They pulled into a long driveway that wound through a forest of trees. When they came to a clearing Gloria saw a large house that looked like a mansion. A name edged in the stone said "Wyman Land Children's Home." This was the home for bad kids—everybody in town knew that. The kids that lived here were violent and they had criminal records. What was she doing here?

"Excuse me, sir, why are we here?" she asked.

"This is where my papers tell me you are supposed to go," he replied. Neither he nor Gloria had any idea of the truth—that the paperwork on her had been processed incorrectly; it indicated that she was the abuser, rather than the abused.

"I take you where I am told to take you," he said, as he walked her to the door. "You will have to work this out after you get settled."

Gloria was terrified all the time. The kids living here were cruel; they were angry at the world, and she sensed that she herself would become violent if she did not get out of here soon.

She kept to herself and her temper remained in check. She was awarded special privileges for good behavior and told herself this nightmare would be over soon. She hated the boarding school. She tried constantly to convince her counselors that she did not belong at Wyman Land.

"There has to be some mistake—I don't understand why I was sent here," she told her counselor. "I am well behaved, I do what I am told and all I ask is that you look into why I was sent here. I don't understand what I did wrong." She said with tears in her eyes, "I do not even know who my real mom and dad are."

She wiped her tears, gathered her feelings and stopped crying. Gloria had learned quickly not to show emotion in this place or the young hoodlums would take advantage of her vulnerability.

The woman who counseled Gloria every week felt sorry for her. Every child who came into the home said the same thing—they did not belong there. However, she knew Gloria was different from the others.

It took a while because of her workload, but the woman investigated Gloria's situation and the mistake was finally corrected. Just shy of turning fourteen, Gloria was taken out of the boarding school and placed with another foster family.

The couple knew she came from the Wyman Land Home, so, even before they met her, they had concluded that she was a troublesome child; they took her into their home for manual labor. These people had her working night and day, and kept her home from public school quite a bit to work in the fields.

When she went back to class, there was a lot of makeup work to do to pass the grade. She had no friends; it was a small school and the children knew she lived in a foster home and came from the Wyman Land. They were as cruel as the kids in the boarding school. She kept to herself and preferred not to go to school, although she liked learning.

It was awful living with these people; again, there was no love or affection in this home, but at least they did not hit each other or her, she thought. The day she turned sixteen, she packed some clothes, a bit of food, and a canteen of water and ran away. She was going to take care of herself from now on.

"I don't need anyone!" she said aloud.

Gloria never graduated from high school, so it was hard for her to find decent employment. She would do just about anything to earn money, work any odd jobs she could find. There were people in town who would help her out, feeding her and giving her a place to sleep in exchange for her taking on chores. She was a hard worker. Gloria begged many times on a street corner; it was a hard life for her.

She always wondered, especially when she was cold and hungry—which was most of the time—how her life could have taken such a bad turn so quickly. How could a mother give her baby away? And she had experienced this twice in her life: the birth mother she had never known and a mother who gave her away after twelve years. She would never understand.

Gloria spent a lot of time on the banks of the Erie Canal. She would sit and watch the boats go by and think how much she wanted her life to be different. What would her life have been if her mother had kept her at birth?

There were places to rest under the bridges along the canal that kept her out of the rain and snow. She had a place she went to twice a week that was easy access for her to wash herself: a clear running stream, with water crisp and cold but clean. She used a piece of soap that she had taken from the bathroom of a local restaurant.

An elderly couple was walking home from their weekly trip to the market one afternoon and saw this strikingly pretty young woman begging on a street corner. They approached her and told her that if she helped them carry their bags home, they would feed her a decent supper.

"Would you be so kind and help us with our market supplies," the man said. "We will repay you with a hot meal." Gloria never hesitated. She gingerly took the bags from the elderly woman.

"My name is Joseph Moore and this is my wife Sara."

That night, Sara made a delicious beef stew filled with vegetables in brown gravy, and there was warm bread for dipping in the stew. The Moores gave Gloria a blanket and told her that she could sleep in their shed.

"There is a mat in the shed, it is clean, and on the wooden crate there is a small lamp you may use."

She helped the couple out frequently and slept in the shed regularly. They let her bathe and furnished her with some personal items that she was able to keep in the shed with her. They had boxes of old clothes they kept in storage from when they had their own children, and they allowed Gloria to go through the boxes to find things to wear. The woman also gave her a warm winter coat that had barely been worn.

The Moores enjoyed helping Gloria because she was pleasant and appreciative. They felt sorry for her and wondered how this beautiful young woman had ended up on the streets. Gloria liked working around their home. There was plenty to do and, whatever they asked her to do, she did it and did it efficiently.

After many months of getting to know Gloria, they allowed her the use of the spare bedroom in their home. All they asked was that she help them with tasks around the house that they could not do themselves.

Eventually, Gloria told them how she had come to live on the streets. Sara hugged Gloria and cried. They had helped her through the hardest time of her life. Gloria loved them and knew that she could never repay them for their kindness.

Christmas morning, Gloria woke up in a warm bed for the first time in many years. She smiled, and when she went downstairs, Sara and Joseph were waiting for her in the living area.

"Good morning. It's about time you got up!" Joseph said.

"I'm sorry. Is there something you needed me to do?" Gloria went to them quickly.

"Yes, you can open this. Merry Christmas, Gloria!"

She stood there holding the wrapped gift that they had handed her and began to cry. "You should not have done this. You have done so much for me already." She wiped away her tears.

"Well, are you going to open it or just cry all over it?"

They all laughed. She sat down on the floor and ripped open the wrapping paper. They had bought Gloria everything she needed for sketching, all assembled in a nice leather case.

"Now when you sit by the canal, you can sketch what you see."

Gloria was crying as she hugged and thanked the people who had helped turn her life around.

Chapter Nine

1942—Emma Jean's Story

There were times when Rose could get her daughter to sit down with her. She would brush and braid Emma Jean's long, thick, dark brown hair. They both enjoyed this time together. Her daughter loved the attention and having her hair brushed, plus it kept her in one place for a while, which Rose enjoyed. The two talked about everything: life before she was born, how her mom and dad met—all the things that kids want to know about when they are growing up.

"How come Daddy is so much older than you?" Emma Jean asked curiously one day.

"Well, dear, when your mom and dad met at a Christmas party, we started talking and enjoyed each other's company. We didn't see the age difference between us and we had a conversation about wanting the same things in life. We danced and talked together the entire time we were at the party, despite our age difference. We knew there was something between us that first night," she told her daughter honestly.

"How come I'm so much younger than my brothers and sister?"

"That's a good question. We didn't think we were able to have any more children. You were what we called a surprise—a pleasant surprise," she said as she kissed her daughter's cheek.

Rose wondered whether she should tell Emma Jean about her twin. This would be a good opportunity to explain it to her but, at the age of ten, was she old enough to comprehend what had happened? How could Rose expect a ten-year-old to appreciate the situation at the time she was born? She could not bring herself to disclose what she and Albert had done. Emma Jean would not be able to grasp why they had given her twin sister away. Maybe someday soon there would be another opportunity.

"You got awful quiet, Mom."

Emma Jean seemed to grow out of her clothes quickly. She usually wore hand-me-downs from a neighbor next door. That family had three girls who were older than Emma Jean, so when the youngest girl outgrew her clothes, Rose would pick through them to find something for her daughter to wear. She could even sew different pieces of clothing together to make Emma Jean something decent. She usually did this while the kids were in school, so as not to embarrass her daughter.

Occasionally, Rose would bring home a dress or skirt for Emma Jean that she had made from scrap material at the tailor shop. Rose could work magic on a sewing machine, and she made it look remarkable. She took her daughter to work with her periodically because she wanted to spend time with her and teach her how to sew. Emma Jean just sat in a chair in the corner of the room and read her book, not paying any attention. Rose tried, but did not spend enough quality time with her youngest child. She had found that spending time with Emma Jean brought back heartbreaking memories, and it made her sad knowing there was a young girl out there who looked just like her daughter. Their relationship diminished quickly as Emma Jean grew older.

The boarding house property was large, and during the summer months they were able to plant a vegetable garden. Gert took it upon herself to help look after the garden for Rose, and the man in room 2 helped tend it on weekends. Rose continued to feed their boarders because they desperately needed the income. She was able to stretch a dinner and make it taste delicious.

The fresh vegetables helped bring their costs down during the summer. Rose's favorite vegetable from the garden was the corn. She never knew which boarders were going to be present for supper each night, and, if they were short portions, Rose, Albert and Emma Jean went without because their boarders were paying. Rose would make something for the family later.

Rose asked her daughter several times to help in the kitchen while she cooked dinner.

"Come with me, Emma Jean. We'll go pick vegetables from the garden, and then we can make a nice stew together," she said one day.

"No thanks," her daughter said sharply. "Can I go now?"

"Yes, supper will be ready at six," her mom said softly. Her daughter was not willing to make an effort and Rose did not have the heart to force her to do things.

"I know what time supper is. You tell me every day. Am I going to *get* any supper tonight?" Emma Jean asked sarcastically. She didn't wait for an answer and she walked out.

When their daughter turned sixteen, Rose and Albert made it a special birthday for her. Rose brought her breakfast in bed and later made her favorite dinner with a delicious chocolate cake for dessert. Her brothers stopped by the house to help their sister celebrate, and Marla was also invited to dinner.

Rose bought Emma Jean a stunning skirt and blouse from the department store and a brand new pair of Buster Brown, Mary Jane shoes as well. Everything fit perfectly and Emma Jean loved her gifts. Marla bought her a beautiful hairbrush with a matching mirror, Peter gave his sister a new book, and Harry gave her a jewelry box that played music. This was the best birthday Emma Jean could ever remember.

Rose continued working at the tailor shop, as well as taking care of their boarders. Now she was taking care of her husband, who was seventy years old, as well. Albert could no longer work on his clocks and, occasionally, they would sell one of many they had hanging in the house. He told Rose never to sell the jeweler's regulator clock he had made especially for her.

For a few nights during the week, Rose was able to sit and relax with Albert, although she had to find the time, and they would catch up on everyday life. Albert would update her on the news he listened to during the day and Rose would tell him about what was going on with their daughter.

Emma Jean spent very little time with her parents when she was home. Her siblings seldom came around to visit and she barely knew her sister Ruth. Emma Jean was a lonely, angry daughter and Rose blamed herself. She could see now that God had given her daughter a twin sister for a reason and that she was not supposed to have separated them. Emma Jean was not supposed to be lonesome; she was meant to grow up with her sister and live with her as best friends. Rose should have brought home both babies, and she would regret her decision for the rest of her life.

As he did every day now, Albert rested in his chair, listening to the radio and thinking. He was disappointed that he could not teach Emma Jean the things he taught his older children. He felt regret that he had not gotten the chance to spend more time with her and taken her fishing along the canal when she was younger. When the twins had been born, Albert knew his age would be a factor in raising them. Emma Jean had turned out an unhappy child, and he felt they should have given up both babies, giving them both a chance at a better life.

Emma Jean saw a difference in her parents when her siblings and their families came to visit. Their eyes lit up and they responded to their other children in a different way than they did to their younger daughter. They shared laughter and happiness among them. They would sit and tell wonderful stories about the earlier days growing up in the tiny apartment they had started out in—Albert's old "bachelor pad." Rose and Albert had had enthusiasm for life back then and it had showed.

Emma Jean never experienced those parents. They were different now, tired and subdued. Her mom, especially, seemed withdrawn and submissive and never appeared happy. The connection between her siblings and parents made Emma Jean jealous and angry because she felt that she had missed out on so much by having older parents.

The worst part was that, because she was the youngest, she had to endure the role of taking caring of her elderly parents. She didn't have the same genuine, loving relationship with them as her brothers and sister had, and she resented all of them. Emma Jean saw her parents as an obligation.

Her dad was not in great health, and his age and his work had strained his eyes. He was nearly blind, so they kept his living area dark all day to relieve the pressure on his eyes; he could not work magic on clocks or watches any longer.

"Would you check on your dad while I am working at the shop?" Rose asked her daughter. "Make sure he eats and please help him get to the bathroom. Maybe sit and listen to the radio with him and keep him company. Emma Jean, please do this for your dad." Rose worried about Albert sitting there for several hours a day while she was away.

"Okay," Emma Jean said harshly, and then she quickly left the room. She did not check on her dad the entire day; she saw him as a nuisance—her own father!

Albert took it slowly and carefully and made it to the bathroom on his own and to the kitchen to get something to eat.

Rose was upset when she got home and found that Emma Jean had never checked on him. "He could have fallen and been seriously injured!" she yelled. "He was there for you when I was not, Emma Jean. You do not know," Rose said, crying.

"He has supported you your entire life—we both have—and you have been nothing but ungrateful. It's the least you could do for him. He is your father, for God's sake." She was shaking and could not continue. She held her tongue for fear she would blurt out something in anger. Her daughter showed no emotion.

Emma Jean did well with her schoolwork. That was the one thing her parents did not have to persuade her do because it came easily to her. She struggled a little in math but worked hard on it and brought home good grades.

One afternoon when she went to her mother's desk to get a piece of paper so that she could finish her schoolwork, she found a poem under a pile of papers. It was not addressed to anyone and she looked around the room apprehensively before she read it. The poem was signed *Rose* and dated February 22, 1932. One line included the words "having to bequeath the other."

My mom wrote this right after I was born; was it about another baby? Emma Jean wondered. "I am deeply torn by my babies' love, as two seeds have grown," the poem went on. *Why would she write something like this? Did my parents have another baby, and why would they not tell anyone?*

The poem raised many questions for her. What should she do with this? She decided to take it. She folded it up and put it in the middle of her math book. She would show it to Marla.

The next day, at school, Emma Jean showed her friend the poem.

"What do you think it means?" she asked Marla. "Do you think they had a baby that they gave away?"

"I don't know why it would say something about giving someone to another," Marla replied.

"Maybe it means the baby was given to God," Emma Jean said slowly.

"I bet you're right. What are you going to do with it?"

"I'm going to hide it somewhere in the house and then confront my mom about it sometime."

Later that day, Emma Jean folded the paper very small and hid it inside her mother's jeweler's regulator clock. She knew her mother would never sell the clock. She opened the front glass door and there was a metal plate inside on the back of the clock, near the bottom. It had a space between the wood and the plate into which she slid the paper; it fit perfectly.

No one will find it there, she thought, *not even when Mom needs to wind it up*. Emma Jean forgot about the poem as the years passed.

She did well her last year of school, well enough to get into a good college. However, her parents did not have the money to pay for a college education. Her friend Marla was working and saving her money so that she could go and she tried to get Emma Jean to do the same. The two girls had been friends since the first grade and they told each other everything. Marla was always the level-headed one and tried to help her friend because she knew what Emma Jean's family life was like.

"I'm not going to college! The first chance I get, I am going to marry a man and get out of the house!" Emma Jean declared.

"Going to college will get you out of the house."

"No, Marla, I don't want to waste my time going to college!"

When they graduated from high school, Marla headed to college while Emma Jean worked at a local department store. One afternoon, a young man walked into the store. Emma Jean thought he was very nice looking, so she smiled at him.

"Hello, my name is Walter Wilkinson," he said.

Emma Jean blushed when he spoke to her. *He must be new to the area because I don't remember him coming into the store before,* she thought.

"Hello, I'm Emma Jean Sterling," she said, smiling.

"Maybe you can help me," he told her. "I'm looking for a nice outfit for a woman." That disappointed Emma Jean because she thought that he must have a girlfriend.

"Sure." She was losing interest, but she helped him pick out a skirt and blouse. He knew what sizes he needed, and they were clothes for a rather large woman.

"Are you sure this is the size you are looking for?" Emma Jean asked.

"Yes, I think my mother will like this. It's her birthday," he said as Emma Jean rang the sale.

"Yes, I think she will like it," Emma Jean said, perking up. "It's one of our most popular skirts."

Chapter Ten

1950s—Emma Jean's Story

Walter was smitten with the attractive young woman that he had met at the department store. She was behaving in a playful and alluring manner and Walter was flattered. It was Emma Jean, though, who asked him to go out with her after she got off work. Even though he had been dating another girl for a year, he accepted.

Emma Jean made sure she was available whenever Walter called to see her. She would not show up for work on those days, and she wouldn't come home until very late at night.

"This sort of behavior is not respectable for a young woman," her mother told her.

But there was nothing Rose and Albert could do, because Emma Jean would not listen to them. Her parents knew she wanted to get out of their house and they were ready for her to go, as she did nothing to help them.

They liked Walter; he was a decent, nice looking man with a good job. However, Walter's mother Betty, a widow, didn't like Emma Jean; she was suspicious of her, and for good reason.

Betty was fond of Iris Mead, the girl her son had been dating before he met Emma Jean. Iris was a polite, well-mannered young woman and came from a good family. Walter's relationship with Iris seemed to end abruptly. No one ever knew that Emma Jean intimidated Iris to stay out of Walter's life. She would show up where Iris worked or she would happen to be at the grocery store when Iris was there.

"If you ever tell anyone I was here for a 'visit,' I will deny it and I'll make your life difficult," Emma Jean told her.

Iris was afraid of her, but she saw Walter one last time to ask him about the other girl.

"How could you have brought that unstable woman into our relationship?" Iris said to Walter. "I love you, and I thought you felt the same way—you have told me so."

"I do love you, Iris. I'm sorry."

"Then why would you go out with her?"

"I don't know what I was thinking," Walter said sincerely. "Please forgive me. I made a mistake."

"It's too late for that," she told him.

She didn't want to risk telling Walter about being shadowed by Emma Jean. She was angry and disappointed with him, and she bowed out of Walter's life forever.

Emma Jean had just turned twenty and Walter was twenty-six when she convinced him they should marry. They had only been dating six months, so their announcement was a surprise to everyone, especially Walter's mother. This was not like her son; he was cautious and intelligent and he was focused on his career. How could this woman sweep her son off his feet so quickly? Could Walter not see how selfish and needy Emma Jean was?

"This is not like you, Walter," his mother told him. "She is not a nice girl in many ways."

"Mom, you're speaking of the woman I'm going to marry. The decision has been made and we will wed in a few months."

"Is she pregnant?" Betty asked.

"Mother!" Walter knew it was a reasonable question due to the fact that things were progressing so quickly. "No, she is not pregnant."

"I don't like it, Walter. Your dad would be disappointed," she told him and walked out of the room.

Several days after Walter and Emma Jean decided to marry, they went shopping for a wedding ring; he picked out several she could choose from. She stopped by her house to show her parents the ring.

"Is this not the most beautiful ring you have ever seen?" Emma Jean held her hand in the air. "You have to make me a dress for my wedding," she told her mother.

Rose was tired. She was in her mid-fifties and still taking care of the boarding house and working at the tailor shop, trying to earn a living for her and Albert. Still, she made her daughter a spectacular gown. In her heart, Rose knew she was doing this for her daughter out of guilt.

The day Emma Jean and Walter married, Albert was seventy-seven and very close to being blind. He was unable to walk his daughter down the aisle to give her away, so Emma Jean asked her oldest brother Harry to escort her to the altar.

When the minister asked the question, "Who gives this woman in holy matrimony?" her father slowly stood up from the pew and in a whisper of a voice said, "Her mother and I do."

The newlywed couple moved into a new apartment immediately after they were married. Emma Jean did not want to live in Walter's place because Iris had been there. The apartment he picked was a decent size—big enough to start a family when they were ready.

Walter was working at Harrison Radiator, a division of General Motors. Emma Jean quit her job at the department store before they were married. Walter persuaded her to take secretarial courses at a local community college. After she finished, he found her a position at Harrison's.

Walter advanced through the company quickly and Emma Jean was doing well herself as a secretary when she realized she was pregnant. She was having an easy pregnancy and she wasn't sick or tired, so going to work and sitting at her desk all day wasn't a problem, her doctor told her.

Rose and Betty, Walter's mother, held a baby shower for Emma Jean a month before her due date. Rose made her several charming outfits, plus a beautiful gown for the baby's baptism and a blanket that matched the infant's room. Betty purchased a stroller for her grandchild.

No one knew if the expectant mother was having a boy or girl, but because of the way she carried the baby everyone expected her to have a boy. Rose was the only one who thought her daughter was having a girl.

Emma Jean had everything a mother could desire to bring an infant into the world; she read "how to" books that explained what she needed in preparation for the new infant. Everything that she and Walter had was new, clean and sterilized.

It was the end of summer and the first cool day the North had had in months; it had been a long, sweltering summer. Emma Jean was two weeks past her due date and she was at the doctor's office once again for an appointment. He told her it should be any day and he suggested that Walter take her for a ride in the car on a bumpy road.

"Really, that is what the doctor told us to do?" Walter questioned.

"That's what he said."

When they left the office they took the long way home on several bumpy dirt roads. Walter and Emma Jean laughed as they bounced around in the car. The next day her labor pains started.

"This has to be a coincidence," Walter said as he drove her to the hospital.

"I don't know … that's why he's the doctor. It was fun though." They both laughed thinking about it.

Walter nervously waited with his mother and Rose in the waiting room. He was hoping for a boy, and he had a name picked out: Alvin. It was his father's name. They had decided on Alice if it was a girl, after his grandmother. Walter was a little disappointed, but only for an instant, when he found out the baby was a girl. She was healthy and perfect and that was all that mattered. As Emma Jean was waking up after giving birth the first thing she wanted to know was the sex of the baby.

"What did I have?" she asked. Then she wanted a cigarette; at that time, she was a smoker. Alice was a healthy weight at six pounds, one ounce.

Emma Jean and the baby remained in the hospital for a week after she was born, which was normal. Every day Walter stopped by to see his daughter through the nursery window and then went to visit his wife.

When they brought Alice home, she received a lot of attention from her parents, grandparents and her parents' friends. She was the first grandchild for Walter's mother, who couldn't get enough of baby Alice. Walter and Emma Jean occasionally took the baby to visit her grandpa Albert since he was unable to get around, and Rose took the opportunity to fuss over the newborn when they came for a visit.

Walter and Emma Jean both went back to their work routine. They were doing well, with good jobs in Lockport making a good income. The company they worked for was prosperous because the automobile industry was doing well. One afternoon, when Emma Jean was at her desk, she got a call from her friend Marla, who took care of Alice during the day. Emma Jean got nervous when she realized it was her friend calling.

"Is everything okay?" she said quickly.

"Yes, don't worry. Alice is fine," Marla said. "I know you have been in search of a house to buy, and I wanted to tell you about a place that just went on the market. It's right across the street from us on Chestnut Road. It's a nice three-bedroom house with a large backyard," she said. "You know the one—it's next to the Huskey cemetery."

"I like that house," Emma Jean told her friend. "I'll tell Walter right away. Thanks for calling and give Alice a big kiss for me."

Emma Jean called her husband at his office and they made an appointment for that evening to see the house. It was perfect and just what they were looking for: three bedrooms, loads of closet space, a large kitchen with appliances and plenty of space for a growing family.

However, there were two things they didn't like about the house. First, Chestnut Road was a busy main road with a lot of traffic. Second, there were old scary stories told about the house next to Huskey cemetery. Emma Jean and Walter had heard them all when they were growing up. They decided to purchase the home despite the road and the stories. They moved in when Alice was two years old.

They both continued working full time. Marla continued taking care of Alice, which was now more convenient because she lived across the street. Emma Jean spent as much time as possible with her daughter in the evenings. After she made dinner they had playtime and then it was off to bed for both of them. Sometimes Walter was there, but there were many nights that he had to work late.

Weekends seemed to fly by because Emma Jean had to catch up on the household chores as Walter did the yard work. When Monday morning rolled around, it was back to Marla's house for Alice. They paid Emma Jean's friend weekly for her help. Marla didn't work outside her home and she and her husband Vernon had two children of their own, both boys: one a year older than Alice and the other a year younger. It was an odd twist that Marla had gone to college for a secretarial degree and Emma Jean was the one with a top secretarial position at Harrison's.

Alice was in her "terrible twos" and she liked getting attention. She was very close to Marla and her two boys, and was at their house more than she was home. Alice would sit by the front door looking out the window, crying because she wanted to go over to Mrs. Marla's.

"No, Alice, you can't go over there today, but you will see Mrs. Marla in a few days. Come here and play with your toys," Emma Jean would tell her. Alice would cry harder when she heard the word "no."

She was a very determined child. Emma Jean and Walter had to keep a constant watch on her, especially after the first time she got the door unlocked, opened it and went out; she was heading to Mrs. Marla's house. Alice was very close to the busy road. Emma Jean saw her just in time.

Emma Jean ran out the front door screaming at her little girl, "Stop, Alice, stop!" The next day Walter installed bolted locks high on both the front and back doors so Alice couldn't reach them, even with a chair.

"I think I might be pregnant again," Emma Jean told Walter one day. She made an appointment with her doctor and he confirmed her suspicions: she was expecting. "I was never sick like this with my first pregnancy," she told the doctor. "I'm nauseous and not just in the mornings. I am tired all the time, and I feel awful. Is there anything you can give me?"

"Every pregnancy can be different. The symptoms you're having will subside soon, and they usually last only through the first trimester," he replied. Emma Jean quit smoking but it only made her feel sicker.

During the time they were expecting their second child, Walter's mother became very ill. She had had diabetes for years, but her health had deteriorated quickly over the last several months. Walter was not as close to his mother after he married. Emma Jean and Betty didn't like each other, even though Rose and Betty were friends. It put a strain on Walter's relationship with his mother and he didn't see her as much as he felt he should have. She passed away just before Emma

Jean gave birth to her second child. It devastated him when she died, not only for the loss but for the guilt he felt.

Emma Jean's labor pains started quickly in the middle of the night, two weeks before her due date, and the contractions came on fast and strong. Walter called Marla, who rushed over to get Alice so he could take his wife to the hospital.

The nurses in the delivery area immediately prepped Emma Jean and rushed her into an operating room. When they checked the baby's heart rate, the pulse was weak. The doctor was already there because another woman was also giving birth that night. Within one hour Emma Jean gave birth to their second little girl.

This time it was just Walter in the waiting room, which brought up memories of his mother. He felt he should have taken Alice over to see her grandmother more often. When Emma Jean woke up in her hospital room, Walter was allowed in and he brought up naming the baby. He suggested naming their new baby girl after his mother out of respect, and Emma Jean became irate.

"We are *not* naming our little girl after a woman who hated me."

"She didn't hate you, Emma Jean. You never gave her a chance to get to know you."

"She never gave me a chance!" she snapped back.

"I'm not going to argue with you right now about my mother, for Christ's sake! Just think about it, would you please?"

Emma Jean did not have to think about it and she decided to name their new baby Aimee without discussing it with Walter. She filled out the paperwork that evening after Walter left for the night.

A lot of the attention Alice had received from being an only child for three years now diminished. Walter and Emma Jean tried to explain to her that they needed to give her sister the same caring attention she had received as an infant, but Alice took it as rejection.

They knew it was not uncommon for an older child to try to get attention, positive or negative, from parents when a new baby came home. Alice opted for the negative attention and she cried and had temper tantrums. Her parents had to watch their daughter around the new baby. She would wake Aimee while she was sleeping and make her cry. She took all of her sister's toys, hid them and then told her parents that she didn't know where the toys were. They found them in Alice's closet. Walter and Emma Jean sat her down many times and told her the things she was doing to the baby were naughty.

"You are supposed to help us take care of your little sister, not make things more difficult," Walter told her.

Alice was sent to her room with a spanking and no dinner on many occasions. Her feelings didn't subside even as she grew older—she merely learned to be sneakier so she wouldn't get caught.

Walter and Emma Jean liked having the three-year age difference between the children. Walter wanted to have a third child, but he had to talk Emma Jean into it.

"It will be different when we have a boy," he told her.

Emma Jean knew right away when she became pregnant. Walter was desperately praying for a boy, but, at the end of summer, three years and two months after Aimee was born, they had their third baby girl. They named her Alexandria, and her father nicknamed her Lexi.

Emma Jean was definitely finished having babies; three children were enough even though Walter wanted to try one more time for a boy. She secretly made an appointment with her doctor to discuss getting a new medication that had just come out on the market that was known as "the pill." She understood that it helped regulate a woman's menstrual cycle and also could keep a woman from getting pregnant. She did not want another baby, boy or girl.

"You are here without Walter. Does he know you want to take this medication?" The doctor sounded skeptical.

"Of course he knows I'm here. I'm here alone because he had to work today," she lied, with a bit of sarcasm in her voice.

Her doctor had delivered all three of their children and he had known their family for many years. He intended to fulfill her request; however, he was obligated to do a few tests prior to that.

"I'll have your test results in a few days," the doctor told her.

Emma Jean was restless waiting for the doctor's call. Three days later he called and told her to come to his office. She had Alexandria with her so the doctor could give the baby her six-month check up. It also gave her an excuse for going to the doctor. Emma Jean went there thinking she would get her new prescription, but when the doctor entered the room he checked the baby and got that business out of the way—she had a clean bill of health. He then turned his attention to Emma Jean.

"Emma Jean, I cannot give you the prescription that you requested," he told her. "You are pregnant."

"What!" Emma Jean said in disbelief. She was in such shock that she almost dropped Alexandria. "I'm not having another baby," she told him.

"As they say, my dear, the rabbit has died. You are having another child," he said.

"I can't go through another birth, especially so soon after this last one. Isn't there something you can do?" She began crying. "Please, can't you just take it out of me? I'm not that far along."

"I won't do anything of the sort, Emma Jean. You will have to discuss this with Walter. Maybe once you calm down and let this sink in, you'll see it won't be so bad."

She drove home from the doctor's office crying uncontrollably. When she walked through the back door her eyes were swollen and her face was red.

"What is it? What's the matter? Is there something wrong with Lexi?" Walter asked. He was frantic as he took their little girl and looked her over.

"She is fine. It's not her, it's *me.* I'm pregnant," she told him. He was shocked and surprised.

"I didn't know you'd been to the doctor. Weren't you feeling well?"

Walter could see that she was obviously not happy about the pregnancy. He wasn't going to let his wife know how excited he was, not right now anyway. This was going to be his last opportunity to have a son. Emma Jean was still weeping and verging on hysteria.

"You need to calm yourself," Walter said. "Come and sit down. I'll get you something to drink." He brought her back a glass of water and she took a few sips.

"How about something stronger?" she asked. She got up off the couch and went to get herself a shot of Southern Comfort. "We are going to have two babies in diapers," she said as she sat back down. "I'm not getting around very well. My hip and back hurt me constantly and being pregnant is not helping. I sit at a desk all day, and if I get up to stretch my legs, my boss gets angry. He's a demanding, overbearing, goddamn son of a bitch."

Emma Jean had been transferred to a different department when she returned to work after having Aimee and didn't like the man she was working for. She took another swig and raised her voice.

"We both work full time; Marla is the one raising our children. I come home from work stressed out because of my boss. I pick up the kids, make dinner, get them into bed and do it all over again the next day," she said. She wasn't crying quite as hard now. "Where are you when we get home? I make dinner while you sit and relax in front of the television. You do nothing to help me."

Walter did help with the kids when he was home. He also did the yard work and fixed things around the house; however, he was not going to start an argument about that right now. Emma Jean decided she was going to lie down and rest.

Emma Jean was correct when she said Marla was raising their girls. The kids were at her friend's house all week and with Marla's children—three of them now—she had a house full. However, Marla adored the girls and, of all the kids, Aimee was the one who helped her the most. Aimee liked taking care of the animals Marla and her family kept in their barn in their backyard. They had three dogs, several chickens and a pig named Oscar.

They also had many cats to help keep the mice away. Aimee was there when one of the cats had a litter of kittens. Every day after school she ran over to help the new mommy cat take care of her five kittens. For Aimee's fifth birthday, with Walter and Emma Jean's permission, Marla gave her one of the kittens she had helped care for. She brought her a big box with holes in it.

"What is it?" Aimee asked.

"Open it and find out," Walter told her. She screamed when she saw her favorite: the black and white kitten with the beautiful green eyes. It started meowing and Aimee picked it up and hugged it.

"Thank you, Mrs. Marla, thank you. I love her and I will take good care of her."

"I know you will," Marla said. Aimee ran over and gave her a big hug and kiss.

"I'm going to name her Oreo because she looks like an Oreo cookie." Aimee giggled as the kitten started licking her ear. "Do you want to see my kitten?" she innocently asked Alice, who was sulking in a chair.

"Yeah, I see it," Alice said and then looked at her mother. "Is the party over? May I go now?"

"I don't care," her mother said.

Alice left the room thinking, *Why would Mrs. Marla give her a kitten? I don't have one and I'm older.*

CHAPTER ELEVEN

1950s—Gloria's Story

GLORIA HAD OVERCOME the hardships in her life. It had been difficult for her not to feel sorry for herself but there was nothing she could have done to change her childhood. If Sara and Joseph Moore had not offered her a hot meal and a warm bed when they saw her on the street corner, she would probably have died. Gloria truly believed that she would have frozen under the bridge by the Erie Canal because that winter had been one of the worst that Western New York had ever seen. The blizzards, cold winds, and blowing snow had gone on for months.

She had focused on the future and moved forward. The devastating childhood she had experienced made her a strong, independent woman.

Gloria worked odd jobs but she was always in search of better employment. She had to concentrate on making a living for herself; however, without a high school diploma it was difficult. Gloria was an attractive young woman with a charming personality that benefited her during interviews.

She applied to a local supermarket and they hired her to stock shelves and bag groceries. She had a good work ethic and a positive attitude, and she quickly worked her way up to a cashier position. During this time, Gloria had the opportunity to go back to school and obtain her general equivalency diploma.

She continued her schooling and received a two-year business degree. The supermarket offered her a manager's position and she gladly accepted the job; she received a generous raise and medical benefits. Gloria had worked hard to turn her life around and, finally, at the age of twenty-nine, she had accomplished her goal: she was making enough money to support herself and live a decent life.

Gloria had done what she could for Sara and Joseph, the elderly couple who had gotten her off the streets. They were getting old and could hardly care for themselves so she checked in on them regularly. The couple had had two children, but they both lived out of town and were unable to visit them often. However, the Moores' children had kept in touch with their parents and Gloria to make sure that all were well.

It had become a tradition for the couple and Gloria to spend the entire day together on Christmas. She brought a small Frasier fir tree to the house for them all to decorate with the couple's most memorable ornaments, the ones their children had made when they were young.

Gloria brought all the groceries needed, and the women cooked a large turkey, bread stuffing, yams, green beans, mashed potatoes, and gravy. Gloria had also made Joseph his favorite dessert, a mincemeat pie.

Each year Gloria brought them a special gift, and they would reprimand her at first, telling her to save her money; then they would open their presents with joy and excitement.

This Christmas, she surprised them with a sketch of the locks on the Erie Canal. She had drawn this with the drawing kit they gave her the first Christmas they spent together. She had signed it and had the impressive picture framed.

Sara and Joseph smiled when they saw the special thank-you message written on the back.

"This picture is beautiful and remarkable," Joseph said as he held the sketch up. "You have real talent and should sell your artwork."

"I'm glad you like it," she said. "I'm much too busy these days, but maybe someday I'll be able to spend more time on art."

"God made you a special person, Gloria, and we love you as if you were one of our own children," Sara said. "The things that you do for us are beyond what a daughter usually does for her parents. We don't know why your life turned out the way it did, but we are blessed you came into our lives." It was the nicest thing Gloria had ever heard and she hugged them both.

"I love you both more than you will ever know," she said.

In the earlier years Gloria had lived with the Moores. Finally Gloria had been able to afford her own apartment. She found a place close to the supermarket. It was clean and it had a kitchen, a sitting area, one bedroom and a bathroom.

Sara and Joseph had provided her with many items she needed to furnish her new place and Gloria found other things at flea markets and second-hand stores. She had framed several of her sketches and hung them on the walls. Her apartment was charming and she finally had a place she could call home.

Not long after she moved in, she was grieved by a great loss. Sara and Joseph both passed away within months of one another. The only people who had ever loved her were gone, and once again Gloria was alone.

Gloria became friends with a co-worker named Julia and they started spending their lunch breaks together. Their friendship grew and expanded to outside the workplace. Gloria had dated periodically, but never found a man who she wanted to marry. She had trouble committing to a relationship and she knew it.

However, she had met a man who shopped at the grocery store on the days she worked. John asked her out and the two occasionally went places together. He would take her to dinner and sometimes they would see a movie together at the Palace Theater. Their courtship lasted quite a few years; they were taking things slowly and enjoyed spending time together.

It was a Sunday evening and she was not very busy at work, so Gloria decided to go home a little early. If there was any problem at the store she could be back quickly. She headed home in her used two-door Ford Falcon. She had decided she was going to cook pasta with fresh vegetables for her supper that evening.

Gloria was unaware that a man had been watching her and had followed her home from work. She got out of her car and just before she reached the door of her apartment, the man grabbed her from behind. He clamped one hand over her mouth and with the other arm around her waist, he dragged her behind the garbage dumpsters.

She tried to scream, but with her mouth covered, it only came out as a muffled shriek. As she tried to fight him off he punched her repeatedly.

She was still struggling, when he threw her to the ground, ripped her clothes off and raped her. The terrifying, brutal experience felt like it went on forever, although it had only been a few minutes. He took hold of her hair and slammed her head against the rocks.

"Please don't kill me," she mumbled, not realizing that she had said it out loud.

"Bitch!" He muttered the one word in a low raspy voice. He stood and zipped up his pants as he stared down at her with a disgusting grin on his face. Then he turned and walked to his car, looking around to make sure that no one saw him.

He left her there, battered and cold with shock. Gloria's head was bleeding and she was dizzy. She could not move for several minutes after she watched him drive away. As she tried to gather her thoughts, her mind was numbed by the nightmare memory of the disgusting man and what he had done to her. He had smelled of body odor and his breath stank of alcohol and stale cigarettes.

She rolled her head to the side and vomited. Then she slowly pulled her bruised body off the ground and searched for her purse and keys. She staggered through her front door and locked it immediately. Gloria could not get her tattered, filthy clothes off fast enough and she threw them into the garbage.

She went into the bathroom, avoiding the mirror over the sink, and climbed into the shower. She stood there while steaming hot water burned her skin. Then she dropped down to her knees and put her head in her hands and wept.

"What have I done to deserve this?" she cried. "Why, God? What have I done? I hate my life! *I hate my life*!" she screamed.

After a while the water turned cold so she turned off the shower, reached for a towel and gently dried her sore, bruised body. She put on her warmest pajamas and climbed into bed.

Gloria called her boss the next morning and told him she had influenza.

"You take all the time that you need," he told her. "We can manage a few days without you." He could not remember any other time when Gloria had called in sick.

She stayed home in bed for an entire week after the attack. She barely ate and didn't answer the phone or door when Julia came to check on her.

She never told anyone about the rape. There really was no one she trusted enough to tell, not even Julia. She grieved for Sara and Joseph. She desperately needed their love and support right then.

Gloria withdrew from everything in her life. She stopped going places with John, without explanation. She cut back on her hours at work and seldom left her apartment. She was constantly afraid and she was suspicious of everyone. Her depression began to affect her health and she was constantly sick and tired.

Julia was concerned and asked her, "What's going on?"

For well over a month she had been seeing a different Gloria, subdued and quiet. "I am your friend, Gloria, and if you need help

I'm here for you. Please tell me what I can do to help you," she said. "You are not yourself."

Gloria looked away and began to cry. "There's nothing anyone can do. I'm just not feeling well. It's probably just a cold and I'll be fine shortly," she lied. She could not bring herself to tell Julia what had happened; she was embarrassed and ashamed.

After the change in Gloria had gone on for several more weeks, Julia finally convinced her to see a doctor. "If you will not let me help you, please see if a doctor can find out what is wrong," Julia had pleaded. "Please go see one, Gloria. You don't look well."

Gloria took her friend's advice and went to a doctor. After a full check up, the physician advised her that she had a mild concussion that was causing the headaches. It could also be the cause of her personality change.

The doctor hesitated a moment as he looked over her paperwork and noticed she was not married. "The pregnancy test result indicates that you are pregnant, which is why you are feeling nauseous and tired."

"What?"

"You are pregnant, Miss Michaels," he said again.

Through tears she told the doctor about the attack that had resulted in her pregnancy. The doctor took her hand gently and let her cry until she was calmer.

"You are the first person I have told about the attack," she told him. "This cannot be happening! I had finally put a terrible part of my life behind me."

She told the doctor about her childhood. "Now I am pregnant with my rapist's baby," she said, still weeping.

The doctor gave her a mild sedative to calm her nerves. He explained that she was too far along in her pregnancy to abort the fetus. However, there were many couples willing to adopt a baby, if that is what she decided to do.

"I will have to think about it," she said.

"You have time," he told her. "I want to see you in a month."

Gloria told Julia all about her conversation with the doctor and she explained what had happened to her on that terrible Sunday evening. Julia was speechless.

Gloria's pregnancy was difficult. Not only did she fight nausea and fatigue, but she also had to tolerate the way people treated her when they saw she was pregnant. The people who knew her had been shocked because she wasn't married, and some of them even made snide remarks.

It was devastating to her. She did not want people to know about the attack, and she had let everyone except Julia think she was promiscuous.

John had been surprised when he realized that she was pregnant. Then he became angry.

"So this is why you stopped seeing me," he said. "You could have been truthful with me and told me you were intimate with someone else." Gloria said nothing. "I had much more respect for you than you obviously had for me," he continued.

She had tears in her eyes, but could not reply—telling John the truth was too hard. He shook his head and walked out the door. He stopped coming into the store and she never saw him again.

Gloria contemplated suicide. Who would care if she ended her life? Her own birth mother had given her away and her adoptive parents had been physically and mentally abusive to her and then decided they did not want her either. She had no family and the only two people who had ever loved her had died.

I could be with them again, she thought. She cried herself to sleep that night, as she did many nights.

A few weeks before Gloria's due date, Julia and the girls at work threw her a surprise baby shower at the store. The party was a wonderful gesture and she received many lovely baby gifts. She was grateful to everyone, but she was still not sure whether she was going to keep the baby or put it up for adoption.

Gloria was at home when her water broke and her labor pains started. She felt scared and alone. She knew Julia's mother was a midwife, so that was where she went. Both Julia and her mother told Gloria she should go to the hospital but she didn't want to go there, so they agreed to help her. Gloria was in labor for hours, which allowed Julia's mom time to get the items she needed for the birthing.

Those hours were terrifying for Gloria, since she was weak and exhausted, unable to get to the hospital at that point, even if she had wanted to go. Julia's mom injected her with a combination of morphine and a muscle relaxant. In no time at all Gloria went into a "twilight sleep." When she woke, Julia presented Gloria with her beautiful, six-pound three-ounce baby girl.

"Is she okay? Is she healthy?" Gloria's voice was shaky with worry.

"She is perfect," Julia told her. "She may be a bit hungry, though," she said with a smile.

Gloria could not take her eyes off her precious newborn. "I cannot thank you both enough," she told them softly.

"The first thing we need to do is to get you and your new baby to the hospital and get you both checked out by a doctor," Julia told her. "What are you going to name her?"

"I am going to name her Sarah Jo Michaels," Gloria said without hesitation, looking down at her daughter, "after the two people who saved my life—the wonderful couple who took me into their home when I was living on the streets. Naming her in their memory is the least I can do." Julia and her mother looked at each other with surprise, since they hadn't known about Gloria's childhood.

When they arrived at the hospital her doctor was already there. He examined both Gloria and the baby and arranged to admit them to the hospital for a few days. He pulled a chair up to Gloria's bedside and sat down.

"Have you decided what you want to do with the child? Are you going to put her up for adoption or raise her yourself?" he asked.

Gloria had thought long and hard these past months about what would be best for her and the baby. This would most likely be her only opportunity to have a child since she was thirty-three and not married.

"I was not sure how I was going to feel about the baby after it was born because of how she was conceived," Gloria said, "but I have decided to raise her myself. I fell in love with her the first time I laid eyes on her and I could not give her away now. I have a good job with benefits so I'll be able to provide for her." She looked at the doctor sitting next to her. "I named her Sarah Jo Michaels after the elderly couple I told you about."

"Well, it sounds like you have put a lot of thought into this. I think that is a lovely name," he said as he stood up. "You are going to make a wonderful mother." Smiling, he patted her hand.

"Thank you for everything," she said.

"I'll see you and Sarah in the morning. Get some rest."

A few minutes later a nurse brought Sarah into Gloria's room so she could feed her. Sarah had been born with a full head of dark black hair, and Gloria brushed it and put bows in it every day. She watched her newborn as she nursed her and came to the conclusion that her own birth mother must not have held her as a baby. If she had, she could not have given away such a precious gift.

This little girl would grow up never knowing her father or how she was conceived, but she would certainly get all the love and affection her mother had to offer. This new chapter in Gloria's life was devoted to caring for baby Sarah. She had a completely fresh outlook on life and she was excited to begin their life together.

Chapter Twelve

1961—Emma Jean's Story

Walter and Emma Jean were in their thirties and expecting their fourth child. Emma Jean complained about her boss every day. When she came home from work, she would have a drink, make dinner and then go to bed.

"Do you want to quit your job?" Walter asked. "Your coming home complaining and drinking every night is not good for any of us, especially our unborn baby."

"Yes! I do want to quit," she said quickly.

"That's fine. We'll discuss it more this weekend."

But the very next day, Emma Jean went to work and gave her overbearing boss a two-week notice. They replaced her after one week, and Emma Jean never worked again.

Walter, on the other hand, was advancing through the company quickly. He was promoted to director of Electronic Data Processing, responsible for all of the computer operations, programming and the keypunch documentation library. Walter was in charge of seventy-five employees in that organization. He was put in control of all the computer equipment, not just in his department but also throughout

Harrison's facility, as well as the network that kept them up and running, which at the time was an IBM system.

It was a very lucrative but demanding job. There were many times during the night when he was called in to work because of a problem with one of the computers. He would spend all night in the loud, massive computer room, supervising the job of getting it back up and running. He had a lot of responsibility and was paid well for his hard work; therefore, Emma Jean's not working and staying home with the girls wasn't a strain on their finances.

Emma Jean constantly complained about her hips and back throughout her entire pregnancy, and she remained in bed most of the day. Alice's job after school was to take care of her mother; her sister Aimee was allowed to go across the street to help Marla take care of Lexi.

Alice, angry that she had to stay home, had started showing a lot of animosity, especially toward her sisters. One afternoon while Aimee was across the street, Oreo was asleep in her little bed. Alice woke the kitty and fed it something from the garage to make it sick. She wanted the kitty to vomit so that Aimee would get in trouble and have to clean up the mess; however, that wasn't what happened.

Walter picked up the two girls from across the street; Emma Jean and Alice were in the kitchen making dinner when they walked in. Aimee called for Oreo, who always came running when she heard Aimee's voice, but Oreo didn't appear. Aimee went all around the house searching for the kitty, but she was nowhere to be found.

"Where is she? What did you do to her?" Aimee yelled at Alice.

"I don't know where she is," Alice yelled back.

"Daddy, I can't find Oreo anywhere!" Aimee ran over to her dad and climbed on his lap crying, "I know Alice did something to her."

"She wouldn't do anything to your kitty, Aimee. Maybe Oreo got out the back door," her dad said, trying to reassure her.

"Now that I think about it," Emma Jean said, "I haven't seen that cat for hours."

"I'll go outside and look around. You girls sit down and eat your dinner." Walter grabbed a flashlight and headed out the back door. He called for the cat and looked everywhere she could be hiding. Finally he walked into the Huskey cemetery, where he spotted a small, fresh pile of dirt behind one of the headstones. Walter found a stick, pushed some of the dirt away and saw Oreo's tail.

"Oh, dear God!" he said out loud. He covered the tail back up and went into the house. Aimee came running over to him.

"Did you find her?" she asked with a look of hope in her eyes.

"No, I didn't, honey. I'm sorry, but it's pretty dark outside. I'll look again in the morning."

"She's gone forever, I just know it." Aimee ran to her room crying.

Walter stared at his oldest daughter, who never looked up from her dinner plate. "Alice?"

"I didn't do anything," she responded quickly.

"What's the matter? What's going on?" Emma Jean asked, confused.

"It's nothing. I just need to speak to Alice when she's finished with her dinner." He sat in his chair at the kitchen table. Neither Walter nor Alice said a word all through dinner.

Afterward, he escorted his daughter into the family room and sat her on the couch. "So why don't you tell me what happened?" he said firmly.

"Dad, I didn't know what to do when I saw it with its tongue out and not moving. I got scared. The kitty must have eaten something. I didn't want Aimee to see it so I buried it." Alice showed little emotion.

"Why didn't you tell your mother?" he asked.

"Because she is having a baby, and the kitty looked gross." Alice wanted to snicker when she thought of the dead kitty with its tongue out. Walter didn't think she was telling the whole truth, but he couldn't prove she was lying.

"We aren't going to say anything to anyone about this. Do you hear me, young lady?" he said in a stern voice.

"Yes."

"The kitty wandered off and got lost. Got it?"

"Yes."

"If anything like this ever happens again and you don't tell anyone, you will get the buckle end of the belt. Do you understand?"

"Yes, I get it."

"Now go to your room!" he told her. "I don't want to see you for the rest of the night!"

Alice got up and walked out of the family room. *Oreo is never coming home,* she thought. Her father couldn't see that she had a grin on her face.

Emma Jean went into labor a few months after the kitty incident and gave birth to their fourth child, a boy, who was born on Christmas Day. Walter was thrilled, thinking of all the things he wanted to teach his boy. He wanted to name his son Alvin, after his father, but again Emma Jean snubbed the idea.

"That name is so old-fashioned." Emma Jean chose the name Conrad David.

Walter didn't want to fight about a name, and let it go. He was thankful he got the boy he desperately wanted.

Walter decided the house they were living in on Chestnut Road was much too small for the six of them, and looked for a larger home. A wooded area not far from where they were living was being cleared out. A builder was breaking ground for production of new homes in a neighborhood called Plantation Estates. Walter and Emma Jean purchased a large corner lot and both agreed it was the best location in the entire neighborhood. In 1963 Walter and his family moved into their brand-new home.

The house was the first in the new neighborhood to be completed, a typical two-story home with four bedrooms and one bathroom upstairs, and a half-bath downstairs off the large family room. It had a beautiful fireplace, which the family used often on cold winter nights. On the same floor were a sizable dining room and a spacious kitchen. The basement was also large; Walter used one wall and built a workshop and, at the other end, they installed their washer and dryer.

Their unique in-ground pool in the backyard was made out of an old water tower that had been located in the front of the neighborhood. The builder had contacted Walter and explained that the tower had to come down. He gave him the option to take it off his hands and Walter agreed to the proposal.

The tower was cut on a diagonal, making two pools; they had rounded sides, each with an eight-foot deep end and a three-foot shallow end. Emma Jean's friend, Marla, and her husband acquired the other half and kept it for many years.

Every spring Walter had to prepare the pool after the long harsh winter, with a small window of opportunity to accomplish this task. There couldn't be any rain in the forecast because the rainwater would get under the pool and lift it out of the ground. He started by empting out the green murky water, with Aimee and Lexi helping. A garden hose was filled with water and one of the girls took the end of the hose down the escarpment lower than the pool, while their father put the other end of the hose in the murky water. When the person down the escarpment uncovered that end, the flow began. It usually took twenty-four hours to empty. Next the small rust spots that had developed during the winter months had to be sand-blasted. The interior of the pool was then painted and once again filled with fresh water.

The oldest sister, Alice, had thick, dark red hair and bright blue eyes and was the skinniest of all the girls as they grew up. She was very obstinate around people she didn't know and very dominant around her family. She told her mother and sisters what to do when her father wasn't around and was very compliant to him when he was around.

Alice did very well in school; she brought home good grades and was rewarded and praised for her achievements, especially by her mother. Alice went to the public library often; she read dozens of books with a diverse interest and was able to retain information easily.

"What were you reading about at the library today?" Emma Jean asked one afternoon.

"I was reading about poisons. Did you know there are a lot of plants that are poisonous and have been used to kill other plants, animals and even people?"

"I didn't know that—very interesting," Emma Jean said, taken aback. "Is that the project you went to research?"

"No, actually, I saw a unique plant the other day and wondered what it was. When I was looking to find out about it, I ran across the stuff about poisonous plants and their uses. It was very enlightening," she told her mother with a grin.

Aimee had black, curly hair and dark blue eyes; she was the feisty child growing up, the prankster. She pulled pranks on her mother and sister that made her father howl with laughter, although neither Emma Jean nor Alice had much of a sense of humor.

While the two were making dinner one evening, Aimee came running into the kitchen with a fly swatter pretending to be after a fly. She swatted and yelled, "I got it!" As they turned to look, she picked up a raisin and ate it.

"That is disgusting!" Alice said. "You are repulsive."

"You did not just eat a fly!" her mother said sternly.

"They have a lot of protein," Aimee told them.

"Get out of here—you're sick," Alice told her. Aimee couldn't hold it any longer; she laughed so hard that she was rolling on the floor.

Aimee convinced her young brother, Conrad, to do the legwork for her mischief. Lexi had learned better than to do this because, when Emma Jean fell for the practical jokes, she impulsively yelled at the person standing there. Now, this was usually Conrad.

Alice would console her baby brother after he got reprimanded and tell their mother, "It was Aimee who put him up to it."

They were harmless pranks but Emma Jean would send Aimee to her room with no supper. Later in the evening, Walter would give Lexi a plate of food to take up to her sister.

Aimee also had a lot of friends in school. Their parents went out to dinner every Friday night and then over to a friend's house to play cards. Because Alice was in college, Aimee had to stay home and keep an eye on Lexi on Friday nights, which she heartily disliked, so she invited her friends over to the house. Lexi never said a word to their parents because she liked her sister's parties. Sometimes she and her friend Denny sneaked beers and drank them in the shed in her backyard.

One weekend, Alice decided to come home from college because her roommate was out of town and she didn't want to be in their room alone. She saw that Aimee was having a party and kicked everyone out.

"You can't kick my friends out! You don't even live here," Aimee said angrily. "We never cause any trouble. We sit around, play music and swim. What's the big deal?"

"There is underage drinking going on and I won't have it," Alice said in her high-and-mighty tone. "Do Mom and Dad know what's going on?"

"Who the hell are you to tell me you won't have it? Go back to college—you're not wanted here, you cat-killer."

There was a surprised look on Alice's face. Although only the two of them knew what Aimee meant by the remark, all Aimee's friends began to laugh. Lexi and Denny were also standing in the distance laughing. Aimee had never actually known what happened to her kitty, but she always believed her sister had something to do with it.

The look of hate on Alice's face was scary. "Get your friends out of here," she said in a low, angry tone.

"You sounded just like Mom when you said that." Everyone laughed harder. "Come on, let's go," Aimee told her friends.

As they were driving away, she yelled out the window to Alice, "Keep an eye on your sister." Aimee and her friends headed to the sand pits to drink their beer.

"Well, that sucks for us," Lexi said to Denny.

Lexi, as she liked to be called, refusing to answer to the name Alexandria, had been three when the family moved into their new house. Lexi's features were very different from her sisters'. She had shiny brown hair with auburn highlights; the texture was thin and straight. Her eyes were a light hazel and sometimes took on a golden hue.

When they first moved into the new house she and Aimee shared a bedroom while Alice and Conrad had their own rooms. Lexi didn't get a lot of attention as a child; she and Conrad were only fifteen months apart and her little brother was sick a lot of the time, so she became independent at an early age.

Lexi loved to be outside and would leave the house right after breakfast, climb down the escarpment and spend all day in the quarry behind her house. The wooded area she explored stretched for miles; there were trails, ponds and a freshwater creek. Lexi and her best friend, Denny, who lived next door, were always together.

Denny was the youngest of seven children. His parents were divorced and his mother worked a lot of hours as a nurse and wasn't home very often. The two friends decided to be "independent together." They investigated the miles of forest every day they could, making campfires near the creek and cooking the hotdogs they had brought with them. During the summer months, they packed picnic lunches. The two built the best tree forts. They searched for the perfect tree and took wood, nails and hammers from the construction sites of the houses being built in the neighborhood.

They both collected matchbox cars, and between the two of them they had well over a hundred. They played in the dirt with their cars, using rocks and scrap wood to build cities. Lexi's dad rang a loud bell that echoed through the escarpment when it was time for them to come home for the day.

Lexi helped her dad around house whenever he needed her. She mowed the lawn and helped him with the pool. Every so often, Walter climbed into the large, wooden box that held the pool filter unit when the filter needed to be cleaned or fixed and it seemed like every time he climbed in, there would be a snake in the corner. Walter was deathly afraid of snakes. He had always hoped it would have been his son climbing in the box to do this task.

"Lexi, come kill this snake!" he'd yell.

"Okay, Dad!" Lexi came running; she'd climb in and pick up the snake by the tail and then tease her dad with it.

"Stop that!" he would say in his gruff tone.

"What's the matter, Dad? It won't hurt you," she'd laughingly tell him. She'd take the snake back down the escarpment and let it go near one of the ponds; she would usually stay down there and explore.

The last child, Conrad, was small for his age; he didn't eat well as an infant because of digestive problems that caused him to cry a lot. Conrad had a full head of dark hair and he had beautiful blue eyes the same color as Aimee's. He was three when his eating troubles subsided; however, the doctor determined that he had severe allergies. Conrad was a needy child because of this and he was used to getting attention. Alice was the one who took care of him the most, keeping him inside the house with her. All Conrad wanted was to follow Lexi and Denny.

Alice was babysitting Lexi and Conrad one afternoon while her parents were shopping for new furniture. As soon as Emma Jean and Walter left, Lexi quickly headed down the escarpment with Denny for the day. Because they knew every inch of the woods, they knew exactly where to go, and when six-year-old Conrad couldn't find them, he would go home crying. Lexi and Denny would then meet up at their secret hiding place when he was gone.

"Stay here with me, Conrad. I'll turn on the television and you can watch the Road Runner," Alice told him. "Mom and Dad will be home soon."

Alice ran upstairs to get dressed so she could go to the library when her parents returned. She was in front of the mirror going through her mother's makeup case practicing applying blush, eye shadow and lipstick. She heard a noise downstairs and, thinking that her parents were home, quickly ran into the bathroom and washed her face. She went downstairs and could see that Conrad was not sitting in front of the television.

"Conrad?" she yelled. "Where are you?"

She started searching the house, looking in and under everything, thinking that he was playing hide-and-seek. "You need to come out, Conrad!" Alice was starting to get nervous.

She ran out the front door calling his name. When she walked around to the side yard, she saw that the gate to the pool was open. A wave of fear went through Alice. She looked toward the pool and saw Conrad, floating face down.

"Oh, my God!" She ran to the pool and stood on the deck for a moment, not knowing what to do. "Help! Somebody help me!" she yelled.

She jumped into the pool and pulled her baby brother's lifeless body out of the water and onto the deck. She was crying hysterically, holding her little brother on her lap, rocking him as she continued yelling for help.

"Someone, please help me!"

A neighbor finally heard Alice and ran over to see what the trouble was. "Call the police," she told the woman. "My brother isn't breathing." The neighbor ran into the house and used their telephone to call the police.

Emma Jean and Walter saw the police cars and rescue equipment at their house when they pulled up. Emma Jean immediately started crying as she and Walter quickly got out of the car. Walter saw Lexi sitting on the porch curled up into a ball rocking and crying with Denny's arm around her. Alice was with a policeman.

"What happened? What's going on?" Walter asked the uniformed officer walking up to him. "Where is Conrad? I don't see my son," he said as he looked around. He knew Aimee was at her friend's house, where she had spent the night.

"I'm sorry, sir, there has been an accident. Your child was found floating in the swimming pool," the officer said softly. "They transported him to the hospital, but he didn't make it. I'm very sorry."

Emma Jean fell to her knees, with her hand covering her face and began to scream. A policeman helped her into the house.

"No, not Conrad!" Walter began to cry. Lexi ran to her dad when she saw he was home. He picked her up and hugged her tight as Alice watched in the distance.

"Daddy, I'm so sorry," Lexi told him. She could barely catch her breath as she spoke. "It's my fault. I didn't let him follow me into the woods. I should have brought him with me." Lexi couldn't breathe and Walter tried to calm her down.

"Lexi, it's not your fault—it's nobody's fault," her father told her. "It was a terrible accident." He looked over at Alice, "Where were you when this happened?"

"I was upstairs only for a few minutes, Dad. He was supposed to be watching television. It happened so quickly. If only Conrad had been with Lexi in the woods then maybe—"

"Alice!" Walter interrupted. He put Lexi down; he grabbed Alice's arm and "escorted" her to the side of their car so that it was just the two of them.

"Don't you dare put the blame on your sister," he said in an angry tone. "If this is anybody's fault, it would be yours. I left you in charge," he told her. "*You* ... were responsible for the two of them." He choked out the words.

"It was an accident," he said again. "Now go inside and check on your mother."

Alice went into the house as her father requested. She knew he blamed her; the look in his eyes said it all. Her relationship with her father was never the same after that terrible day.

Walter and Emma Jean had a small funeral ceremony for their only son. Friends and family paid their respects and little Conrad was laid to rest in Cold Springs Cemetery, the oldest cemetery in Lockport.

Emma Jean's depression got much worse after her son's death. Walter tried to get her help, but she refused. Her aches and pains never seemed to go away and there were doctor visits constantly. She went through the motions for many years of being a housewife and mother, but she did less and less as her daughters grew older.

Alice finished college and married a man she met at school, Drew Dickson, who was also from Lockport. Aimee went to college for two years and married her high school sweetheart, Blake Matthews.

They were living their own lives and starting their own families while Lexi was still in high school. She watched as her mother became withdrawn and bedridden while her father worked all week. Lexi and her dad went boating on the weekends. Walter was at peace when he was on his boat in the middle of Lake Ontario.

Lexi would come home from school and her mother would still be in bed. Emma Jean didn't get up until just before her dad came home from work and acted as if she had been up all day. Lexi told her father, but he already knew.

The day Lexi graduated from high school, her father had troubles at work in the computer room. He couldn't get away to make her graduation ceremony and her mother didn't feel well enough to attend. Alice and Aimee also came up with an excuse not to go. It didn't bother Lexi that she didn't have family attend until after the ceremony, when everyone was standing outside. She saw her friends and their families celebrating and taking pictures. She felt very alone.

After high school Lexi moved to Syracuse and went to an art school in the area. She moved into her own apartment with two roommates.

It was the winter of 1985; Walter knew something was medically wrong but procrastinated getting help. By the time he saw a doctor, it was too late; he was diagnosed with cancer that had spread to several organs. He kept the information to himself for a time, not knowing how to tell his family—not after what happened to Conrad—and he got his affairs in order.

Walter went into the hospital for treatment and one month later, in January, he passed away. The day of his memorial service was sunny but extremely cold, with two feet of snow covering the ground. His funeral service was held, but his burial was delayed because the ground was frozen. Months later, Walter was buried in Cold Springs Cemetery near his son's gravesite on a rise under a beautiful Scotch pine tree.

His death left a huge, devastating hole in his daughters' lives. He had been the bond that kept his family together—the generous and supportive father they all turned to for guidance and understanding.

After Walter's death, Emma Jean became even more self-absorbed and stayed in bed all day. Alice and Aimee checked on their mother periodically. Lexi continued attending art school in Syracuse during the week and commuted home to Lockport on weekends to help her mother take care of the house.

During that busy year for Lexi, she met and fell in love with a man in Syracuse. Chase Morgan was an air traffic controller. Lexi and Chase dated six months and decided to move in together. Lexi continued helping her mother by going home several times a month. One year after moving in together, Lexi and Chase married. Her husband was transferred to Jacksonville and fifteen months after their nuptials, Lexi and Chase Morgan moved to Florida.

The first thing Emma Jean did after Lexi moved was get rid of the pool. There were terrible memories and it was too much upkeep. She gave the pool to Marla's son, who had bought the land next to his parents' house on Chestnut Road. She said that he could have it if he paid the expense of digging it up and moving it. It took two days for the huge flatbed truck to pick up the half of a water tower and move it four miles down the road.

Several months later Emma Jean was determined to sell her house. It was too big and she was tired of the long, cold winters. Four years after Walter died, Emma Jean sold the family home and moved to Florida.

Chapter Thirteen

1967

Rose and Albert were still taking one day at a time. All of their children were living their own lives with their own families. Emma Jean had married a good man and had her own children, whom Rose and Albert didn't see often. If it wasn't for Walter stopping by the boarding house with the kids to check on them, they would never have seen their grandchildren. Emma Jean didn't help her parents much when she was growing up, and Rose and Albert didn't expect much from her as an adult.

At ninety-one, Albert was very frail; he could not get around very well but his mind was still strong. Rose made him comfortable day after day. The two were devoted to each other and had a bond that showed every day they were married. They had kept their boarding house, so they had a little income coming in to cover food and personal needs. They only rented three of the six rooms now; all three tenants have been there for many years.

Rose didn't cook for them anymore. Several years back, she and Albert hired a friend to put a mini-kitchen into each of the three rooms; they were able to ask twenty dollars a month rent.

The older children, who had remained in Lockport, came by the house occasionally with the grandchildren to visit. The doctor would also come by periodically to check on Albert—and on Rose.

Most days, the two would sit and watch television, although Albert now could not see the pictures, or listen to their old radio. They would laugh about many thing and sometimes Rose would cry when she talked of the baby they had put up for adoption. She always wondered what her life had become. How could she have separated her babies and, to this day, not told anyone? Had she ever come face to face with the child? Would she have even known her if she had? It was a small town, after all.

"I hope she had a good life, Albert," she said, a remark she had made many times over the years. "We should have tried to manage. We could have asked for more rent at the time. The baby did not even have a name." She cried.

"You cannot keep doing this to yourself," he said. "It has been too many years, and what is done is done. We gave her a chance at a decent life."

Years ago, when Rose was going through her deepest depression, he had suggested that she express how she was feeling, put her emotions in writing, and get it out of her system.

"Did you ever write down your feelings on paper? You never told me," he said.

"I did," Rose said. "It helped. I wrote a poem, but when I went to get it out of my desk one day to read it to you, it was not there. I couldn't find the poem anywhere. It must have been thrown away, but it did help me at the time."

It had been many years and she remembered the poem word for word and told it to Albert. She still wondered what could have happened to it. She looked over at her husband and saw that he seemed pale.

"What can I get you, Albert?" Rose asked as she covered him with his blanket.

"Nothing, my love, just sit next to me," he said as he held her hand. So that is what they did, the two of them sitting in the dark room listening to the radio, together.

They were married for fifty-four years, and they stayed in their boarding house, in the back residence, until Albert passed away in 1968, at the age of ninety-two. Rose continued to live there until she could no longer care for herself or the home. Her family put her in a nursing home when she was eighty-six.

During her remaining years, her thoughts were of the children she raised, her wonderful caring husband she missed every day and the newborn baby girl she had given away so the child could have a better life. Rose Sterling died in 1992 at the age of ninety-six.

Chapter Fourteen

1970s—Gloria's Story

Gloria had been permitted to hire and train an assistant manager at work, which allowed her to spend as much time as possible with Sarah. She loved watching her daughter grow up. Sarah had an exuberant personality and when she smiled she could light up a room. She was not afraid of anything.

Gloria enjoyed spending time with her little girl. During the winters they went sledding at Country Club Hill, and in the summer months she taught her how to swim. Gloria celebrated every holiday with her daughter and made them all special; Sarah's favorites were Halloween and Christmas.

The days that Gloria had to work, Julia or Julia's mom always helped out. Sarah liked spending time with Ms. Julia and Gammy, as she called them, and they loved her in return.

Gloria and Sarah had lived in the same apartment for the first several years. Gloria's dream was to find them a home, a real house where her daughter could grow up. She had a substantial amount of money saved, more than enough to make a down payment on a house.

Finally she found the perfect one. It was a three-bedroom ranch, with two and a half baths, a large eat-in kitchen with all new appliances, a new roof and carpeting, and a comfortable family room with a fireplace. The house was on a large corner lot with a white picket fence around the property. The homeowners accepted Gloria's offer and she and her daughter moved in four months later.

It was perfect for them; Sarah had her own room with a Jack-and-Jill bathroom, which connected to the spare bedroom. Gloria had allowed her to decorate her bedroom. Sarah had wanted bright pink and white with flowers; she did a great job picking out everything and the result was charming.

"You may have a career in interior design," her mom told her and Sarah giggled.

Sarah grew up a happy and contented child. She did well in school and her report cards were typically straight A's, although she had a little trouble in math. She would work on a question until she solved the problem, sometimes staying after class to get help from her teacher.

Sarah had many friends at school, and on weekends, she and her friends would go to the Palace Theater to watch a film and then off to get pizza at Pontillo's. Sarah understood that her mom worked hard at the store to provide for them—Gloria was top management—so Sarah helped around the house as much as possible. She learned to cook and had dinner ready for her mom when she got home. Sarah was particular in everything she did, and when she cleaned the house it was spotless but done quickly. She actually enjoyed it and the sense of satisfaction it gave her.

Unlike most teenagers, Sarah liked spending time with her mom; the two got along well and they talked about everything. Gloria had never told her daughter the truth about how Sarah was conceived—and she never would. There were only two people who knew this secret:

her doctor and Julia. When Sarah asked about her dad, Gloria told her a "white lie"—she didn't want her daughter ever to know she was conceived through violence.

Sarah was a well-adjusted young woman and Gloria never wanted her daughter to question who she was. Her explanation for her unmarried pregnancy was that she made a bad decision with a young man.

"We hadn't been dating very long and one night while we were at his house, he convinced me to sleep with him. I knew it was wrong and against my better judgment, I did it anyway," she said, holding Sarah's hand gently. "I found out a month later I was pregnant. We were going to do the right thing and get married, but he became ill with a staph infection. He died a few months later." Gloria told her he was buried in Cold Springs Cemetery but she couldn't remember where.

"Oh Mom, I'm sorry you had to go through that."

"To be honest with you, Sarah, I didn't love him," Gloria said, "but I want you to understand something—I am so grateful this man blessed me with the most precious gift." She took her daughter's face in her hands and kissed her cheek.

"You have been the best thing that has ever happened in my peculiar life. You give me a stability and purpose." Gloria had tears in her eyes as did Sarah. They hugged each other.

"I love you, Mom." Sarah gave her a big grin. "My friends tell me how lucky I am to have a mom like you."

"They've told you that?" Gloria asked, surprised.

"Yes, think about it, Mom. You let my friends raid the refrigerator … of course, they're going to like you." They looked at each other and laughed.

"If that's what it takes, I'll go grocery shopping tomorrow," Gloria said jokingly.

The two decided to splurge and go out to dinner at their favorite restaurant, Garlock's. They often ate there when they were celebrating something special. The small restaurant's décor was very calming and comfortable. The tables were dressed in white tablecloths with candles flickering as centerpieces. The lights were dim for atmosphere and original artwork by local artists covered the walls. The food at Garlock's was exceptional, making it popular with the people in town.

It was busy when they arrived and the two had to wait a few minutes for a table. They were finally seated in the corner, one of the best tables in the place. Sarah began updating her mother on school and Gloria told her daughter about happenings at the store.

"Any cute men come into the store today?" Sarah asked. She asked this question frequently; she was always trying to fix her mom up on dates. Just then, the server placed their meals in front of them.

"Everything looks delicious as always," Gloria told the waitress.

"Is there anything else I can get you?"

"Not at the moment, thank you."

Then Gloria noticed a picture hanging on the wall across the room. It looked familiar somehow. She had an odd look on her face as she slowly got up from the table.

"Mom, what's the matter? Where are you going?" Sarah asked.

Gloria walked over to the picture and looked at it closely. There in the bottom right corner was her signature. It was the sketch she had given to Sara and Joseph for Christmas many years ago.

"Where did you get this?" she turned and asked her server.

"I don't know, ma'am, but I can find out for you." The server walked into the other room to find the owner.

People were looking at Gloria, but she didn't notice. Sarah walked over to where her mom was standing.

"What is it?" she asked.

"This is a sketch I drew years ago as a gift." As she said it, the owner of the restaurant, "Gig" Garlock, walked up to them.

"Is there a problem?" he asked.

"No, of course not—I was just wondering where you bought this sketch."

"I bought it years ago at an auction. I was assured a local woman was the artist. It is one of my favorite pictures."

"May I be so bold as to ask how much you purchased it for?" Gloria asked. Everyone around them was listening, including Sarah.

"No, I don't mind telling you," he said. "It was auctioned off for $260. I knew it was a bit much for an unknown artist, but the work is superb."

"Thank you," Gloria said with a smile. Mr. Garlock just looked at her, as did everyone else. "I sketched that picture when I was in my late teens. It was a Christmas gift for an elderly couple I knew." Gloria could not stop staring at the drawing; it brought back so many memories.

"There is a message written on the back," she told him. The restaurant owner smiled broadly. She was clearly telling the truth, since very few people knew about the message.

"The picture is really good, Mom," Sarah said. "Did you sketch any others?"

"I did a few more," Gloria replied. "May I ask a favor of you?" Gloria addressed the owner. "May I show my daughter the message I wrote on the back of the picture?"

"Of course," he said as he took the picture off the wall. "Let's look at it in a better light." They followed him to the front room. He held the back of the picture to the light as Sarah read the message.

To Sara and Joseph, *12/25/51*

I do not know where I would be today if not for your kindness and generosity. This is a small token of my sincere thanks to you both for aiding me through a very tough time and helping me become the person I am today.

Love, Gloria

"That was nice, Mom," she said. "I can't get over what an artist you are." Sarah stared at the picture. She turned to her mother with an odd look on her face. "Sara and Joseph were the names of the older couple you told me about? I was named after them?"

"Yes, you were. I named you after the two most wonderful people I've ever known."

She turned and shook Mr. Garlock's hand. "Thank you so much. I appreciate you taking the time."

"My pleasure—after all these years I have finally met the artist."

Gloria put an arm around her daughter and they walked back to their table.

Their meal was on the house, compliments of "Gig" Garlock. They thanked him again on their way out and headed home. They walked through the gate of their white picket fence and sat in the Adirondack chairs on the back porch. They were silent for a few minutes, enjoying the crisp air.

"You are a talented artist, Mom! You've had one of your pictures sell for quite a bit of money. That is so cool," Sarah said. "Why don't you paint anymore?"

"I don't know—maybe I will take it up again."

"Do you have other sketches, or did you give all of them away as well?"

"I have a few. I'll show them to you tomorrow."

"You still have them?" Sarah asked excitedly. "I can't wait to see them! What else have you sketched? Where are they?"

"I'll show them to you tomorrow," Gloria repeated. "You have school in the morning."

"I have a little studying to do before I go to bed," Sarah said. "I'll see you in the morning." She stood and gave her mom a kiss. "Your picture was beautiful and you should be proud."

"I am, thank you. I love you, darling." As she sat on the back porch of her own home, Gloria thought back on her difficult life:

the hardships she had endured and how far she had come to get to where she was today. She got up slowly and headed to the attic in search of her sketches.

As high school graduation grew near, Gloria tried to convince her daughter she needed to go to a decent college. Sarah's choice was going to the local community college. She wanted to live at home and find a job, to earn and save money. Deep down she didn't want to be far away from her mom.

"I'm a big girl, Sarah, I can take care of myself," her mother told her, laughing. "You need to earn a degree at a good college so you'll be able to make a good living when you graduate. I don't want you restricting your education because of me."

"This is what I want to do, Mom," Sarah replied.

"Okay, let's compromise," Gloria said. "There is a Jesuit school called Canisius College. It's a very good business school and you will be able to commute from home, and if you to decide you need to work, you could." Sarah agreed to think about it.

Sarah graduated in the top ten in her class. Gloria was so proud of her daughter when they called her name and she walked across the stage to receive her diploma. Ms. Julia and Gammy were also there to watch Sarah graduate. Gloria organized a small party for Sarah on the back porch at their home. The place was decorated with signs and balloons, and many of the people Gloria invited from work were at the party, as well as several of their neighbors and many of Sarah's friends.

"There's plenty of food on the kitchen table." Gloria directed the statement to Sarah's friends. Sarah looked at her mother, knowing exactly why she said that to them.

"Trying for more brownie points, Mom." They both laughed. It was a memorable day.

Gloria wanted to give her daughter something special for a graduation gift. Sarah had made excellent grades and had worked hard to help her mother around the house all those years as well. The two had taken occasional trips to Niagara Falls in the past. They had ridden on the *Maid of the Mist* tour boat and had seen the falls. Although they had both enjoyed it, Gloria had decided a trip to Key West, Florida, for a week would be a vacation that Sarah would never forget.

The flight to Florida was the very first plane ride for both of them and it was more thrilling than they could have ever imagined. The weather in the Keys was perfect the whole week they were there. They stayed at a quaint bed and breakfast just off Duval Street, rented scooters and drove all around the two-by-four-mile island. They tanned at the secluded pool, watched the sunset at Mallory Square and ate fresh seafood every night. It was hard for them to go back home to the "real world."

Sarah started at Canisius College in the fall. As a Jesuit college, it strove to educate the whole person spiritually, intellectually and emotionally. There was also an emphasis on the physical well-being of the students. Sarah hadn't had much contact with any church as she grew up because her mother had not been interested in attending church. She had been baptized but that was the extent of her religious upbringing.

When her mother had suggested Canisius College and Sarah looked into it, she liked the idea of some spiritual teaching. She majored in business management and told her mother she was going to own her own business someday.

Sarah started cleaning houses to make extra money. It worked out well for her since she could schedule cleanings around her school schedule and still have time to study in the evenings. She made some good money. When word got around town about the quality job Sarah did, she wasn't able to keep up with the requests for her services and she was forced to turn potential clients away.

Sarah opened a bank account and deposited most of the money she made cleaning houses. The first thing she bought with her money was a used two-door Buick Skylark. After graduating from college with honors, she had a four-year top business degree and was ready to start her own company.

"Are you sure this is the business you want to go into?" Gloria asked her.

"Yes, I am. I'm very good at cleaning, if I do say so myself," Sarah laughed at herself. "I can make a lot of money with a cleaning business. I wouldn't have to clean only houses. I could clean apartment buildings, restaurants and newly constructed buildings. There is a demand for this type of service, especially in this area."

"Well, if anyone can be successful in that business, Sarah, it would be you," her mother told her.

Sarah had all the details worked out. "A lot of my initial expense will be obtaining a license and insurance," she said. "I will hire and train the girls myself and will do background checks and drug tests. I've calculated what I will have to charge in order to make a profit. The fees will be based on the size of the place, how many people I would have to employ, what I would pay the girls and how many places they will be able to clean in a day."

Sarah continued, "The best part is I already have quite a few clients, plenty to get me started and I have picked out the perfect name for my company: Clean-N-Pristine. What do you think?"

"I love it, Sarah, I think it's catchy."

Sarah kissed her mom's cheek and headed to her room to begin the basics of starting her company.

Chapter Fifteen

1990—Emma Jean's Story

Emma Jean put her belongings in a climate-controlled storage unit when she moved to Florida and stayed with a friend for many months until she found the perfect place to live. After purchasing a double-wide "manufactured" home located on Swan Lake, she moved in and started living life as a Floridian.

Her children visited periodically and after one of Alice's visits, Emma Jean moved into a new home in a fabulous gated retirement community called Grand Manor. It was a surprise to Aimee and Lexi, who had had no idea their mother was looking for a new place to live. Her new three-bedroom home was in a community that had all the amenities: an Olympic-size pool, an eighteen-hole golf course and a restaurant with outstanding food.

"I found this beautiful home for you so that you could be comfortable in your retirement years," Alice had told her mother the day of the move.

"I was content in my previous home," Emma Jean said. "I don't need a house this large."

"Dad left you financially comfortable, and he wouldn't have liked where you were living. He would have wanted you to live better than in a mobile home, Mom. Besides, those places aren't safe in Florida because of the destructive hurricanes they have." Alice gave the same explanation to her sisters.

Lexi's husband, Chase, worked at the Federal Air Traffic Control Center in Hilliard, just north of Jacksonville. His schedule consisted of four days on and three off. He decided to take several vacation days, which gave him a week off. He suggested to Lexi, since he was off for the week, "You should drive to south Florida and visit your mom."

"You're not going to fly me down?" Lexi giggled.

Chase had a recreational flying license and had bought a Cessna 172 airplane several years back. A man he worked with had owned the aircraft, but when he later couldn't make the payments, he convinced Chase to purchase the airplane for a great price. Chase hangared his plane at Craig Field in Jacksonville.

He enjoyed flying his family for weekend excursions; they had been to Key West and the Bahamas several times and up north to visit family. He also flew them down to visit his parents on the Gulf Coast of Florida. His mother and father lived reasonably close to Lexi's mother.

It had been a while since Lexi had last visited her mother in her new home.

"Don't let her know you're coming and surprise her," Chase said. "Leave the kids with me."

Lexi and Chase had two children, four years apart. Their daughter, Chloe, was a striking, petite young woman, who had dark hair and dark eyes and her father's features and personality. Their son, Lucas, was the complete opposite—tall and slender with light hair and green eyes. He resembled his mother.

"Good idea," Lexi said. "I just finished several paintings. I'll take them to the gallery and Jessie will get them ready for display. I'll leave from there if that's okay. I could use a few days away, maybe it will help get my juices flowing again," she laughed.

Lexi was an artist who dabbled in different types of art, but she mainly painted watercolors, usually bridges and lighthouses. Her work was displayed at a gallery in San Marco, Florida, called The Art Montage. Her good friend Jessie owned the gallery and helped Lexi with the business aspect of her company.

When Lexi arrived at her mom's house, she was shocked when she walked in. The smell made her gag, and when she saw the condition her mother was in she was taken aback. Her sister Alice had just been there a month before. *Mom could not have gotten this bad in a month*, Lexi thought.

"Hi, Mom, it's me, Lexi," she yelled.

Emma Jean came out of her room with a surprised look on her face when she heard her daughter's voice. "Why didn't you tell me you were coming? I would have had the cleaning girl come a day earlier. She just called an hour ago to tell me she was on her way." She saw the look of disgust and concern on her daughter's face.

Emma Jean's hair was matted and greasy from lying on it constantly and she smelled like she desperately needed a shower. Lexi didn't know what to say to her mother—she hadn't seen her in months and didn't want to distress her right away.

"Are you hungry?" Lexi grabbed the crusty dishes that were on her mother's bed and carried them to the kitchen.

"I'm okay right now." Her mother went back in her room and climbed back into bed. Lexi loaded all the dishes in the dishwasher, thinking how disgusting the situation was. She could see and smell that her mother had not been taking care of her dog, Mercedes, properly.

When she put her suitcase in the blue spare bedroom, she saw where the dog did his business—in the yellow spare bedroom. Her mother evidently thought that was acceptable: it was her house, and he only did it in one area, on the papers laid out on the floor in that one room.

Mercedes was a cute little multi-colored Shih Tzu. Emma Jean talked to him as though he were a person and the dog seemed to understand everything she said. She loved the dog, and it was obvious that she felt he was all she had. She hand-fed him twice a day; he sat on her bed as she fed him his food piece by piece. The problem was that she never let the dog out to go to the bathroom, due to sheer laziness on Emma Jean's part.

My mother lives like a pig and she doesn't care, Lexi thought. The whole situation disgusted her.

Thirty minutes after Lexi arrived, a young Mexican woman walked through the front door using a key. She was carrying several Publix shopping bags.

"It's Meg, Mrs. Wilkinson," she said loudly in a Spanish accent. Emma Jean heard the door open and jumped up out of bed quickly. Lexi was in the kitchen when her mother came out of her room; she hadn't seen her mom move that fast in a long time.

"That's Meg," she told her daughter. "She's the girl who cleans my house for me. Meg, this is my daughter, Alexandria; we call her Lexi. She lives in Jacksonville and she drove down to visit for a few days. Her husband usually flies her here in his airplane," Emma Jean said proudly. The two cordially said their hellos.

Lexi was determined to talk to Meg before she left for the day. She wanted some insight on her mom's living habits and Meg would be the one to ask. She had plenty of time to get her alone because Meg was going to be there a while.

A polite young woman in her early thirties, Meg wore no makeup and her long, black hair was pulled up in a bun on top of her head. She had on khaki shorts and a white T-shirt with something Spanish written on the front.

Meg certainly had quite a job cleaning this three-bedroom house every two weeks, and Lexi was going to help her out this week. Not only did Meg do all the standard cleaning, she also threw out the old food in the refrigerator, changed the sheets on all the beds, and did a couple of loads of laundry. Meg had the disgusting task of cleaning up the papers in the spare bedroom that the dog dirtied. She vacuumed the carpet and put down fresh papers, every two weeks. She also stopped by the grocery store to pick up items for Emma Jean. Meg went "above and beyond" her duties and was reimbursed for the groceries as well as paid generously for the cleaning.

"I'll clean out my mother's refrigerator and you can put her dirty sheets in the washer. I'll get her laundry done this week," Lexi told Meg.

"Thank you, ma'am."

Emma Jean seldom got out of bed or went out of the house. She drove herself to the grocery store when necessary or to her doctor's office when she had an appointment. The doctor had told Emma Jean at her last visit that she had to eat and drink more. She only weighed seventy-nine pounds.

"Eat high-calorie foods like hamburgers and french fries, milkshakes, things like that," he told her. "You need to put some meat on your bones."

"I can do that," she said. "I like to eat, but I'm lazy when it comes to feeding me."

"There are drive-through eating establishments, Emma Jean," the doctor reminded her.

In her lovely retirement community, all she needed to do was get in her electric golf cart—Alice had found it for her—drive it up to the restaurant, and enjoy a delicious meal. She could put it on her account and would be billed monthly. It was easy, but too much effort for Emma Jean.

She wasn't hungry most of the time anyway. The medication she took affected her appetite. She took pills to wake her up, to make her sleep and for headaches, arthritis, blood pressure, cholesterol and pain. She was overly medicated.

Lexi called her sisters and told them how bad their mother had gotten.

"Mom is much too skinny. Her coloring is gray, she doesn't shower and when she talks she slurs her words," Lexi said. "There were dirty dishes on her bed and the dishes in the kitchen sink had bugs. It was so disgusting. The worst part was that the dog had been pooping in the spare bedroom, and the cleaning girl told me this has been going on for a very long time. Mom's living habits are disturbing and we need to help her before she kills herself."

When Lexi talked to Alice, she wanted an explanation: "You were just here a month ago—she couldn't have gotten that bad in four weeks. My God, Alice, why didn't you say anything to anyone?" Lexi asked angrily.

"Mom didn't seem that bad," Alice said quickly. "She got out of bed and we did things together."

Alice had been misleading her sisters about their mother's condition. She had found her the perfect home and wanted her to stay there. Alice enjoyed her vacation getaways; she visited her mom at least four times a year, sometimes more, and "persuaded" her mom to reimburse her for her roundtrip airline tickets.

"Your refunding my tickets is between us. I don't feel like fighting with my sisters. You do it so I can come down to take care of you," Alice told her mother as if she truly meant it.

She never went out of her way to help her mother while she was visiting, although she brought her meals from the restaurant and bought the groceries. Otherwise, Emma Jean never saw her daughter—Alice was at the pool or the restaurant or shopping.

While Lexi was visiting, she shamed her mom into taking a shower, putting on clean clothes and brushing her teeth. She helped her mom out as much as possible the several days she was there. She did all her laundry and took the dog outside several times a day for long walks. She also gave him rides in the golf cart and Mercedes loved it.

"Want to go for a ride?" The dog would run and stand by the back door with his tail wagging. Lexi bought him doggie "pee pads" to replace the newspapers, for use later on, when she would not be there. She cooked her mother delicious meals each day and they actually sat at the kitchen table and ate. She purchased easy-to-prepare foods from the grocery store for her mom and stocked her freezer and cupboards full.

When it was time for Lexi to go back to Jacksonville, she sat on the side of her mom's bed to talk to her before she left.

"Thank you for all your help," her mother said sincerely. "Do you want me to pay for your gas?"

"No, Mom, you don't have to pay me to help you. I just want you to take better care of yourself," Lexi said in concern.

"I feel bad, though. I pay your sister to fly down and she doesn't help me half as much as you."

"You don't have to pay me … Wait! You do what?" Lexi exclaimed.

"Nothing … I misspoke."

Lexi was persistent and finally got the information out of her: Emma Jean reimbursed Alice for her airline tickets every time she flew down.

"Let me ask you a question: whose idea was that?"

"Your sister's. She did all the work to find me this *wonderful* place to live." Emma Jean said this with sarcasm in her voice.

"She told you that you owe her for that?" Lexi wasn't sure what she was going to do with this information.

"I talked to my sisters," she said. "We're trying to figure out what we need to do for you, Mom, because you can't keep living like this."

"Why don't you all just leave me alone?" Emma Jean snapped. "Weren't you leaving?"

"Yes, I'm sorry to be so concerned."

Lexi got up and left her mother's room. She didn't understand why she bothered; you couldn't help someone who didn't want to be helped. She grabbed her suitcase and shut the front door behind her.

Several weeks had gone by since Lexi had seen her mother. She and her kids were planning their yearly two-week summer vacation to Lockport to visit her family. They arrived on Thursday and the three sisters got together on a Saturday afternoon to discuss their mother's situation. It was a warm day late in July, and they met at Alice's house on Willow Street.

Their mother was not taking care of herself and they needed to figure out what they should do to help her. They discussed many options and decided on a meal service delivery. That would give Emma Jean one good hot meal a day that she wouldn't have to fix herself. Alice spoke with the management at the complex and discussed their mother's condition; they allowed it to be delivered to her front door since it was a legitimate company to help the elderly. The girls also hired an aide for an hour three days a week to make sure that Emma Jean was eating properly and showering and to make sure there were no dirty dishes that could attract bugs.

"Let's see if that works for a while," Aimee said.

"When I visited her several weeks ago, I got the cleaning girl's telephone number. I'll call her and see if she can clean once a week, instead of every other week," Lexi suggested. "I'll be able to drive down in a few months to check on her," she added.

"Are you planning any trips to Florida in the near future, Alice?" Lexi asked in a strange tone. Aimee looked at their sister curiously, because Lexi had never mentioned Alice's "paid" vacations to Florida. Lexi figured it was over and it would only stir up trouble.

"No, not any time soon," Alice said, staring at her sister. The way that Lexi had asked, Alice knew that their mother must have told her.

Lexi's two-week vacation with her family went by quickly. The weather was perfect: sunny and in the low eighties. They did their usual sightseeing, taking the Canal Cruise Tour through the locks of the Erie Canal, visiting Niagara Falls (on the Canadian side) and taking the kids on the *Maid of the Mist* boat tour.

They ate at all their favorite restaurants; Chloe's choice was Sub Delicious, Lucas's was Mighty Taco and Lexi's was Garlock's. Lexi also spent a lot of time at Aimee and Blake's restaurant called "Shenanigans." It was a very popular place to eat in Lockport. The furnishings were dramatic: dark cherry wood tables and booths, the cushions on the high-back chairs and benches a rich, dark navy blue color in soft, luxurious leather. The décor was a vast assortment of antiques that Aimee and Blake had collected throughout the years.

Aimee and her daughter, Skye, had developed a variety of items on their menu. After helping out in her parents' restaurant for many years, Skye had been inspired to go to culinary school and had become a chef. Aimee and Blake allowed Skye to run the kitchen. Having a restaurant in western New York meant that certain items on the menu were absolutely necessary, such as "Buffalo" chicken wings. Skye included a secret ingredient in the wing sauce, which added a unique twist.

Then, of course, they had the "beef on weck" sandwich, made with thinly sliced roast beef on a kummelweck roll. The roll is topped with kosher salt and caraway seeds, which give the sandwich its name and unique taste; the bun is usually dipped in *au jus*, but Skye grilled it and the *au jus* was presented on the side.

They offered a variety of quality homemade foods. Skye also made fresh soups daily and a seafood gumbo that was one of their best sellers. The restaurant and the bar were always busy.

Lexi painted her sister and her husband a watercolor likeness of their restaurant for their anniversary one year and Lexi also had prints made of the same picture for every menu jacket. The original artwork still hangs in the restaurant today.

It was going to be a year before she saw her family again, unless they came to Florida, so it was a tearful goodbye.

Chapter Sixteen

1996—Sarah Stevens

Sarah's company, Clean-N-Pristine, had been established in Lockport for many years and was doing incredibly well. It provided top-of-the-line service for properties including homes, apartments, condos and small businesses. Each two-woman team (she had five teams) was trained by Sarah, and they were fully licensed and insured. Wearing uniforms, the team arrived at the client's property in a company-marked van. The women brought all necessary cleaning equipment and non-toxic cleaning supplies; harsh chemicals were not used in any of the homes or businesses that they cleaned. Their work was guaranteed: they would re-clean any area within twenty-four hours if a client was not completely satisfied. Sarah randomly inspected clients' homes for quality of service.

Sarah had bought a small home on West Avenue and turned it into an office for her company. The house was where cleaning supplies were stocked and company vehicles parked. It had all the amenities of home for her employees to make use of throughout the day. She had modernized the upstairs as well and made it into a two-bedroom apartment that she rented out.

Sarah herself didn't clean many houses, although she kept a few special clients. She liked to stay behind the scenes to do the training of new hires and make sure that everything in the company ran smoothly.

When she was in her early thirties, she purchased a home for herself on Day Road. The house was on several acres of land, with a guest house that she had renovated and then asked her mother to live there.

Sarah could see that the maintenance and upkeep on her mother's home were too much for her mom to handle. Gloria would be turning seventy soon; she loved the idea of moving close to her daughter but it was hard to think about letting her house go. There were so many wonderful memories of Sarah as a young child growing up there.

"You will finally be able to relax, Mom," Sarah explained. "You can do your gardening and painting without having to worry about the work and expense of taking care of your house. Think of the money you'll save," she said, trying to convince her mother. "I won't charge you too much rent," Sarah said jokingly.

"That would be nice," Gloria said. She thought about it and finally agreed.

Gloria's home sold quickly. On a cool Saturday morning, she and Sarah advertised a huge moving sale in the *Union Sun and Journal*: "Everything must go!" Gloria sold just about everything she wasn't taking with her, and the rest went to Goodwill.

She moved into her daughter's splendidly remodeled guest house. It had everything she needed: a comfortable bedroom with a walk-in closet and a bath with a Jacuzzi tub. The family room had a fireplace and the kitchen had all updated appliances. Sarah's home was the perfect setup for the two of them and Gloria liked living closer to her daughter.

For too many years Sarah had focused all her time and energy on her company, her mother and her properties. Although this had paid off, once her business was established and her motivation settled down, she realized that she had no one special in her life except her mother and a few close friends. She had never given herself a chance to date.

She was thirty-six years old and couldn't believe how fast the time had flown by. Sarah thought she would have had plenty of time in her life to do it all.

A good college friend of Sarah's insisted on setting her up on a blind date and she agreed. Sarah arranged to meet Garret at Garlock's restaurant for dinner. As she walked in the front door, she saw a nice-looking man sitting at the bar. He turned to the door when he heard it open. They both smiled.

"Hello, I'm Garret Stevens," he said as he held out a hand, "and you must be Sarah."

"I am. It's a pleasure to meet you, Garret." Still smiling, she shook his hand. She liked his looks—he had thick, dark hair with a little gray at the temples and light brown eyes with long eyelashes.

"Our table is ready, but would you first like to order a drink from the bar?" Garret asked.

"Sure, I'll have a glass of Cabernet."

They started a light conversation about their experiences dining at Garlock's and discussed the history surrounding the establishment. They spoke of their lives, and Sarah learned that Garret was five years older than she and had been divorced for many years. He and his ex-wife had an amicable divorce for the sake of their children—two daughters, Ella and Nicole, who were now fourteen and fifteen. He had spent as much time as possible with his girls while they were growing up, but not as much lately because they were teenagers.

Sarah talked about her business and a lot about her mom. Garret could see that she adored and respected her mother. They had a wonderful time and as they left the restaurant she showed him her mother's sketch hanging in the main dining room.

"Your mother sketched this?" Garret's voice showed his admiration.

"Yes. She was a young girl living on the streets, and she sketched it for an elderly couple who helped turn her life around," Sarah said.

Garret could appreciate exactly what Sarah was talking about, as he knew how children can get caught up in a flawed system. He was a lawyer for Children's Rights Law and safeguarded children, their well-being and their individual rights.

"How did Garlock's get your mom's picture?" he asked.

"They bought it at an auction years ago. My mother had written a note on the back of it thanking the elderly couple, Sara and Joseph, and I was named after them. My mom had no family of her own."

Sarah and Garret continued seeing each other after that evening. Although both had busy lives, they spent as much time together as they could. They met for a quick lunch or a late evening dinner; they couldn't wait to be together to discuss their day. They became best friends, telling each other everything with no reservations. They planned their days off together and spent them at places such as Artpark in Lewiston, New York. They walked on the nature trails and did some fishing on the docks. Other days, they sat and listened to the free concerts in the outdoor amphitheater.

They spent time with his daughters as well, and Sarah and his girls got along very well. They liked her and thought that she was good for their father because she made him happy. Sarah and Garret took the girls with them to fun places that they all enjoyed; in the winters, they skied at Kissing Bridge Ski Area. When summer rolled around, they all went on the Whirlpool Jet Boat Tours. This boat ride took them through the Niagara River Gorge. The time they all spent together bonded their relationship as a "family."

Sarah had a special evening planned and asked Garret over for a home-cooked meal—baked stuffed clams as an appetizer, freshly baked tilapia with a lobster thermadore sauce accompanied by au gratin potatoes and, for dessert, bananas Foster. She set a magnificent table and had candles flickering throughout the house. The lights were dim, soft music was playing and she opened an expensive bottle of red wine to let it breathe. Everything was ready; she had about thirty minutes before Garret was due to arrive. Sarah ran over to her mother's house.

"Will you come and see my table setting?" Sarah asked excitedly. "Garret isn't expected for a little while yet."

"Of course." Her mother got up from her favorite chair and followed Sarah outside, through her back door and into the kitchen.

"It looks beautiful, honey. You did a wonderful job," Gloria said. She was happy for her daughter, who deserved someone special. "I'll make sure I won't bother you in the morning," her mother said with a smile and a wink.

"Mother ..." Sarah laughed. She pulled out a plate of food that she had been keeping warm in the oven for her mom. "Here, take this and I'll see you in a few days." They both looked at each other and laughed again.

"Have a wonderful time!" Gloria gave her daughter a kiss on the cheek and walked out the door, back to her favorite chair with her warm plate of food.

Sarah was starting to pace, waiting for Garret to arrive. She hadn't been with a man in quite a long time, certainly not anyone who had meant as much to her as Garret did. She was ready to commit to this man and she hoped he felt the same way about her.

The doorbell rang and Sarah quickly went to answer it, butterflies in her stomach. Garret wore a dark blue button-down shirt with black pants, and he smelled so good, Sarah thought as he walked in.

"Wow, you look remarkable!" He leaned in and gave her a kiss. They headed into the kitchen, where Garret poured them both a glass of wine while Sarah took the clam appetizer out of the oven.

"It smells wonderful in here," he told her, as she placed the clams in the center of the table. Garret took her in his arms, holding her tightly and kissing her with passion.

"I should have cooked dinner for you a long time ago," she said, and they both smiled as they sat down at the table.

They continued talking as Sarah plated the tilapia and poured the sauce over the fish.

"Is there anything I can do to help?" he asked.

"No, thanks, I'm just about finished. Maybe a little more wine."

"This looks incredibly delicious," Garret said as she set the plate in front of him, and he poured them each more wine. They continued talking about the times they'd spent with Ella and Nicole and laughed about silly things they had done in their lives.

"This meal was better than any I've ever had in any restaurant," Garret said. "If you ever sell your cleaning business, you can always go into the restaurant business."

"I don't think so—too much work," she replied. After they cleaned the kitchen together, they took their wine into the family room.

"You amaze me, Sarah. Is there anything you can't do?" He stroked her hair and touched her face. He leaned in and kissed her gently, barely touching her lips. She melted inside when he kissed her that way. Sarah was falling in love with this man, but she wasn't sure if he felt the same way. Their touching was getting passionate.

Sarah abruptly stopped and stood up. "I'll be right back." As she walked to her room she turned and looked at him with a smile on her face.

Garret sat holding his wineglass, as though he was not seeing it at all. He was so in love with her, and it seemed impossible that this amazing woman did not have anyone in her life. Tonight he would show her his deepest feelings—not because it was going to be their first time making love, but rather because he had already fallen in love with her months ago—the first time he had laid eyes on her at the restaurant. He never wanted to pressure her into taking their relationship to the next level if she wasn't ready; he would wait for her forever.

Sarah opened her bedroom door, and he drew in a quick breath as he saw her in a gorgeous black silk nightgown. The flickering of light from the candles behind her showed the outline of her slender body through the silk; it looked as if she was glowing. He stood up and walked toward her. Her breathtaking loveliness and warm smile excited him more than even he could have imagined.

"You look stunning." He held her close and kissed her hard. He picked her up and carried her to the bed, where he gently laid her down on the silky-smooth mauve comforter.

Sarah's heart was beating fast as she watched him slowly unbutton his shirt and let it fall to the floor. In a moment he had tenderly placed his body over hers. He started kissing her neck, then brought his lips to hers. Garret stopped for a moment as they looked deep into each other's eyes.

Sarah felt her desire rising to match his, and the passion overwhelmed her and continued for hours.

"I love you, Sarah," Garret whispered in her ear. She smiled and looked into his eyes.

"Are you saying that because that's what you think I want to hear?"

"Of course not," he said, holding her close. "I have wanted to tell you that ever since the first moment I saw you walk into the restaurant, but I didn't want to scare you away." He kissed her again, softly.

"You are a beautiful person, Sarah. You're smart, caring and generous … I am so blessed to have you in my life."

"I'm glad you feel the same way I do," she murmured. "I love you too, Garret. You have my heart."

Garret rolled her over and they made passionate love … again. They lay in bed holding each other close for hours afterward.

The next morning Garret woke up reaching for Sarah, but she was already out of bed and in the kitchen making breakfast. She wore a matching silk robe over her black nightgown. Garret walked into the kitchen wearing only his black pants.

"Good morning," he said as he walked over to give her a kiss.

"There's some fresh brewed coffee—the mugs are above the coffee pot."

"I could get used to this," he said with a smile.

"I hope you're hungry. We worked up quite an appetite last night," Sarah grinned.

"We had quite an appetite for each other," Garret responded and they both laughed.

As they ate pancakes with fresh strawberry sauce on top, they planned to spend the whole day together.

That evening as they finished a delicious dinner at Garlock's, Garret pulled out a small box from his jacket pocket and looked into Sarah's eyes.

"I have loved you from the very first moment I laid eyes on you." He opened the small red box and presented her with a dazzling two-carat marquise-cut diamond ring.

"Will you marry me?" Sarah's eyes were wide with surprise. "I know we've only been seeing each other for a short time," he said, "but I knew from the moment I saw you I wanted to spend the rest of my life with you."

There was silence only for a moment, and then with tears of joy in her eyes, Sarah said, "*Yes!* Of course I will—I love you."

He took the ring from the box and placed it on Sarah's finger.

The two decided on a small wedding ceremony because Sarah didn't want anything elaborate. Garret tried to change her mind but she insisted on a simpler wedding.

"All I want is an intimate wedding—just a few friends and family," she said.

"If that's what you want, it's your decision," he said.

They waited nine months to be married. When their wedding day arrived, it was a lovely spring day. They were married at the Emmanuel United Methodist Church; it looked spectacular, with lush red roses displayed along the pews and two glimmering candelabras on each side of the altar.

Their reception was held at the home of a friend of Garret's, who also was a lawyer. The reception began with a cocktail hour followed by a six-course sit-down dinner.

Their hosts escorted the newly married couple and their guests onto the back patio for after-dinner drinks with live music.

"This evening is like a dream come true," Sarah told Garret as they danced under the stars.

"You are incredibly beautiful, Mrs. Stevens."

"I like hearing that," she said.

The next morning they flew to Hawaii for their honeymoon.

When they returned to Lockport, they had to decide which house they wanted to live in. They agreed to sell Garret's house and he moved into Sarah's home, which was definitely larger, with plenty of room when his daughters wanted to stay over. The property was spacious, with a yard twice the size of his and much more secluded. Also, her mother's home was there.

Life soon got back to what the couple now considered normal, and the best part of "normal" was at the end of the day, when they came home to each other.

Chapter Seventeen

1999

It had been three months since they had implemented the help for their mother; again, Lexi drove to her mother's house, again wanting it to be a surprise. When she arrived, Emma Jean didn't look any better than she had the last time Lexi had been there.

"Are you checking up on me?" her mother asked.

"Yes, you could say that. It's a good thing I'm here," Lexi said. "You don't look any healthier, Mom."

Emma Jean told her that the food from the meal delivery service was okay. "I pick at it. I do like having it brought right to my door, though. They usually won't allow food deliveries past the gate."

"That's because it's a special food delivery service and we worked it out with management," Lexi replied.

"As for the aide you hired to check on me, she never stayed the full hour. She would only stay about thirty minutes, so I fired her."

"Why didn't you tell anyone about this, Mom?" Lexi was frustrated.

"I did—I told Alice."

"I should have known; Alice never tells us anything. Mom, she knew I was coming down to visit you and she still said nothing.

When will you learn that she doesn't have your best interests at heart?"

Lexi checked with the guard at the gate, to confirm her mother's story.

"Our log book shows that when the aide first started, she logged in for the full hour, which lasted about a week. Eventually it got less and less; toward the end, she was clocking in around at eleven and clocking out about thirty to forty minutes later, three days a week. She stopped coming after a month."

Lexi called the agency and they told her that Emma Jean was verbally abusive to the aide. When the aide tried to get her out of bed to shower and brush her teeth, she became stubborn and irate.

"Your mother was billed only for the time the aide was there. You can check our records," the agency representative told her. "The situation only lasted a month."

Lexi had called Meg several months back to see if she could clean for their mother every week, but Meg's schedule was full and she was not willing to give up any of her other clients, even though Lexi offered her a raise. They had to leave things the way they were—every other Thursday. Meg mentioned to Lexi that she might be moving; she would give them plenty of notice.

"By the way," Emma Jean said to her daughter, "Meg is moving, so this will be her last week to clean."

"You're telling me this today! Did you tell Alice that the cleaning girl was leaving?"

"No, I forgot to mention it to anyone."

Lexi called her sisters and updated them on their mother's decline.

"Well, that's it," Aimee said. "She will have to sell the house and we'll find her a place up here to live." Finally, they all agreed, although it took Alice longer to approve because she thought that her mother could keep the house in Florida and rent it out.

"Mom can't manage a rental. Hell, she can't even manage her own life!" said Lexi.

"I could help her with it," Alice said.

"I don't think so," Lexi said with disdain. "I know why you want her to keep the house."

"What is that supposed to mean?"

"You know exactly what I mean. Mom reimbursed you for your airline tickets when you flew down to visit her … how many times a year?"

"I went down there to help her, Lexi!" Alice said sharply.

"That's bullshit! She told me you did a few things for her—but it was a vacation for you that she paid for," Lexi continued. "You would love to continue that ritual, wouldn't you? She flies you down, you can care for her rental house as if she *owes* you and you have your little vacation."

"We could all use the house, you know," Alice told her sister.

"No, Alice. You need to call Mom and tell her she is selling it and moving back up North," Lexi said firmly. She'd had enough of her oldest sister's dominance over their mother.

The next day Alice called her mom and told her they were finding her a place and moving her back to Lockport so that her family could take care of her. Surprisingly, Emma Jean didn't need convincing. She didn't care if she moved from her amazing retirement community because she had never wanted to live there to begin with, but Alice had picked it out. The house was too big and the community fees for the many amenities, which she didn't use, were expensive. She had been perfectly content in her "manufactured" home, but that hadn't been good enough for Alice.

The sisters began moving their mother back to Lockport. Alice and Aimee were searching for a place that would accommodate Emma Jean, while Lexi was down getting her mother's house ready to sell.

"Nothing fancy," Aimee told Alice. The two had already looked at several independent living places when a friend of a developer told Aimee about a new development under construction. It was an adult community on a lake, and forty homes were to be built. Aimee mentioned it to her sister and the two went to tour the model home.

The place was excellent, not too big—a two-bedroom, two-bath home with an open floor plan and a gas fireplace as the focal point of the living space. Sliding glass doors opened up to the large patio.

"It will be perfect for her," Aimee said, and their mother agreed.

While Emma Jean's new home was being finished, she bought tickets for her girls to come down and she paid for Lexi's gas, as well as a lobster dinner because the airline tickets cost more. They all helped their mother with her move. Aimee made sure that the dog got outside and the house stayed clean. The realtor showed the house to many potential buyers; it sold in two weeks to an active retired couple.

While Lexi was there, she cleared out everything her mother was not taking with her and called Goodwill to pick it up because the community didn't allow yard sales.

Alice flew down for the last time. She reprimanded her mother for not taking care of herself and having to move out of her magnificent home. She helped her mother finalize the sale of the house, banking documents, and her medical files. Alice also told her that she had to do something about her dog.

"I have a doggy carry-on bag for him, so he can be brought onto the plane when we fly up."

"That's not what I mean. He doesn't go to the bathroom outside, Mom. Even when someone takes him out, he won't go," Alice lied.

"Yes, he does," Emma Jean snapped back.

"If you take him up North, he will ruin the carpeting in your brand-new house. Is that what you want?"

"What are you saying? I can't take him with me?" Emma Jean was shocked. "He'll be fine. I will have a leash right by the back door for him," she said desperately.

"Are you really going to get up every few hours to take him out? You're certainly not going to let him run in the spare room to poop!" Alice said sharply. "What about during the winter? That dog hasn't had to go to the bathroom outside for years in nice weather and you think he's going to run out in the snow to pee?" Alice knew exactly what to say to control her mother.

"I don't know what you want me to do," her mother said, confused. "Do we have enough time to find him a new home?" Emma Jean said innocently with tears in her eyes. She was holding and petting her little Shih Tzu.

"Really, Mom, think about it: what sane person would take in a nine-year-old dog that has to be hand-fed and pees and poops all over the house?" Alice had no compassion.

"We will take him to the veterinarian's office tomorrow morning and have him put to sleep." When Alice turned to walk out of her mother's room, Emma Jean was in shock.

"Alice, no!"

Emma Jean couldn't believe what her daughter wanted to do. Most of that night she held Mercedes and cried; she talked to him and told him how sorry she was. The next morning, Alice woke her mother early.

"Time to get up, Mom. We have to take the dog."

"The 'dog' has a name," her mother snapped. "Can't you take Mercedes and do this for me?"

"No, he's your dog."

"Exactly. I won't be able to do this."

Alice put the leash on the dog while her mother procrastinated.

"We need to get going, Mom. I have things to get done for you today," Alice said harshly.

The veterinarian hesitated to euthanize the dog; he tried to convince Emma Jean to take the dog with her when she moved.

"Do you have any friends or relatives that can take him? He seems like a very loving dog."

"She doesn't," Alice spoke up quickly. "She can't take him with her. The place where my mother will be moving won't allow animals and I can't take him because my daughters are allergic," she lied.

Emma Jean couldn't believe what she was hearing. She stared at Alice, not speaking, only crying. Alice told the doctor about Mercedes not being housebroken and how disgusting the situation was, which embarrassed her mother. Emma Jean signed some papers and the doctor took Mercedes into the back room for the last time.

When they arrived back at the house, Emma Jean's eyes were swollen from crying all morning and she felt sick to her stomach. Everything in the house was packed and her little friend that had kept her company for nine years was gone. She took two sleeping pills and climbed into bed. Alice got her book and jumped into her mother's golf cart and headed to the pool to get some sun for a few hours.

Alice drove to the airport to pick up Blake, who had volunteered to drive his mother-in-law's car north. The car was packed, and the moving truck was loaded. Blake dropped Alice and Emma Jean off at the airport to catch their flight and he headed north.

Emma Jean moved back to western New York in the summer of 2000. She had lived in Florida over ten years and was back where she had begun her life, in the small town of Lockport.

Emma Jean was shocked when she saw her new house for the first time. It was amazing and she was glad to be "home."

"You did a wonderful job matching everything, Alice," her mother told her.

"The cabinets were upgrades and so was the tile flooring," Alice said proudly.

It had been a long, emotional week. A brand-new bedroom suite was all set up when Emma Jean arrived and she couldn't wait to climb into bed.

The following day, Lexi and Chase flew up to Lockport in the Cessna with their kids, Chloe and Lucas. Blake arrived with Emma Jean's car, the moving truck arrived and Aimee and her children,

Nathan, Skye and Brooke, came by, as did Alice, Drew, Kayla and Layla. It was the first time in many years that the entire family had been together. The family reminisced about Walter and Conrad briefly and how much they each missed them. Emma Jean couldn't wait to put their pictures up on her bedside table. Everyone helped get her moved in; they ordered Pontillo's pizza and Buffalo wings. They drank wine, took lots of pictures and caught up on each other's lives. It was an enjoyable day for everyone.

Emma Jean had an appointment with her lawyer the next day to sign the deed to the house. She had paid cash for her home, so she had been allowed to move in before signing all the documents. She said goodnight to her family.

"Stay as long as you wish," Emma Jean told them and she went to her bedroom; Alice followed her to her room.

"What time is your signing tomorrow?" Alice knew, but asked anyway.

"One o'clock. Why? Are you going with me?"

"I want to talk to you about the deed to the house. Can the four of us meet in the morning before you go?"

"What now, Alice?" Emma Jean was tired and frustrated.

"I think the three girls should have their names on the deed to the house. If something happens to you and you have to go into a nursing home, the state won't be able to take your house."

Alice always had something up her sleeve when it came to her mother's money. "The state will get the rest of your money, but they won't be able to touch the house if our names are on the deed. Of course, you will have lifetime use," she said, patting her mother's shoulder reassuringly. "I'm bringing this up now because if we try to change it later, there could be complications. What do you think?"

"Well, I don't know. I paid cash for the house, so there's no mortgage, so in that aspect it won't make a difference. We should discuss this with your sisters first. Have you said anything to them about it?"

"No, I haven't. I wanted to run it by you first and then meet with them in the morning before you go. It's good timing because Lexi is here right now."

"You're not giving them very much time to think about it. You bring this up the day before I have to sign the papers." It was late in the evening and Emma Jean didn't want to deal with this right now.

"All right, I'll call in the morning to delay the signing a day or two until the papers are changed. Lexi will be here for a week." Emma Jean sighed, thinking at least she could rest tomorrow if she didn't have to go out.

"I've already taken care of that," Alice said. "I knew you would agree because it's the right thing to do. I didn't want there to be any delay for you."

"You did *what*?" Emma Jean said loudly as she sat up in bed. "You had them changed without saying anything to me? You once again took it upon yourself to run my life!" She was furious. "What if your sisters don't want to go along with this?" By now, Emma Jean was shaking with rage. "Why do you do these things without discussing it with anyone?"

"I'm only looking out for you, Mom. I'm trying to make your life easier, doing what is best for you. I am taking care of you because that is what Dad asked me to do," Alice snapped back.

"You always have it all worked out, don't you?"

"I'll tell the others to be here around noon." Alice didn't wait for a response.

"Does it really matter what I think?" Emma Jean asked under her breath, as Alice closed the door.

The next day, the sisters arrived at their mother's house. Aimee and Lexi were wondering why Alice had summoned them to be there. She had told them nothing the night before—only to have a few hours available. Chase, Blake and Drew went golfing early and then picked up the kids and gave them a flight in the Cessna.

"So, what's up?" Aimee asked her mother as she walked into the kitchen where the others were waiting.

"Well," Alice started, "I talked to Mom about putting the house deed in our names. Then, if she were to go into a nursing home, God forbid, the state wouldn't be able to take her house. She will have life use, of course." Aimee and Lexi looked at their mother.

"Is this okay with you, Mom?" Aimee asked, surprised.

Emma Jean hesitated for a moment; she didn't seem very enthused.

"Yes, it's fine." She shrugged. "Everything goes to the three of you anyway."

Chapter Eighteen

2001

It was early in the morning and the light of dawn was just starting to break through the dark sky. Drew Dickson was dressed and ready for work. He stood in the kitchen, leaning against the counter enjoying his morning coffee. Alice walked in the kitchen, reached for a mug from the cabinet, poured herself a cup of coffee and put an English muffin in the toaster. This was their routine every morning.

"Good morning," Drew said as he took a sip of coffee. "What are your plans today?"

"I really don't have much planned. I thought I'd go to Eastern Hills and do some shopping because several of the stores are having big sales today. Why?"

"Please don't spend a lot, Alice—the credit cards are getting close to their limit," he said. He had discussed her spending habits with her several times but she never seemed to listen.

"That's why you wanted to know what I'm doing today?"

"No, it's not. If you could do me a favor and find some time this afternoon, about four o'clock, I have something important I wanted to talk to you about."

"What is it? It's not about my spending, I hope," she said in a dismissive tone.

"Just meet me here, at four," he said. "I'll be in Toronto most of the day, so I'll let you know if I get delayed." Drew was usually very punctual. "It will depend on the traffic going over the Peace Bridge in and out of Canada."

"What is this about? Can you give me a hint?"

"I'll see you at four," he said and then filled his coffee mug, grabbed his briefcase, and headed out the back door.

When Drew arrived back at the house at three-thirty, Alice was not home yet. He set the cheese and fruit platter he had bought at the grocery store on the kitchen table. He grabbed two wine glasses and one of Alice's favorite bottles of Cabernet Sauvignon from the wine rack in the family room and set them on the table as well. Alice arrived home right at four, bringing a few shopping bags in with her. The rest were in the trunk of her car and she would bring those in when Drew was not around.

"They had some great sales!" she said in excitement

Drew just shook his head. "You really have to stop with the spending."

Alice didn't have enough closet space in their large walk-in closet in their master bedroom, so she had started using the spare bedroom closet for the overflow of outfits and shoes. She took her shopping bags upstairs and threw them on the bed and then rejoined Drew at the kitchen table. She took a seat on the bench at the bay window and Drew sat next to her on one of the high-backed kitchen chairs.

"Wow, this is all set up so special! Are you trying to get me drunk with the wine?" she said jokingly. "What we need to discuss must be very important."

"It is." Drew poured them each a glass of wine. "I am up for advancement at work. It's a promotion that would allow me to oversee the inspections on buildings with asbestos. I would instruct others in the use of the company machines, and the best part is that I wouldn't have to do the concentrated cleaning myself. This is a management position and comes with a huge raise, but it means that I'd have to travel during the week." He finished with a sigh of relief because he had been trying to find the right opportunity to tell Alice about this promotion for weeks.

Drew worked at a company called Asbestos Debris Sanitation that removed asbestos that had been used as insulation in older buildings all over the United States and Canada. The government had put a stop to its use after it was found that inhalation of asbestos fibers caused serious illnesses, including malignant lung cancer and mesothelioma.

Drew's job was very time consuming and demanding, and he used great caution not to allow the asbestos fibers to become airborne. His company also recycled this hazardous material by transforming it into harmless silicate glass. Drew's territory was the western New York area and Canada, and the company wanted his expertise in training others all over the country.

"Drew, you haven't taken this promotion yet, have you?"

"No, I'm discussing it with you first, of course, but I have to make a decision soon." Drew had a few beads of sweat on his forehead; he wanted this advancement desperately. He was not looking forward to the traveling but the raise would come in handy. He wasn't sure how to read his wife's reaction.

Alice hesitated a moment and then she began. "I can't be in this big house by myself all week. You know that I hate being home alone, especially at night," she said. "Kayla and Layla can't leave Rochester during the week to stay with me when you're gone."

Kayla and Layla had been born prematurely; Kayla was born two minutes before her sister. Alice and Drew had had many problems conceiving a child and, just before they gave up on having children, Alice discovered that she was pregnant. The doctor had told them that she was carrying twins, and he also told them that twins usually ran in certain families.

"I understand your reservations," Drew said. "That's why I wanted to sit and discuss it with you, to go over all our options. This position means a lot to me—it's what I've wanted and worked for, for many years."

"I know it's a better job and that we could use the money, but what will I do all week without you?"

"Well, maybe a part-time job during the week would help fill some of your time," Drew suggested. "I also would like for us to install a security system for the house."

Alice just shrugged. "I've been searching for part-time employment," she lied, "but I haven't found a job out there that agrees with me." She hadn't looked for a job in many years.

After their marriage, Alice had held a secretarial position at a law firm for several years, until the twins came along.

When the girls were born, she had returned to work, and she and Drew hired a nanny to care for the girls during the week. A year later, though, Alice no longer wanted to leave her baby girls every day and decided to be a stay-at-home mom. She didn't discuss this with her husband until after she had put in her two-week notice.

Alice took her daughters to the park near their house most days, to play on the swings and slides. In wintertime, she took them sledding. Kayla and Layla were very well dressed, wearing the cutest matching dresses, adorable sweaters, coats and boots. They never wore the same outfit twice. Alice's spending addiction started during those early years.

Several years after the girls started school, Alice got bored during the day and took a part-time job at a prestigious realtor's office in town. They hired her to work the front office, greeting potential clients, typing, handling the company mailing, answering the telephones and taking messages for all fifteen selling agents in the office.

Alice had been at the firm a number of years, when her job took a turn for the worse. Three of Alice's co-workers were caught giving added benefits to special clients, additional discounts in sales and pocketing the money. The realtors did the discounting and Alice processed the paperwork; she had questioned office procedure but was told that it was fine doing it that way.

The company secretly hired an investigator to go over the files. All those involved were reprimanded. The owner of the company could have brought criminal charges against them for theft of the money that he had lost, but they all agreed to pay it back. They were all suspended and a letter was placed in their files.

"All I did was process the paperwork they gave me, sir. I questioned their procedure," Alice had said, trying to plead her case to the owner of the company, but to no avail.

"If you thought to question the paperwork, you should have come to me and asked me," he told her.

Alice put in her resignation a month after she returned from her two-week suspension. She did not tell Drew that she had quit until her last day.

"I don't need that crap. People at work look at me like I'm a criminal," she told him. "I was told to do it that way, for God's sake. It's so unfair."

Alice never told her husband that the realtors involved were giving her cash under the table for her "assistance." Drew was surprised when his wife had to contribute and pay back a percentage of the money lost.

"Why are they making you pay money back?" he asked. "It was the three realtors who benefited and stole the money."

"I'll just pay it. I don't want the company pressing charges against me."

"But we can fight this," Drew said.

"I just want to put this all behind me, Drew. Let it go." She had not worked since.

Now, the two of them sat at their kitchen table for hours discussing their options. They had finished one bottle of wine and were on their second.

"I hate being alone at night without you!" she kept telling Drew. The wine was making her tipsy, so she finally had the nerve to bring up a subject that she had wanted to discuss with him for some time. She hesitated for a moment; her mind was going a mile a minute because this was her chance—finally, the opportunity that she had been waiting for fell right in her lap.

"I have a solution," she said as she took a deep breath. "My mother has that terrific, new house. It's only two years old and everything in that house I picked out because she was in Florida. When I called to ask her about the cabinets or the flooring, she would tell me 'Whatever you think, Alice,' so I chose what I liked. The house is totally paid for, there is no mortgage, and I have already convinced my mother to put all three of her daughters' names on the deed. Technically, it's ours."

Confused, Drew asked, "Where are you going with this?"

"What if we sell our house and move in with my mother?"

Drew, who was in the middle of taking a sip of wine, choked. "You want to do what?"

Alice put up her hand and said, "Hear me out. I've thought about this for a while. First, we would have no mortgage to pay. We will split all the bills with my mother and pay only half the property taxes. We'll be able to save thousands," she told him with a sparkle in her eye.

"It will be perfect, especially if you're planning on being gone a lot. That way I won't be alone. When you get home after a long week, you won't have to worry about spending the weekend doing yard work. It will have already been done because the association takes care of all that."

Alice had made up her mind that she wanted this particular house the day that they had started building it. Drew was speechless, so Alice continued.

"She has a cleaning lady that comes in every other week. We can pitch in for that, plus we can split the cost of all the food we buy."

Drew was still in shock. His wife had every detail worked out down to how much money they would save a month. Drew knew that she must have thought about this for quite some time—definitely before he was up for his promotion.

"We can save thousands, Drew," she said again.

The house they lived in was a beautiful two-story home on Willow Street, one of the most sought-after residential streets in Lockport because of its Old World charm. Most of the homes there were over a hundred years old; theirs was one of only two original brick streets left in Lockport that had not been paved over. A house on Willow Street didn't stay on the market long if the price was right, so once they made up their mind to sell, it would go quickly.

This was where they had lived for over twenty years, and their daughters had been born and raised there. How could Alice give it up so easily? Drew wasn't ready to downsize yet, especially moving in with his mother-in-law.

"No!" Drew said. "I don't want to do that."

"What do you mean 'no'? You haven't even thought about it!"

"I don't have to think about it. I'm not selling our home and moving in with your mother."

"Then forget about your promotion at work because I'm not going to stay here by myself all week."

"What did you just say? Are you serious?"

"You won't even think about it—how perfect the situation would be."

"I don't want to move. This is our home, our retirement," Drew said, slamming his hand down on the table. "We've talked about this and agreed that, when we're finally ready to retire, we will sell the house and with the money we make we will buy a place somewhere warm.

"I have at least fifteen years left before I retire, and I'm not spending it living with your mother. I just told you about my promotion today; I don't even have the job yet. Why don't we see if I get the new job before we think about making a drastic move?"

"Listen to me," Alice interrupted. "We'll be able to take the money from the sale of the house and invest it for our retirement.

Who knows what the housing market will be like in ten or fifteen years when we want to sell? If we sell it now, we won't have all the continued expenses of owning this money pit. We'll be able to put money away and save."

"I am sure that you can convince your mother of this whole situation, but it's not right!"

"Living there I can help care for her," Alice said. "Isn't that what we all wanted for her in the first place? That's why we had her move back up here—to make the end of her life comfortable. Besides, the way she lives, she won't be around much longer."

"Your mother will last forever; both her parents were in their nineties when they died."

"Listen to what I'm saying, Drew. We can live there during the summer and have a winter home in Florida—that's how much money we will save," Alice reiterated. "My mother lies in bed all day; she doesn't use the rest of the house. I will make it into our home."

Drew couldn't believe that they were having this conversation. When this day had started, all he wanted was to talk to Alice about his promotion. Now they were talking about selling their home and moving in with her mother.

"I'm not going to do it," Drew said sternly. This was a huge decision and he was the one who worked to pay the bills. "I like this house, Alice. I've worked hard to make it a home and I've worked hard for this promotion. I shouldn't have to compromise by selling our home and moving in with your mother because you're afraid to be alone a few nights during the week. It's an unreasonable request. We will have plenty of money when we retire, if you don't spend it all."

"I knew you would bring up my spending," she snapped back.

"What bothers me, Alice, is that you have had this planned for quite some time—from the day they started building the house. It's your mother's home, for Christ's sake. Just let her live her life for once."

"What the hell is that supposed to mean?"

"It means that you're out of control over this whole house situation. If you want to live there, then go ahead," he told her.

Alice jumped up from the table. "Maybe I'll just do that!" she yelled. She walked out of the kitchen and headed upstairs. *He won't even consider the move, but it would be an ideal situation*, she thought to herself as she put away her new clothes.

She was determined to change his mind.

Two weeks later, Drew was awarded his promotion and started two months of training. Neither Alice nor Drew talked about the move again, but Alice was just waiting until she was ready. Drew was hoping that the whole moving situation was over. Besides, he had a lot going on the next year and he didn't need the stress.

First things first, Alice thought. She started by "convincing" her mother to upgrade the basement in her house.

"It will bring the value of the home up immensely," she told her family. "When Lexi, Chase and their kids fly up to visit, they will have plenty of room to stay comfortably." Alice got her mother involved in designing the layout and actually got her excited about it. "Why don't you call Lexi and tell her what you're doing for her?" Alice said and Emma Jean called her daughter in Florida right away.

Construction was under way; Alice convinced her mother that the basement should have a large bedroom with a walk-in closet, a full bath, and a family living area with a big-screen TV hooked up to cable. A separate room was made into a huge office, with a wall-to-wall desk and shelving. Emma Jean paid over twenty thousand dollars for the cost of the basement, not including the furniture. While construction was going on, Alice also "persuaded" her mother to have the landscaping professionally done.

"You know, Mom, when you drive into this amazing neighborhood, all your neighbors have a good-looking, landscaped yard and then there's yours, which looks so dull." She hoped this would embarrass her mom and it worked. "You pay to have them tend it each week, so you might as well have something for them to take care of."

Six thousand dollars later, a quaint, decorative, hand-laid stone patio was in place, adorned with colorful perennials. Several truckloads of dirt were brought in to make islands in the backyard, and unique plants and pine trees were added. Along each side of the house were exotic plants, all picked out by Emma Jean—under Alice's supervision.

"You should get an awning so that the rain and snow don't ruin the patio furniture that you brought up from Florida," Alice told her mother. "You want to be able to sit out there and enjoy your picturesque landscaped yard without the sun bothering you, don't you?"

"What's going on, Alice? First the basement, then the landscaping and, if that wasn't enough, now an awning?" Emma Jean asked.

"What are you talking about?" Alice answered.

"You're getting pretty good at spending my money," her mother said. "I'm not going to sit outside, so it isn't being put up for my benefit."

"I'm doing this for you."

"I'm so tired of you telling me that. I'm not an idiot, Alice. Everything you do has a motive behind it, and I've learned that the hard way throughout the years."

"I was helping you out so that your daughter and her family had a comfortable place to stay when they come to visit. I'm trying to keep this family together as best I can," Alice said.

"Things have been fine with our family—it's you who adds the stress and pressure on everyone."

"How dare you say that to me!" Alice started crying, pretending her feelings were hurt. She left her mother's house—with the credit card her mother had given her to order the awning.

Stage one of my plan is accomplished, she thought. The crying stopped immediately and an overconfident grin appeared in its place.

Chapter Nineteen

It was a snowy morning in late February and Alice couldn't sleep. All the upgrades to her mother's house were complete and a few months had passed. Alice was ready to convince her mother to agree to their moving in. Once Drew saw the changes to his mother-in-law's house, he would agree to the move, Alice thought. She used her key to get in the front door. She and her sisters had each received a key to the house.

"Hi, Mom!" Alice said loudly as she shut and locked the door behind her.

"Is that you, Alice?" Emma Jean asked from her bedroom.

"Yes, Mom. Who were you expecting?" Alice rolled her eyes.

"Actually, Blake is due to stop by and pick up my grocery list," Emma Jean said as Alice entered her room. "Sometimes Brooke stops by on her way home from school."

Brooke was the seventeen-year-old daughter of Aimee and Blake. She had always been very mature for her age and did very well in school in the honors program.

"Can I talk to you about something?" Alice asked.

"Of course, sit here on the bed." Emma Jean sat up and straightened out her comforter.

"Why don't we talk in the kitchen?" Alice replied. "I'll make you something to eat." It was mid-afternoon and she knew that her mother probably had not eaten yet.

"Okay, give me a few minutes to freshen up."

As Alice made her way to the kitchen, she sauntered over to the thermostat and turned up the heat; she then headed to the fireplace and flipped a switch that turned on the gas flame. She stood there a moment and let the flame warm her.

"I have some lasagna leftovers in the refrigerator that you can heat up for me," Emma Jean called from her bedroom. "Aimee brought the lasagna by from Shenanigans yesterday—it was made with homemade pasta noodles. Just pop it in the microwave for a few minutes."

"Yes, Mom, I know how to do it."

When Emma Jean walked out into the kitchen, using a cane to steady her, the lasagna was ready and waiting.

"Do you want a glass of milk with that?" Alice asked.

"Sure," Emma Jean responded suspiciously. Her daughter's behavior was out of character. Emma Jean was a little apprehensive about their "talk" because she sensed that her daughter had something up her sleeve again.

"As you know, we all decided that you needed to move back to Lockport so that we could take care of you, to make sure you're eating properly and to get you to your appointments on time," Alice said. "Drew and I think that you could use more assistance. We're worried about you—we all are."

"I thought I'd been doing fine; I've been back for two years." Emma Jean took a big bite of her lasagna and continued, "I drive myself to my appointments, most of the time, and you come by to make sure that everything is okay." She took another bite.

"Blake gets my groceries every week and sometimes, if I have to—not on a day like today, of course—I'll go out and get what I need myself. I certainly eat well, as you can see. Aimee brings me food, and I meet Marla for lunch once a month. As a matter of fact, we went to lunch a few days ago. I've gained fifteen pounds since I've been back. What's the problem?"

"You have been doing well, Mom, really you have, but Drew and I thought we could make things much easier for you."

"How?" Emma Jean did not like where this was going.

"We would like to move in with you. We want to take care of you, so you don't have to worry about anything. Even better, we'll save you a lot of money. We would split all your expenses with you—you would pay half your property taxes, half the electric, groceries, cable, everything." Alice spat out a bunch of numbers, which only confused Emma Jean.

"I do fine financially," Emma Jean said quickly. "I don't have any trouble paying my bills."

Alice pretended that she didn't hear her mother's comment and kept talking.

"I will buy your groceries so you won't have to burden Blake with that anymore."

"I don't think he feels burdened by it, Alice."

"He would never complain to you directly, Mom," Alice lied, making it sound as if Blake did complain.

"Why, what does he say to you?"

Alice ignored her question again. "I'll take you to the doctor and to your hair appointments because I know that you're not very comfortable driving, especially on days like today. Our winters have been pretty bad since you've been back. You could even sell your car because you wouldn't need it."

"The car is paid for," Emma Jean said in almost a whisper.

"Drew will be here to do all your maintenance around the house." Alice didn't want to tell her mother that Drew wouldn't be in town during the week. Her mom liked having him around, and if she knew that he wasn't going to be there, she might not agree.

"He does most of my maintenance anyway," Emma Jean commented.

"I cook dinner every night, and Aimee won't have to go out of her way to get food to you. She and Blake are very busy with the restaurant."

"Alice, I don't think they consider it going out of their way. I'm not a burden and that's how you're making me feel. They visit with me and we enjoy our time together," Emma Jean said firmly.

"That's not what I meant." This wasn't going as well as Alice had expected.

"What are you going to do with your house? You have a beautiful home."

"We are selling it," Alice said as if the decision had already been made.

"You *will* be selling it," Emma Jean corrected her.

"Yes, it won't be hard to sell once it goes on the market."

What scared Emma Jean the most about the possibility of their living with her was that they would make her get up every day. She liked her rest and her solitude.

"If you move in, are you going to make me get up if I don't have an appointment or have to go anywhere? I like to lie in bed and you have a big problem with that."

"The only time you'd have to get up is to eat dinner with us at the kitchen table—how's that?" Alice would say anything to get her mother to say yes. "That's exactly what I'm talking about, Mom. You won't have to get up, and I will do everything for you—your laundry and your banking and pick up your medications at the drug store—everything."

"Are you going to make me get rid of my cat?" Emma Jean spoke with a bit of disdain because of what had happened to her dog Mercedes.

Several months after she had moved back to Lockport, her friend Marla had given her the cat after she'd told her friend about Mercedes being euthanized. Marla was appalled because she was an animal lover and couldn't comprehend that there was no other alternative.

When one of her cats had kittens, she decided to give one of them to Emma Jean. She thought her friend could use the company and a cat was easier to care for than a dog. Emma Jean loved the little gray kitten and had named it Flagler.

"I don't believe you just said that!" Alice pretended that her mother's comment had hurt her feelings. "I felt horrible about Mercedes."

"I like having my own space, Alice. I am able to do what I want, when I want. I have been on my own for many years and I like it that way."

"To be very honest, I'm usually not around very much," Alice told her. "I visit with Kayla and Layla in Rochester, and I'm usually busy running errands most of the day, and I'll be adding yours to my list."

"I need to think about it for a few days."

"Sure, of course, just do me a favor and don't mention this to anyone right now," Alice asked. "It's no one else's business but ours."

"Of course I won't say anything. I never do," Emma Jean said. "I'm finished with my lunch; I've lost my appetite." She stood from her chair to take her plate over to the sink.

"I'll take care of that for you." Alice took the plate, rinsed it off and put it in the dishwasher.

"I will call you," Emma Jean told her as she went back into her bedroom.

"Okay, let me know soon, Mom," Alice said as she left her mother's house with a smile on her face. "Stage two accomplished," she said softly.

Emma Jean was angry; she didn't want anyone living with her—she liked things just the way they were. What was it about Alice, she thought, that she was always interfering in her life!

It had been several days since Alice had talked to her mother. *If she doesn't call soon, I'm going over there*, she thought.

She stopped by Tops grocery store to pick up a few items, and her mind was elsewhere as she turned the corner and almost bumped into Aimee. They both were surprised.

"Well, hello," Alice said quickly. "I haven't seen you in a while."

"We've been busy; we have a big party at the restaurant tonight, so I needed to get a few things for it."

"It sounds like things are going well at Shenanigans. Drew and I were thinking about stopping by for dinner Friday night."

"Good, you haven't been there in a while," Aimee said, smiling. "Skye has put a few new items on the menu."

"Sounds good. We'll see you Friday." Telling her sisters was going to be the hardest part of her arrangement with her mother.

Emma Jean lay in her bed wondering what she was getting herself into if she allowed Alice and her husband to move in. She didn't want things to change. Alice was the one who was never satisfied with the way her mother was living. Emma Jean loved her new place in Lockport and moving back was working out great. She needed help during the winter months, but the whole family pitched in and they weren't burdened by it, as Alice tried to make her believe.

After two years, Alice and Drew have to move in to help care for me and save me money? Bullshit, Emma Jean thought to herself. Alice wanted to move in for her own benefit, to save herself money.

"Oh, my God!" Emma Jean said aloud. "That's why she had me upgrade the basement."

The thought of it made her furious. It was a good time to call her daughter and tell her she was not moving in. As she picked up the phone, Alice was walking through the front door.

"I was just going to call you." Emma Jean would have preferred talking to Alice over the phone instead of in person but she continued, "I don't think that you moving in here is a good idea. I like things just the way they are, and I like living alone."

"We already have an offer on our house, Mom. Now what are we supposed to do?" Alice lied.

"You should have waited for my decision," Emma Jean told her.

"I can't believe you don't see that this will be a good thing for you," Alice said angrily.

"It won't hurt you either, will it?" Emma Jean snapped back. "I figured it out, Alice. Here we are six months after all the improvements to the house and you want to move in."

"What are you talking about?" Alice said with a confused look on her face.

Emma Jean wasn't buying her innocent act. "By applying the rules of logic, my dear, I understand *now* why it was imperative to get the basement finished. Did you honestly think that I wouldn't figure it out? Do you think that your sisters won't figure it out?"

Alice started crying. "I can't believe you think I could be so conniving. Do you honestly believe I could be that devious?"

"Do you really want me to answer that?"

"All I've ever tried to do is to take care of you. I've tried to make you comfortable and make things better for you because that's what Dad asked me to do, and you have the audacity to think that I am devious and calculating." She kept crying.

"You are never happy with the way I'm living."

"In a few years, Mom, you're going to need a lot more help. Drew and I will be here, so we can do that for you." Alice wiped her tears. "I'm trying to look ahead for your future and what would be best for you because that's what I was told to do."

"I'm a big girl, Alice. I can take care of myself," her mother told her.

As the discussion grew more heated, both of them were crying. Alice showed her stamina and dominance as usual, but for the first time she couldn't convince her mother to do what she wanted her to do.

"I like my life right now for the first time in many years. I don't want things to change. If I need help in a few years, we can discuss it then," Emma Jean declared.

"It will be to your advantage if we do it now! Can't you see that?"

"No, Alice, I can't see that. I do just fine."

"Let me at least show you what expenses you can save," Alice pleaded.

"I said *no*! You need to go now. I'm not changing my mind this time."

Alice left her mother's house angry, unable to collect her thoughts. *I will wear her down and change her mind*, she said to herself.

A week after talking to her mother, Alice hired a realtor. She wanted information on selling their home on Willow Street. The realtor told her that she should get the house ready to sell: "You should paint a few of the rooms, depersonalize and declutter the house." Alice did it all while Drew was away and he never noticed when he came home.

He had been very busy the last year, traveling more than he'd anticipated. He was focused on his new job and had no idea what Alice had been up to. When he was home on weekends, he made sure that he and Alice spent their time together. When he inquired about her week, she purposely withheld information. They stopped by Emma Jean's house one Saturday afternoon and he looked around as they got out of the car.

"Your mother had the landscaping done," Drew commented.

"Yes … she finally decided to do something with her boring yard," Alice laughed.

"It looks good."

Alice kept him from seeing the basement while they were visiting. She wasn't ready to show him that project just yet.

Drew was out of town when Alice received an offer on their house. She told her realtor she would discuss it with her husband when he got home. Alice had never put a "for sale" sign on their front lawn because it was a small town and she couldn't risk her husband or her sisters finding out just yet. She still had to convince her husband and her mother what an ideal situation this would be for all of them.

Drew was at Sam's Barber Shop one Saturday morning for a haircut. While Sam was trimming Drew's hair, he brought up the sale of his house.

"I know the couple that put the offer in on your house," Sam told him. "I didn't know you were selling. Where you moving to?"

"I don't know what you're talking about. I think you've got me mixed up with somebody else, Sam," Drew laughed.

"I'm sure it's your house on Willow Street." Sam leaned in and said in a lower voice, "Let me just say, you got a damn good price for it."

Drew turned around in the chair so he could see Sam's face. "What the hell are you talking about? My house isn't up for sale!"

The barber just looked at him and shrugged. Drew got a terrible feeling in the pit of his stomach. He stood from the chair, pulled off the cape that was wrapped around him and took some money from his pocket and handed it to Sam. "I've got to go," Drew said quickly.

"But I'm not done with your hair," Sam said as Drew left the shop.

When Drew arrived home, Alice was cleaning out the refrigerator. He looked around the kitchen and realized that it had been painted and a lot of the possessions she had collected over the years were missing.

"What have you done?" he said, shaking his head.

Alice stood and looked at him for a moment and then said, "What do you mean?" Drew just stared at her, his eyes hard. "How did you find out?" she asked.

"You sold our house?" he said in disbelief. "Without my knowledge?"

"I wanted it to be a surprise. It's an offer, of course. I can't sell it without your approval." Alice was trying to sound excited and upbeat but she could tell that Drew was fuming.

"I can't fucking believe this! I told you that I didn't want to sell the house *OR* move in with your mother."

"Drew, just hear me out for a moment. The last several months my mother has been upgrading her house. You saw the landscaping? Well, she has also remodeled the entire basement. It has a large bedroom and bath, a walk-in closet and a family living area." Alice wanted to save the best for last: "And, Drew, there is a huge office with wall-to-wall desks and shelving—it's spectacular!"

"How the hell did I *not* know about this?"

"You've been very busy," Alice said. "I didn't want to bother you with it, so I thought I would surprise you when the time was right."

"Bother me? You didn't have the decency to tell me what was going on. I think I could have handled your mother redoing her basement. You outright lied to me."

"I didn't lie. I wanted to surprise you."

"Do your sisters know?"

"They think my mother redid the basement so that Lexi's family would have a comfortable place to stay when they come up to visit."

"Their names are on the deed to the house," Drew said. "How is that supposed to work?"

"We all own a third of the house. If something happens to my mother, we can buy their shares at a reasonable price."

"So nobody knows about what we talked about last year. Does your mother know?"

"Yes, and she's still thinking about it, but I believe she will agree," Alice said smoothly. "My sisters don't need to know about us moving in—at least not until our house sells, and then there will be nothing they can do anyway."

"So let me get this straight," Drew continued. "In the last year you convinced your mother to renovate the basement and the landscaping so that, when we move in, it will all be done."

"Yes, and wait until you see the office I designed for you."

"Do you hear yourself? It's dishonest." He was almost shouting, "I'm curious: how much did your mother spend on all of these upgrades?"

"It was about twenty-five thousand for the basement and six thousand for the landscaping, plus a little more for the awning on the back patio."

"Dear God, Alice!"

"She has my father's money just sitting in the bank; she doesn't spend it."

"It's *her* money, Alice! Leave her alone and let her do what she wants with it. Same thing with her house—just let her live there in peace."

"I'm doing this so that we can save money for our future."

"Alice, I don't think you get the big picture. You've manipulated your mother into refurbishing her home and you've lied to me and your sisters for the past year about it! Then you went behind my back while trying to sell our home." Drew's voice was cold now. "I'm glad you needed my signature to sell the house. I wouldn't put it past you to forge it."

"Drew, you think I would do something like that?"

"At this point, I think you are capable of anything," he said harshly. "I said *no* to selling the house. I thought it was understood and that was the end of it."

"Well, you assumed the situation was over, so I let you assume it," Alice replied. "I was hoping that you would change your mind."

"Are you not happy, Alice? Do I not give you everything you want?" Drew continued, "I've worked my ass off to provide for you and the girls, and you have the audacity to go behind my back and practically sell our house out from under me after I specifically told you that I didn't want to live with your mother."

"I wish you could see what a blessing this would be for us. With the money we saved we would be able to buy a summer house on Lake Ontario or maybe a place in Florida during the winter."

"Alice, all these years that we've been together I have sat back and watched as you've manipulated me, your mother and your sisters into getting whatever you've wanted. I'm sure that I don't know half of what you've done throughout the years because you're good at keeping secrets. I will always question what you tell me and wonder whether it's the truth. You have killed my trust in you and I can't stand by and watch any longer. You have gone too far this time." Drew had tears in his eyes.

"What are you saying?" Alice asked in surprise. "You don't mean it! We've been together almost thirty years, and you can't end our love just like that!"

"You're right, I can't. I'm going to have a difficult time dealing with this. I don't know who you are anymore, Alice. You've told so many lies that I don't think that you know what the truth is any longer."

"Everything I've done through the years has been for you and the girls! You can't see that?"

"I married you for your love and generosity toward others, but since your father's death I've watched you change. Your dad left your mother money and you were determined to spend it or get your hands on it one way or another."

"That is not true! How can you say that?"

"It is true," Drew told her. "Now I finally see it because I'm collateral damage and you don't think you've done anything wrong."

"What have I done wrong? You tell me!"

"My point exactly," Drew said as he left the kitchen and went upstairs to pack a bag.

"Where are you going?" Alice followed him.

"I can't stay here tonight."

"You're good at that—running out and leaving me here by myself, only thinking about yourself."

"That's right, Alice. I haven't worked for thirty years supporting you and the girls while you did nothing but spend the money."

Drew grabbed his overnight bag and started down the stairs. Alice grabbed his arm and, as he pulled away from her, he lost his footing and almost fell. They both looked at each with surprise. Drew continued down the stairs as Alice sat on the top step and cried.

"You never loved me if you can leave me like this!" she yelled.

Drew went to his mother's house for a few days. While he was staying there he called his good friend, who was a divorce attorney.

Chapter Twenty

Alice's fixation with her mother's house became a reality, although it cost her her marriage. She would never understand why Drew took such a stand and wouldn't consider selling their home. He had been so obstinate and stubborn; it made her angry that he wouldn't trust her. She deluded herself into believing she'd done all this for him and for the money they could have saved.

The money she received in the divorce would be invested and she would save living with her mother and find her own summer cottage on the lake for her and her girls. She'd show him!

Drew would never understand his wife's obsession. He had tried to talk her out of it, but she stood her ground, as did he, and she ended up choosing the house over their life together. He was bitter and angry over the whole situation. He explained to his daughters the reasons for the divorce, and they understood. The girls also had tried talking to their mother about her actions, but to no avail.

Emma Jean knew nothing except what Alice had told her about the divorce. It seemed hard that after all the years Alice and Drew had been married, he had just left her like he did! Alice used her depression and misery to the fullest extent—crying on her mother's shoulder until she wore Emma Jean down.

"I have nowhere to go, Mom," she cried. "Kayla and Layla offered, but they don't have the room." The fact was, she had never even considered living with them. "Drew wants me packed up and moved out in the next two weeks."

"You can stay here until you get on your feet and find yourself a place to live," Emma Jean finally said.

Lexi flew up from Florida, and she and Aimee went to the house to discuss the situation.

"Mom, can't you see that Alice is using you once again? You didn't want her living there in the first place. Why do you think she and Drew got divorced? She was obsessed with moving in and now you're allowing it," Aimee said.

"Alice got plenty of money from her divorce, Mom. She can afford her own place to live," Lexi explained.

"How can the two of you be so cruel? Your sister is going through a tough time. She is alone because her husband of thirty years kicked her out and kept their house."

"I'm sure that's what Alice told you!" Lexi said.

"She's moving in until she can get on her feet," Emma Jean said. "Now let it go!"

"Mark my words," Aimee said, "she will never leave."

"She is not taking my house. I'm not going anywhere for a long, long time."

"You're in for a rude awakening, Mom."

The two left their mother's house and then decided to talk to Alice about her living arrangement. When they arrived at their sister's house on Willow Street, she was packing.

"Alice, we know Mom didn't want you and Drew moving in with her when you first approached her with the idea," Aimee said, keeping her voice calm. "We know the whole story. Mom paid tens of thousands to have the basement totally refurbished, she paid to have the landscaping done, plus God only knows what else—all because of your persuasion. And then—surprise!—just eight months later, you and your husband wanted to move in and Mom said no."

"It's none of your business what my husband and I were planning on doing," Alice told them.

"Finally, Drew woke up and saw your manipulation," Lexi said.

"Think what you want, you bitches." Alice's voice was harsh.

"There's the real Alice we know! You've had this planned for quite some time, haven't you? I knew there was more going on when Mom had the basement done! Has she even been down there to see her magnificent office that was built just for her?" Lexi asked.

"Screw you! The decision has been made: I'm moving in and there's nothing you can do about it."

"If only Mom could see how distraught you are right now," Aimee commented.

"Did you play on her sympathy to get her to agree to this move?" Lexi asked. "You're grossly taking advantage of her."

"Taking advantage!" Alice shot back. "I have *never* taken advantage of our mother. How dare you suggest that!"

"Oh, please, you've been using Mom for years. You picked out her spectacular house in Florida, the house she didn't want. Then you made her feel as if she owed you so that she'd reimburse you for your airline tickets when you flew down to 'take care' of her." Alice just stared at her sister. "I know a lot more than you think I do, Alice," Lexi told her.

"What? Why didn't I know about this?" Aimee asked Lexi.

"Because it was over and I didn't think Alice would use our mother like that anymore—but here we are again."

"Explain something to me, Alice. What happens if Mom dies or goes into a nursing home and you're living in her house with our names on the deed?" Aimee asked.

"I'm going through the worst time of my life and Mom is helping me out, and that's all the two of you can think about?" Alice asked in a demeaning tone.

"What will happen, Alice?" Lexi demanded.

"The house will be sold and we split the money, or I'll buy it from you at a reasonable price. Will that satisfy you both?"

"No, I'm not satisfied. I don't agree with this." Lexi raised her voice. "I think you should have discussed this with all of us before you went ahead with your plan to move in."

"It's none of your business what Mom and I decide to do with our lives." Alice turned away as if the conversation was over.

"It is when it involves all of us," Aimee said. "You've shown us how easily you can manipulate Mom and now you're moving in with her? What do you expect us to think?"

"I don't care what you think. There really isn't much more to discuss because the decision has been made. You both may leave now. I have some packing to do before Drew gets home."

Alice took a deep breath after they had left. *Okay, that's over*, she thought.

When Emma Jean had first moved back to Lockport, her outlook on life had changed. These had become the most enjoyable years she had had in a long time. At the age of sixty-nine, she was getting out to meet her friend Marla for lunch once a month, and she cooked for herself, even inviting her family for big Sunday dinners periodically. She was even becoming neighborly. She made and delivered a casserole conveying her sympathy to a neighbor who had just lost her husband of forty-nine years. Emma Jean's family stopped by occasionally, spending more time with her. Aimee had been the most pleased with her mother's progress in those first two years.

Everything changed after Alice moved in. She lost her enthusiasm for doing things herself, and she stayed in her room, lying in bed or doing crossword puzzles and watching old movies. She wouldn't leave the house to go anywhere.

She had not changed the household bills out of her name, because that was how Alice wanted it.

"I decided the best way to pay the bills every month would be for you to pay the full amount of each bill from your checking account—the ones that that are in your name—so that we each don't have to send a check," Alice said. "I pay the cable since it's in my name, and I'll buy the groceries. At the end of the month, we will add up the monthly bills paid by each and split the difference. Does that sound fair?"

"I guess so," Emma Jean said, although she was confused. As it worked out, Emma Jean wrote her daughter a check every month for the difference, usually three to four hundred dollars. Emma Jean questioned this for quite a few months, but Alice never showed her any grocery receipts.

"How much are you spending on groceries, Alice? It would have to be at least six hundred dollars a month." Emma Jean asked her over and over to "please" keep the grocery receipts for the month, but Alice always "forgot." After many months of explanations and arguing, Emma Jean got tired of the runaround, so she paid what she was told.

That's the way things went: Alice told her what to do, how to do it and how much money to give her at the end of the month. Emma Jean tried defending herself every day and it was wearing her down. She didn't have much more stamina left.

Her furniture and most of her belongings that she had brought up with her from Florida were sold in a garage sale. With the money Alice made selling her mother's items, she bought new furniture for the family room. Eventually, everything in Emma Jean's house was either sold or given to Goodwill. If there was something Emma Jean wanted to keep, it was put in her bedroom. Alice's possessions, such as table, chairs, lamps, pictures and her piano, were brought into the house, replacing everything of her mother's.

Upgrades were being done all around the house as well. The walls were painted, light fixtures replaced and new blinds and curtains were changed to match the new furniture. Alice added a glass storm door to the front entrance, and, while doing so, she had all the locks to the doors changed.

Alice reminded her mother that she had to split the cost of the upgrades. "We agreed to split all the house expenses. I'll let you know how much you owe me."

Emma Jean had no input on any decisions that were made. She never knew if Alice was home or if she went out.

One afternoon Emma Jean decided to fix herself something to eat. Alice walked into the kitchen and reprimanded her.

"I'm making dinner in a few hours, Mom. Why are you eating now? You know we always eat at six o'clock."

"I wasn't sure; you weren't here last night and didn't make dinner. I never know where you are and I was hungry."

Alice took her mother's plate of food and dumped it down the garbage disposal. "We will eat at six."

Emma Jean stood up gingerly and went into her bedroom, feeling like an intruder in her own home.

Two girls from the Clean-N-Pristine maid service had been cleaning for Emma Jean every other Friday since she'd moved back to Lockport. She was very pleased with the service they provided; they were reliable and quite reasonable for the amount of cleaning they did. Then Alice decided that she wanted them to clean once a week.

"We don't need the house cleaned every week," Emma Jean said.

"You're not the one who has to dust and vacuum because of all the cat hair," Alice replied coolly. "Yes, the cleaning price will double but you won't have to pay any more money because we're splitting the cost."

"You also told me when you moved in I would be saving money, but I haven't saved a dime since you've been here."

"Maybe not right now, but eventually you will see some savings. I'm calling the cleaning company tomorrow, so I need their information."

Emma Jean gave her the phone number. Alice investigated the cleaning service's qualifications on the Internet as a precaution; she was suspicious of everyone. She called the Clean-N-Pristine office and made an appointment with Sarah Stevens to come out to their house for an updated consultation. It had been Aimee who originally had hired Sarah's cleaning service for her mother right after Emma Jean moved back to Lockport.

When Sarah arrived at Emma Jean's house, Alice introduced herself to Sarah at the front door and escorted her into the kitchen. Emma Jean stayed in her room.

"You've been cleaning for my mother for a few years. You charge her seventy-five dollars every other week," Alice said. "We would like to change the schedule and have you clean every week."

"I looked over your mother's contract before I arrived," Sarah told her. "When I was here last, I dealt with your sister, Aimee, on behalf of your mother. I gave Aimee a price quote of seventy-five dollars. Since that time, I understand the basement has been renovated. My team mentioned the upgrade and I let it go at the time, but if my girls come in every week, I'm going to have to raise the price."

"How much?" Alice asked with a bit of dismay.

"Before I make that decision, may I see the basement?"

"Of course, it's this way." She led the way to the basement.

Sarah took notes in her head as she looked around: the stairs to the basement were carpeted, the basement floor was all tile with several throw rugs, furniture in three rooms needed dusting and there was a bathroom to clean.

"The bedroom and bathroom don't get used very often, so it would be a light cleaning down here every week," Alice mentioned. They walked upstairs and back into the kitchen.

"Thank you for allowing me to look around," Sarah told her. "Twenty dollars more a week, which would bring it to ninety-five dollars."

"We are adding another week of business for your company, so how about ten dollars more a week added to the seventy-five, bringing it to eighty-five dollars a week?" Alice said.

"That will be fine," Sarah told her. That was the price she was expecting to get, but she always proposed a higher amount just in case the client accepted. "I'll draw up the new contract and have it for you to sign the next time the girls are due to clean."

"I want to continue our Friday schedule," Alice mentioned.

"My team will be here at nine o'clock Friday."

Chapter Twenty-One

It was mid-morning on a cold and breezy day. Emma Jean sat up on the side of her bed rubbing her face, knowing that she had to get up. "I can't do this today," she said to herself. She could hear the wind blowing against the side of the house and it gave her a chill. She was supposed to have lunch with Marla today.

Marla was the only person Emma Jean confided in. She'd told her friend everything that went on in her house since her daughter had moved in. Marla always listened; she would give support but stayed out of it. It had been months since the last time they'd had lunch together, and at that time she could see a change in her friend's demeanor. Emma Jean's appearance was frail and listless, and she looked jaundiced. This concerned Marla. Emma Jean was going to cancel their lunch date again today. She took a deep breath and dialed Marla's number.

"Hello, Marla, it's Emma Jean. I'm sorry it's such short notice, but I'm not going to be able to make our lunch date. I'm not feeling well today."

"We haven't had lunch in months because you keep canceling," said Marla.

"I know and I'm sorry, but I'm really not feeling myself," Emma Jean told her truthfully. She had been feeling nauseous and sleepy the last several months.

"Do you want me to bring you something?"

"No, but that's kind of you to offer."

"Do me a favor, Emma Jean, and get yourself to the doctor to find out what the problem is. I'll call you in a few days to see how you're doing." Marla knew Emma Jean very well; she could hear in her voice there was something more going on.

After hanging up, Emma Jean sat on the side of her bed for a few moments feeling sick to her stomach. She leaned over and picked up the two-liter bottle of ginger ale that was sitting on the floor by the side of her bed. She poured some into a glass, took several sips hoping that it would settle her stomach and climbed back into bed.

Alice had been up for hours. She was in the office on the computer all morning ordering gifts online for her girls. She hadn't heard movement upstairs and she knew her mother had a lunch date with Marla. She headed up to her mother's room to wake her.

"What are you doing? You have a lunch date with Marla in an hour!" Alice walked over to the window and opened the blinds.

"I'm not feeling well; I have already canceled with her. Would you please close the blinds?"

"You should drink some ginger ale." Alice walked over and poured her a glass. "Do you want some ice?"

"No, this is fine at room temperature." Emma Jean drank the ginger ale and lay back on her pillow.

Lexi and her kids continued to fly up north during the summers; they visited her mother (and Alice), but Lexi didn't stay at her mother's house as they had in the past. Instead, they stayed with Aimee and her family. This upset Emma Jean: she saw Lexi and her grandchildren once a year and she had always liked it when they stayed with her.

"There's plenty of room for all of you to stay here," Emma Jean told her daughter. "Why do you think 'we' had the basement done?"

"I think we are going to stay at Aimee's house this year, Mom, but thanks for asking."

Lexi had voiced her disapproval about having her sister move in and her mother had done it anyway. Lexi hadn't told her the truth about not staying with her, which was that she didn't want a strained situation while she was up visiting.

The one time Lexi had stayed at the house since Alice moved in, her sister planned everything the entire two weeks they were visiting. Alice planned their dinners and sightseeing and she cooked for them most nights. She also went with them everywhere they went. Lexi, Chloe and Lucas wanted to eat out and have their Lockport foods and have fun their own way while they visited. She and the kids agreed that they weren't staying there next year.

In fact, hardly anyone in the family visited Emma Jean much anymore, and Aimee and Lexi didn't see or speak to their mother very often. They had to go through Alice, who controlled everything her mother did.

If anyone called the house to talk to Emma Jean, Alice answered and then let her mother talk while she listened. When Alice wasn't home, Emma Jean wasn't allowed to answer the phone. Alice had told her to let the answering machine pick up, because she didn't get the messages correct. Life for Emma Jean and her other daughters became distant.

Chapter Twenty-Two

IT WAS JUST BEFORE TWO O'CLOCK on a winter afternoon when Lexi walked through the front door of her house in Jacksonville. Early that morning, she'd dropped off several of her newest paintings at The Art Montage. Jessie's gallery as well as Lexi's artwork had become very well known.

"Lucas, are you home?" Lexi yelled out for her son as she entered her front door.

"Hi, Mom. I was just heading out to test ride my BMX bike. I spent all morning putting new wheels on it," Lucas said as he started out the back door.

"Where is your sister?"

"She went to the Town Center with her friends."

"Okay, I want you home by dinner," Lexi said quickly before the back door slammed. She had quite a few things to do around the house; her cleaning people were due in the morning, so she went around straightening up a bit. One thing she always cleaned was her antique clock, a treasure that she didn't allow anyone else to touch.

Her lovely "jeweler's regulator" wall clock was handed down through her mother's side of the family. Emma Jean had acquired the unique, handmade clock when her mother, Rose, went into a nursing home. It had hung in Emma Jean and Walter's home on their dining room wall for years and became a fixture that never worked (or so they thought). When Emma Jean moved to Florida, she had allowed her daughters to divvy up the household items that she wasn't taking with her. Lexi was last to pick and inquired about the clock.

"Does the old clock work?" Lexi asked when it was her turn to choose.

"I honestly don't know," her mother told her. Lexi went over to the clock and opened the glass door; she couldn't believe that the inside smelled exactly like her grandparents' old boarding house. Lexi had only been there a few times and the scent came right back to her. She found the tool that cranked the weight, started the pendulum and it worked.

"I'll take the clock," she said, smiling.

"Wait a minute," Alice said, holding her hand up. "I didn't know the clock was included in the choices."

"I said 'just about everything,'" Emma Jean said. "You should have asked."

Alice's next idea was to get Lexi to trade it for her mother's diamond ring, which Alice had picked.

"Hell, no, I'm not trading … look at this gorgeous thing," Lexi said with a grin as she hugged the clock. This was the first time Lexi could ever remember getting something Alice wanted. Emma Jean always did as Alice wanted, even at a young age.

"Mom, are you going to let her do this?" Alice asked.

"You had your turn," Emma Jean told her. Alice left the room fuming over not getting the clock, and picking out additional items was put on hold until Alice got over her "temper tantrum."

Lexi had had the attractive clock hanging in her own home in Florida for the past twenty years. The clock was nearly one hundred years old and the spectacular key-wound gear system still operated smoothly.

As she did every week, Lexi unhooked and opened the glass door that covered the front of the clock; the inside always smelled the same. As she took the tool from the bottom and cranked the weight, something odd caught her eye. She took her cell phone from her back pocket and used the flashlight application for a light, then moved the heavy pendulum to the side as she took a closer look at the gold plate on the bottom inside of the clock. There was a tiny edge of paper sticking out of it.

She carefully pulled the paper out and looked around for a moment, thinking it was some kind of joke. The paper was yellow and very frail. She carefully unfolded it and began to read:

February 22, 1932

I am deeply torn by my babies' love, as two seeds have grown.
One will fulfill our years, while having to bequeath the other.
I can be with you no longer, thus a better existence you shall have.
I leave your life completely, forever contrite.
You will be in my heart evermore. Rose

Lexi stared at the poem. "What is this? How long has this paper been in there?" she whispered to herself. Grandma Rose must have written this in 1932, but to whom? What did it mean?

She called Chase from her cell phone; it went to his voicemail. Her next instinct was to call her nephew, Nathan, because they talked to and texted each other often.

Aimee's youngest son, Nathan, was soon to finish college with a bachelor's of science dual degree in accounting and finance. He had an internship doing auditing work with a local CPA firm and did taxes during tax season for extra income.

"Nathan, I found an old poem in my antique clock. It looks like it was written by my grandma. It's signed 'Rose' and dated February 22, 1932," Lexi told him. "The paper is very fragile—you can tell it's old."

"Where did you find it in the clock?"

"It was under a plate at the bottom inside the clock," she said. "I have wound that clock for years and never saw that paper sticking out."

"Do you think someone could have put it in there as a joke?" he asked.

"I don't think so. It really looks authentic."

"What's it say?"

Lexi read the poem to him slowly, word for word

"What do you think it means? Do you think there was another baby that was given away?" Nathan asked.

"That's the same thing I thought when I read it," Lexi told him. "It was the Depression, and 1932 was the year my mother was born. What if my Grandma Rose had twins and gave one away?"

"Send me a picture from your phone. I'm at work right now, but I'll look it over and call you later," Nathan told her.

"Don't tell anyone about this, okay?" Lexi asked.

"I won't say a word, and I'll call you later."

Lexi closed her cell phone and took a picture of the poem as well as the plate inside the clock where she had found it, then sent both pictures to Nathan.

Taking the poem into the kitchen, she put it into a clear plastic baggie to protect it and hung it on the refrigerator so that none of her animals could get to it. She continued her tasks for the day, periodically going back to the poem and reading it. *Was my mother a twin?* she thought. *Could there actually be two of her?* She laughed at the thought.

Chase was on a break and saw that Lexi had called.

"What's up?" he asked.

"I was winding the big clock and I found an old piece of paper in it. It's a poem that was written in 1932 by my Grandma Rose; it is signed and dated."

"One of the kids must have put it in there as a joke," Chase commented.

"I don't think so; it looks pretty authentic—besides, I don't think the kids remember my grandma's name. It's about two babies being born and giving one of the babies away. I think my mother might have had a twin."

"That's scary."

"I know, I thought the same thing," Lexi said as they both laughed.

"I would put it into something—" Chase started to say when Lexi interrupted.

"Already done."

"Okay, I'll read it when I get home for night around dinner time, and we can talk about it then. Love you."

"Love you too," she said as they both hung up.

Later that evening, Lexi got a text from Nathan: "I know a guy at the hospital who may be able to get info about the twins. Should I ask?"

"Yes … thanks." Lexi texted back.

Nathan's friend Brad worked for Aztec Computers. The computer company was hired by the hospital to transfer over all its paper files to an advance computer filing system. Brad and three of his colleagues had been working on the project for months.

Nathan had helped Brad out of a jam a few years before when he had been audited. Brad owed Nathan a huge favor and Nathan thought that this would be a great opportunity to collect on it. He put in a call the day after Lexi told him about the poem.

"Hey, Brad, it's been a while. I hear you got yourself a decent computer job that should keep you busy for a while."

"Can't beat it—the money is great."

"I'm hoping you can help me out, but I don't want you to get yourself in any trouble," Nathan said sincerely.

"No problem! What do you need?"

"I'm interested in information on my grandmother. Emma Jean Sterling was her birth name and she was born on January 20, 1932, in Lockport Hospital. Her parents were Rose and Albert Sterling," Nathan told him.

"What do you want me to find out? It sounds like you have most of the information you need," Brad said.

"I want to know if there was another baby born—if Rose Sterling had twins. Can you check it out for me—see if there are any names, dates ... anything you can find, but don't risk your job."

"No problem," Brad said, "but it may take a few days."

Nathan was busy at work doing an audit when Brad sent him a text message. It had been three days since they had last talked: "Call me on my cell when you get a chance." Nathan finished what he was doing and an hour later he went outside to call Brad.

"What's up? Did you find the file?"

"I did, so here's what I found out. There wasn't much in your grandmother's file; she was born prematurely, barely weighing five pounds. The file had her parents' names, the doctor's name and his comments. Other than that, the information you gave me was pretty much the same. For the eight days she was in the hospital, she was known as baby 'A.' Her mother and father named her Emma Jean the day they left the hospital."

"Thanks for checking, Brad. I really appreciate it."

"Wait, man, there's more," Brad said excitedly. "You gave me the birth date of your grandmother, so I looked to see if there happened to be another baby born that same day—and there was! The other file was for a baby born five minutes later, delivered by the same doctor and nurse. This one was known as baby 'B' and was also premature, weighed about five pounds. But the paperwork showed different birth parents: Joan and Earl Michaels. Baby 'B' was named Gloria, but not until she left the hospital eight days later as well."

"The two couples had babies at the same time?" Nathan asked, a bit confused.

"You're not going to have the same doctor and nurse running back and forth to deliver two babies from different mothers, even in the Depression," Brad said. "When I investigated more, I found that when twins are born they are labeled as baby A and baby B so that the staff won't mix them up."

"I don't believe this!" Nathan said.

"Plus, at the very bottom of the paperwork for the Michaels couple who took home baby B, there was the name of an adoption agency—The American Way Adoption Agency. They went out of business in the late '60s."

"That is awesome detective work for a computer guy," Nathan told him. "You won't get in any trouble?"

"No, we're good."

"Thanks, man … now we're even." Nathan and Brad both laughed. "I don't know how to thank you. This helps my aunt out a lot and answers a lot of questions."

"Let your aunt know that I took pictures of the paperwork on my cell phone, and I can send them to her."

"Forward them to me as well." Nathan gave him Lexi's e-mail address so that he could send her the file pictures.

"I'll get those sent to her right away. Let's get together for drinks soon," Brad suggested.

"Sounds good."

Nathan didn't get a chance to call his Aunt Lexi until he was driving home from work. He told her everything Brad had uncovered during his hospital investigation. "You'll be getting an e-mail of file pictures from him," he said.

"I can't believe it! It happened so long ago and I don't think anyone has any idea," Lexi said. "I'm sure my mother has no idea because she would have told us, don't you think?"

"I agree. I don't think she knows. Are you planning on telling her?"

"I will eventually, but I won't do it over the phone, and I'd like to show her the evidence that was found. I'm going to do some investigating myself. Keep this under wraps for now if you would, until I figure out what I'm going to do with the information."

"I won't say a word. Does that mean you're coming up?" he asked with excitement in his voice.

"I might have to."

Lexi received the e-mail from Brad and printed out the nine pages of files he sent her. She was going do some investigating herself from her computer and find as much information as she could.

Chapter Twenty-Three

One Friday morning, Sarah decided to do a spot check on her cleaning team that was at Mrs. Wilkinson's house. She arrived at the house around eleven o'clock and her cleaning team were just finishing. Alice answered the door and escorted Sarah into the kitchen, where Emma Jean was sitting at the breakfast bar eating cereal. Alice introduced the two of them. Sarah turned pasty white and felt a jolt of shock go through her.

"Is everything okay?" Alice asked.

"Yes, I'm fine," Sarah responded. She couldn't stop looking at the older woman who was the spitting image of Sarah's mother. The only difference was that Gloria weighed more, but the features—her eyes, her mouth, her nose—were exactly the same.

"I'm here to do a spot check on my cleaning team," Sarah told them. She was intrigued by this woman and wanted to learn more about her. The best way to do that was to have access to the house. She would figure that out later.

"The girls do a very good job," Emma Jean said.

Sarah walked around the house and talked with her cleaning crew. She thanked Alice and Emma Jean as she walked to the front door.

Sarah got in her car and lit a cigarette; she smoked periodically, usually when she was stressed. The team drove to the office and Sarah drove home, thinking hard.

When she arrived at her house, Sarah went straight to her mother's place.

"I just met a woman that was the spitting image of you, Mom. The resemblance was uncanny. Is there something I should know?" She looked at her mother curiously; she wasn't sure what her mom knew, if anything.

Gloria sat for a moment thinking back to her childhood and what she had been told. It was a long time ago and it had been a very emotional time in her life.

"Sit down, Sarah, and I'll tell you what I know." Her daughter sat down in a chair at the kitchen table. "I've told you about my childhood growing up. I was twelve when the social worker took me away from the people I thought were my birth parents, and that's when I was told I was adopted."

"Could this woman be a sister?" Sarah questioned.

"Maybe she could be. I honestly don't know. They informed me that I was adopted from the hospital when I was eight days old, so I may have siblings."

"Didn't you ever want to know for sure?" Sarah asked.

"Of course, I always wondered. There were many times I was alone and I thought about searching, but I didn't want to bring up the bad memories and have to relive my childhood again."

"I'm going to start cleaning for this Wilkinson woman once a week," Sarah said. "I'm curious about why she looks so much like you, and I'm going to find out what I can."

"You don't have to do this, Sarah. At this stage in my life, it really doesn't matter to me. I'm very happy and content because I have you, Garret, Emma and Nicole—all the family I need."

"Well, I'll clean for a few weeks to see what I can find out." Sarah walked over to her mother and gave her a kiss on the cheek.

"I love you, Mom. I have to get back to the office, so I'll see you later."

Sarah left her mom's house and grabbed a bottle of water out of her own refrigerator. She let her golden retriever out in the yard for a few minutes, then headed to her car. The first thing she was going to do when she got to her office was adjust her schedule so that she was available to clean on Friday mornings.

Alice was finally getting tired of living with her mother and felt as if she no longer had a life of her own. She had not had a date since her husband had left her—and she blamed her mother for that.

She also hated the fact that her mother had the master bedroom, which had a sliding glass door onto the covered patio. She would enjoy using that feature of the house and Emma Jean never used it.

Alice had had enough of listening to her mother's television too. It was on twenty-four hours a day and she was constantly telling Emma Jean to turn it down. She hadn't expected her mother to last this long—not considering the way that Emma Jean had lived her life.

After eight years of cooking, running errands and taking Emma Jean to the doctor and hair appointments, Alice decided she was tired of doing it all herself. *Things are going to change*, she thought. She went into her mother's room to talk to her about their situation.

"Mom, you have two other children and many grandchildren who can help take care of you," she said. "I do everything and it's not right."

"If I'm not mistaken, Alice, wasn't that the reason you gave me when you and Drew wanted to move in here years ago—to help care for me and save me money? It's been a while, but I'm sure that's what you told me."

"Yes, to help you—for a while," Alice said. "But you're not my responsibility alone and, from now on, if you need a ride somewhere, you can call someone else. The time and money I have spent getting you where you needed to go is above and beyond just my obligation."

"How dare you! I do all my own laundry and I clean the kitchen after you cook dinner—and let me just say that you're a messy cook," Emma Jean responded. "We have a cleaning girl once a week, so what is it you do for me? You buy a massive amount of groceries every few weeks, you drive me to the doctor or a hair appointment *maybe* once a month. Otherwise, I ask nothing of you. Why, now, are you bringing this up after all these years—because the money is gone?" Emma Jean was so angry that she wasn't giving Alice a chance to speak.

"Out of sympathy, I allowed you to move in here until you could get back on your feet after your divorce. You're the one who decided to stay and take over my house as well as drain my finances!"

"What did you just say?" Alice narrowed her eyes and frowned.

"You heard me! You want to talk about money? You and your daughters have greatly benefited from my generosity all these years, especially the huge sum of money I gave Kayla and Layla to help them buy the house they wanted in Rochester."

"You 'offered' to help them out," Alice shot back, "because they weren't financially able to do it on their own."

"Yes, offered to 'help,' but I didn't expect you to give them as much money as you did—I practically bought the place for them! To be very honest with you, Alice, I didn't feel I had a choice."

"Well, you helped Skye with her culinary school."

"You're right," said her mother, "I 'helped' her, but I didn't pay the entire cost of her schooling. Plus, when I gave Skye the two thousand dollars, it wasn't a secret. The rest of the family knew I helped her out. I have given you and your daughters considerably more money and gifts over the years and I was sworn to secrecy, not to breathe a word of it to anyone. I knew it was wrong but abided by your wishes and now there's nothing left. I live month to month on my Social Security checks and what do I have to show for the money I had? I live in a twenty-by-twenty bedroom."

"They would have objected and caused trouble if they had known that you'd given the twins and me extra gifts," Alice said, with no remorse.

"Trouble for whom? Trouble for you, me or your girls? Eventually your sisters will find out that all the money your father left me when he died is gone. They had a right to some of that money."

"Is that a threat, Mom? Are you threatening to tell Aimee and Lexi how much money you have given me and the girls?"

"Of course not, I'm just as much to blame for the decisions I've made through your overbearing dominance," Emma Jean said honestly. "They know how much money your father left me and they will figure it out soon enough."

"It's none of their business what you do with your finances."

"It's rather hypocritical of you to say that, when you have put your name on all my bank accounts."

"We live together, Mother. We pay bills together and I do your banking for you."

"I pay the bills. You buy the groceries and, for some reason, I have to give you money at the end of the month. After all these years, I've still never figured that one out."

"I have explained that to you," Alice said sharply. "It's not my fault you can't grasp the concept."

"It's still not fair to your sisters that you have been the only one to benefit from my money." Emma Jean felt her voice rising along with her temper.

"Alice, you came in here to tell me you're going to quit taking me where I need to go and I'm telling you that you will continue taking me. I've paid you quite a lot of money over the years for that service." Emma Jean added, "By the way, I have a doctor appointment tomorrow at eleven."

Alice didn't say a word; she just stared resentfully at her mother and then turned and left the room. Emma Jean felt rather proud of herself for standing up to Alice as she did.

Alice drove her to the doctor's office the next day. She showed her anger by handling her mother forcefully while getting her in and out of the car, making sure that no one saw her doing it.

Emma Jean was scared. After her physical, the doctor had a lot of recommendations for improved health. The most important was to gain weight and take better care of herself, but she had heard it all before. He had the nurse draw blood so that he could run some tests.

"What are you looking for? Is she having a problem?" Alice asked.

"That's what I want to find out," he said. Then he addressed Emma Jean. "I'm checking your vitamins and proteins. You told me that you've had flu-like symptoms for a while now, which makes me believe that you could have viral hepatitis."

"What does that mean? Is it serious?" Emma Jean asked.

"When the liver is inflamed from the hepatitis, it doesn't perform its function, which brings about many of the symptoms you're experiencing. I'll call you in a few days with your test results."

Alice hadn't been able to sleep for quite some time. It was three o'clock in the morning and she had been tossing and turning most of the night. She got up and made herself a cup of coffee. She decided that there was no other choice: she had to do something about the situation with her mother. For hours she sat at the kitchen table planning her strategy.

She turned on her laptop to research various types of medications and found that too much acetaminophen in a person's system caused it to attack the liver. It slowly wore down the immune system and liver failure was the eventual result.

When she was at the store getting groceries the next morning, she bought several bottles of extra-strength Tylenol and, that afternoon, she started dissolving the pills in her mother's food and soda.

The doctor called with Emma Jean's test results, saying the outcome was positive for viral hepatitis, and asked if someone could come by the office to pick up the prescriptions for her.

"Certainly, I can be there in a few minutes," Alice replied.

"If your mother has any questions, just have her call the office," the doctor said kindly.

When Alice picked up the prescriptions, she took them down to her office in the basement and put them in a drawer. She never told her mother about the doctor's office calling with her test results. Several days later, Emma Jean mentioned that they hadn't heard from the doctor's office. "If you haven't heard from them, everything must be fine," Alice said.

Emma Jean was waking up earlier every morning because of her health problems. She could see from the light peeking through her blinds that the sun was up. The nauseous feeling she'd had for the last several weeks was getting worse with each passing day. She sat up, instinctively reaching down for one of the soda bottles that she kept by her bedside.

When she stood up, it took her a moment to steady herself with her walker. Feeling dizzy and weak, she made her way slowly to the kitchen. She looked in the pantry for something to eat, but nothing appealed to her because she didn't have much of an appetite. She stood in front of the open refrigerator door and finally poured herself a glass of orange juice.

It was Friday. *Sarah will be here to clean soon*, she thought. She unlocked the front door on her way back to her bedroom; she didn't want to get up to let Sarah in when she arrived. She decided that one thing she could do was get her birthday cards done for the upcoming month.

She sent cards to her family members on their birthdays; inside each she put crisp new bills in the amount of the age, and anyone under the age of ten received a ten-dollar bill. She heard Sarah knock on the front door.

"Emma Jean, it's Sarah," she called as she entered.

"Come on in, Sarah. Alice is at the grocery store."

Sarah poked her head into the bedroom. "Good morning, ma'am."

"Good morning, Sarah." Emma Jean saw she was alone. "Where is the girl you've been training?"

"She needed the morning off. Her daughter had a performance at her school, so I'm here by myself today; it shouldn't take any more time than usual."

Sarah had changed her personal clients' cleaning schedules after meeting Emma Jean for the first time. Training a new hire would be the perfect opportunity to gain access to the house. However, during the weeks when Sarah had cleaned, she hadn't had a chance to be alone with Emma Jean until today.

"Would you mind cleaning my room first so that I can use my bed to spread my cards on it?" Emma Jean asked. "I try to get all my birthday cards done in advance so that I don't get behind in sending them."

"Certainly, I can clean your room right now." Sarah walked into the other room to get the cleaning supplies.

Emma Jean was in her closet getting her box of cards while Sarah stripped the sheets off her bed. She was quick and efficient and was just about done changing the bed when Emma Jean emerged from her walk-in closet.

"You are already done changing my sheets?" Emma Jean said, surprised. Sarah could see that she was struggling with the box.

"Let me help you with that!" She went over and took the box from Emma Jean and placed it on the bed for her. "Is right here okay?"

"That's perfect; thank you, Sarah." Emma Jean started going through the birthday card section while Sarah cleaned.

"You're looking a bit under the weather. Are you feeling okay?" Sarah asked. She'd noticed that Emma Jean was losing weight—her eyes were sunken in and her skin had a yellowish tint.

"I haven't been feeling well for quite some time," Emma Jean replied.

"I'm sorry to hear that. Is there anything I can get for you?"

"No, thank you, dear. That's nice of you to ask," Emma Jean said, smiling at Sarah. She remembered the first time that she had seen Sarah and thought how much she resembled Lexi.

Sarah held up the picture she was dusting, "Is this a picture of your daughters?" She was desperately trying to get Emma Jean to open up and volunteer some information.

"It is," Emma Jean said proudly. "You know Alice, and after her is Aimee, who lives here in Lockport. She and her husband own Shenanigan's Restaurant."

"Really?" Sarah was surprised. "I've been there many times. It's a great place."

"Yes, they have delicious food," Emma Jean said. "My other daughter's name is Alexandria—we call her Lexi—and she lives in Florida." Sarah noticed a picture of what would have been her daughters at a much younger age, and there was a fourth child in the picture—a boy. Sarah decided not to ask.

"Are you originally from Lockport? I remember that when your daughter Aimee first hired me years ago, she said that you had just moved back."

"I grew up here, but relocated to Florida after my husband passed away," Emma Jean said. "Then my family decided that I should move back."

"Oh, I see." Sarah watched as Emma Jean pulled out a manila envelope from her end table; she could see that it was full of money. It looked like there must be thousands in it. Emma Jean counted out a particular sum of cash and placed it inside the first card, then addressed it and set it aside.

"Did you live near your daughter Lexi in Florida?"

"No, she lives in Jacksonville. I was further south on the Gulf Coast."

Sarah continued dusting the bookshelf that held Emma Jean's books and miniature figurines. "You have a lot of items with a garnet stone. Isn't that January's birthstone?" Sarah kept her voice casual.

"Yes, I was born in January, so my family buys them for me for my birthday and Christmas," Emma Jean said as she licked an envelope. "I'm going to be eighty this January."

Sarah almost dropped the trinket she had in her hand. Her mother was also going to be eighty—in January. She could feel herself breathing heavily but tried to act normally.

"Well, you certainly don't look your age. When exactly is your birthday?" Just as Sarah asked this question, they heard the garage door open and both women turned and looked toward the door. Alice was back with the groceries.

"Alice is home," Emma Jean said, in a fearful tone. Sarah noticed the difference in her demeanor immediately.

"Are you okay?" She was concerned about Emma Jean's reaction to her daughter's return.

"You need to finish cleaning my room," Emma Jean said quietly.

"When is your birthday, ma'am?" Sarah asked quickly, and added in a softer voice, "So I can send you a card."

"Oh, you don't have to do that."

"I know I don't, but I would like to." *Please tell me*, Sarah thought.

"I was born during the Depression on January 20, 1932."

Sarah didn't know what to do or say. She felt her whole body stiffen and couldn't move.

"I'm going to clean your bathroom now."

Sarah slowly set down the object she had in her hand and went into the other room to catch her breath. She felt she was going to hyperventilate: Sarah's mother had been born on the same day. *My*

God, they weren't just related—they were twins! Her thoughts raced and she jumped when Alice walked into her mother's bathroom.

"I'm sorry to scare you," Alice said.

"I'm finishing up your mother's bathroom. It's just me cleaning today but it won't take me any longer than usual," Sarah said.

"Sarah, my mother shouldn't have asked you to start cleaning in her room first. Next Friday, please clean the house the way I have asked you to do it: my room first, the kitchen, the basement, and then her room. I have mentioned that to you several times."

"I will do that. I'm sorry."

Sarah wanted to say, "What's the difference? I just found out that our mothers are twins," but she didn't care to be reprimanded by Alice right now. This controlling, reprehensible woman who treated her mother so horribly couldn't be related to her, could she?

"After you've finished here, you can start on my room and then move on to the basement. By that time, I should have the groceries put away," Alice said, as she left the bathroom to scold her mother.

Sarah finished cleaning the bathroom and was gathering her supplies when Emma Jean came to the doorway.

"I'm sorry, Sarah," she whispered. "I didn't mean to get you in trouble."

"It's not your fault, there's no reason she needed to speak to me *or* you that way."

"I agree," Emma Jean said softly. "Now you know what I have to go through all the time."

Sarah couldn't imagine treating her mother the way that Alice treated Emma Jean. As she looked at Emma Jean, she saw the resemblance to her mother even more.

She cleaned the house as quickly as she could; she had to get out of there. She started on the family room while Alice was in the kitchen, standing at the island. As Sarah worked, she noticed Alice kept looking over at her in a nervous way.

Alice had several soda bottles in front of her, and she took the caps off each of the bottles—again, glancing over at Sarah, who pretended not to notice. Alice quickly poured a bottle of medicine into each of the sodas. She put the caps back on and put the empty bottles of medicine in her pocket.

She went to the cupboard and got herself a cookie, then leaned against the counter as she ate it. Going back to the cupboard, Alice reached into the back for a baggie. She added the three empty medicine bottles to the baggie and put it back into the cupboard.

What the hell did she just do? Sarah thought.

"Are you almost finished in there?" Alice asked. Sarah acted as if she hadn't heard.

"Sarah!" Alice said loudly.

"Yes, I'm sorry, I was deep in thought," Sarah lied.

"Are you almost finished in there?" Alice asked again.

"Yes, I have the kitchen yet to clean and the vacuuming."

"I'll be in the basement on my computer. Let me know when you're ready to leave and I'll write you a check."

On the way to the basement, Alice took the three soda bottles into her mother's room. Sarah couldn't comprehend what she had witnessed and waited to start the vacuum cleaner so that she could hear what Alice said to her mother.

"Here's your soda, Mom. I have plenty more in the pantry when you're done with these. Let me know when you need more and I'll get them for you. They were buy two, get one free, so I got six bottles and I bought you two boxes of your cereal."

"Did you get my vanilla ice cream?" Emma Jean asked.

"Yes, I got your ice cream," Alice said in a sarcastic tone.

Sarah started the vacuum cleaner as Alice headed to the basement. After vacuuming the family room and the stairs to the basement, she moved to Emma Jean's room. While she worked there, she saw the soda bottles next to the bed; there was soda already missing from one of them. Sarah wasn't sure if she should say something to Emma

Jean about what she had seen Alice do to the soda. She decided not to—not yet, anyway.

All that Sarah had left to do was to mop the kitchen floor, which she finished in record time. She had worked so fast that she was sweating. She took all her cleaning supplies to her car, and when she came back into the house, she went to the cupboard to take a look at the baggie that Alice had hidden. There were many empty bottles of extra-strength Tylenol in it. Sarah quickly put it back when she heard Alice coming up the stairs. Sarah turned around instantaneously and tried not to raise Alice's suspicions when she walked into the kitchen.

"Is everything okay?" Alice asked.

"Yes, I'm fine. I stubbed my toe on the corner of the island and it hurts," Sarah lied. "I just finished mopping the kitchen floor, so be careful because it may still be wet." Sarah was leaning on her hands to keep them from shaking, but Alice noticed when Sarah took the check from her.

Sarah quickly put the check into her pocket and said, "Thank you." She grabbed her bottle of water, car keys and cigarettes from the counter where she had left them when she'd arrived. Alice said goodbye and then closed and locked the front door. Sarah lit a cigarette as she got into her car; her hands were still shaking. Alice watched her suspiciously from the front window until she was out of sight.

After Sarah drove away, Alice walked back into the kitchen and opened the cupboard where she kept the baggie of empty medicine bottles. She could see that it had been moved.

Chapter Twenty-Four

Sarah called Garret immediately from her cell phone. She was usually very good about not talking on her phone while driving. The police in town were cracking down on that law and she didn't need a ticket today. In any event, the call went to his voicemail.

"Call me when you get this, Garret, because it's important," she said.

She wanted to call her mother but decided to wait to talk to her in person; she only lived five minutes away and Sarah was almost home anyway. She pulled into the driveway and ran straight to her mother's place. She used her key to get in and saw that her mother was sleeping on the couch. Sarah covered her up with a blanket and decided to let her sleep. Her mother had gone almost eighty years not knowing that she had a twin—one more hour wouldn't hurt.

Sarah stayed outside in the cold to clear her mind. She needed to get a hold of her emotions; she was feeling concerned and anxious. She lit a cigarette as she paced around her backyard trying to make sense of it all. This woman who had been a client for years could be her mother's twin. How could no one have known? All the horrible years her mother had lived, growing up alone in this small town not knowing she had family here.

If that wasn't enough, Sarah had watched a woman—to whom she could be related—drug her own mother. Sarah didn't know what to do. Should she call the police and tell them about what she had seen? It would be her word against Alice's, and maybe Emma Jean knew about it. She desperately needed to talk to Garret.

Sarah didn't realize how long she had been outside walking around. Her mother opened her door and asked her what she was doing.

"Mom, you're awake! I have to talk to you!" Sarah ran over to her and gave her a hug.

"Sarah, you're so cold—what's the matter? You're upset. Come inside and sit down. I just made a fresh pot of coffee."

"I would love a cup."

"Sit yourself down; I'll get it for you." Gloria poured two cups and put one in front of Sarah, who quickly took a few sips. She wrapped her hands around the cup to warm them.

"Now, what is so important?" Gloria asked.

"I told you about Emma Jean Wilkinson and how she resembles you. I was able to talk to her today," Sarah said excitedly. "She is the same age and has the same birthday as you, Mom. She's your twin sister!"

"There has to be some mistake." Gloria couldn't believe what Sarah had just told her. "Are you sure? After all these years in this small town and the people we know, how could I not have known I have a twin sister? I was adopted as an infant. Was she as well?"

"I couldn't get any more information from her because her daughter Alice came home," Sarah said anxiously. "That's why I took this job, Mom. I knew there was 'something' about her, but I don't want to say anything until we know for sure. I don't like or trust Alice."

Gloria shook her head, trying to sort out all of the information, and took a sip of coffee as if to steady herself.

"That's not all, Mom. I saw Alice putting pills in Emma Jean's soda bottles—she was drugging her mother! I watched her do it," Sarah told her. "I can't imagine what goes on in that house when I'm not there. I know Alice is very dominating and controlling over her mother, and she was being abusive to me today over where to clean first. But drugging her mother—your sister! What should I do?"

"Why don't you wait, clean there next week and see if you can get more information from her," Gloria said cautiously. "Maybe get a sample of Emma Jean's soda or take a picture of the baggie of empty medicine bottles. Then you have evidence for the police."

"That's a great idea, but should I wait? I think I may have made Alice suspicious; I had just put the baggie back in the cupboard when she came up from the basement. I told her I had stubbed my toe."

Sarah realized what a lame excuse it was, and she and her mother looked at each other and both laughed. "I was scared—I wasn't thinking straight."

"Then maybe you shouldn't go back there."

"I'll be fine, really. You had a good idea about the evidence."

Garret finally got the chance to call Sarah. He apologized, explaining that he'd been in a meeting all day with social services and two young boys who were taken away from their drugged-up mother. He was representing the boys, who didn't want to be split up and put in different foster homes.

Sarah felt better now that she'd returned home and talked to her mother—as she always did. She told Garret there would be a bottle of wine waiting and she would make him a delicious dinner when he got home.

"I was very upset when I called you earlier," she said. "I hope I didn't scare you. But my mother calmed me down. Wait till you hear …"

"I was very worried when I heard your message. I can't wait to hold you. I'll be home soon," he told her.

Alice realized that she had been careless when she'd put the pills in her mother's soda bottle while Sarah was in the other room dusting. *Sarah saw everything. She pretended not to notice, but she could easily figure out what I was doing.* Alice's thoughts were panicky.

She'd have to proceed with her plan promptly. She would have liked one more month of preparation, but she had to move forward now that Sarah was a witness. She had wanted warmer weather when she went up to her newly purchased cottage with her daughters, but she couldn't wait any longer.

Alice had bought the cottage without her family's knowledge. The checks she'd received from her mother every month had gone into her savings account and she had let it accumulate for years. Her power of attorney had also allowed Alice a fee for her services and she took advantage of that benefit as well, adding to her savings.

Once she'd found the place she liked, she drove to Wilson, New York, to inspect the two-bedroom, one-bath lakefront house. She'd bought it that day—cash. Alice didn't even tell her twin girls; she would let them know soon enough. "It was no one else's business," she always told herself.

Now, she called her daughter Kayla and asked her if she could take some time off from work.

"I purchased a cottage on Lake Ontario and I want you and Layla to help me break it in next weekend. The place is fully furnished; I know it's still cold outside but it has heat and there's a nice big fire pit," Alice told her. "I really need this weekend getaway. I haven't spent much time with you and Layla lately."

"You bought a house on the lake?" Kayla asked in surprise.

"I did! I got it for a steal—I couldn't pass it up."

"I don't think it should be a problem getting the time off work, and it sounds like fun."

"Perfect! I want it to be just the three of us."

Alice called Layla and told her the same thing: how important it was to spend time with her girls this weekend. Layla also agreed to go. Neither of the twins had any idea of the real reason why their mother planned the get-together for this specific weekend.

Alice went into her mother's room to tell her about her plans for the upcoming weekend. When Emma Jean woke up and rolled over, Alice was taken aback by her appearance. Emma Jean looked terrible and she had a yellowish tint to her complexion, but Alice felt no remorse for what she was doing to her.

Occasionally Alice had thought about what her mother had done for her through the years, but then she would snap into a sick rationalization that she was owed for taking care of her. Alice felt she had given up a lot, and over the last decade, her resentment had overtaken any affection she'd ever had.

"I wanted to let you know that Kayla, Layla and I rented a house on the lake this weekend," she said as she stood by Emma Jean's bed. There was no reason to tell her mother that she'd bought a place. "The three of us are going for a much-needed mother-daughter-sister bonding."

"You rented a house on the lake? Isn't it supposed to be cold this weekend?"

"It is, but that's okay. The place has heat and we will sit by the fire pit and drink a lot of wine." Alice smiled.

"Alice, I should tell you I haven't been feeling well. I've been having terrible shooting pains in my lower back. I feel dizzy and weak and I've lost my appetite," Emma Jean said softly.

"Are you doing this on purpose?"

"Doing what?" Emma Jean asked in surprise.

"I'm finally going away with my girls for a few days and you tell me today—two days before I leave—that you're feeling sick? I am *not* going to cancel this weekend with them!"

"I'm not asking you to. I just thought you should know. I think I should see a doctor soon, because I seem to be getting worse."

"I'll make arrangements to have Aimee stop by to check on you, if she's willing to do it. Will that satisfy you?" Alice said sarcastically. "I have too much to do the next few days. I don't have time to run you around town. I'll make a doctor appointment for you when I get home on Monday."

She walked out of her mother's bedroom. Emma Jean poured herself a glass of ginger ale as Alice returned and gave her a bottle of Tylenol and her laptop computer.

"Take two of these every four hours and see if that helps the pain in your back." Her mother immediately took two.

"I have to go out and run a few errands," Alice told her. "Why don't you play on my laptop for a while—find something you'd like to buy for yourself. It will take your mind off your problems. There are a few of those games you like to play on here too." Alice had only one reason for the suggestion: she wanted her mother's fingerprints all over the laptop.

"I will, thanks." Despite her words, Emma Jean wasn't feeling up to doing anything. She couldn't remember the last time Alice had allowed her to use her computer.

Alice's "errand" was a doctor's appointment in downtown Buffalo. She'd made the appointment two months in advance and, even though she'd made plans for the upcoming weekend, she decided to keep the appointment. It was her first visit to a psychiatrist, and she'd made the appointment because she had started having problems sleeping. She'd had confused thoughts and felt she couldn't cope with her daily problems and anxiety. She wanted the doctor to confirm that these were symptoms of menopause.

When Alice sat down with the psychiatrist, he started by wanting a brief history of her life. She told him only what she wanted him to know. Toward the end of the appointment, the psychiatrist began explaining to her what happens with mental disturbances.

"There are disorders that affect your mood, thinking and behavior. Some examples of mental illness include depression, anxiety disorders, schizophrenia, eating disorders and addictive behaviors. Many people have mental health concerns from time to time. But the concern becomes a mental illness when symptoms cause frequent stress and affect your ability to function," he said. "A mental illness can make you miserable and can cause problems in your daily life. In most cases, the symptoms can be managed with a combination of medications and counseling such as psychotherapy."

"Well, I can tell you that I'm not mentally ill!" Alice said firmly. "Unless you consider menopause a type of mental illness." She laughed. All she wanted from this appointment was reassurance that what she was going through was normal. She wouldn't listen when he tried to tell her that what she was feeling wasn't normal.

Her hour was up and the psychiatrist definitely wanted to see Alice again. He gave her a pamphlet that discussed the signs and symptoms of mental illness, such as feeling sad, excessive fears or worries, confused thinking, excessive anger, hostility, violence, problems sleeping, hallucinations and suicidal thinking. As Alice quickly looked it over, she realized that she had quite a few of the symptoms. He insisted that she make an appointment with him for the following week.

"I'll see you next week. Thank you for your time," Alice said as she walked out of his office. She would cancel the appointment later; she was *not* going back there—he just wanted her money.

Alice made a delicious dinner that evening. Emma Jean only picked at her food but drank her large glass of water, into which Alice had dissolved two sleeping pills.

"I'm not very hungry tonight," Emma Jean said. "I might have something later." She told Alice she was going to lie down. By the time her head hit the pillow, she was fast asleep.

Alice placed her laptop next to her mother as she slept. Sitting on the side of her bed, she used her mother's fingers to hit every key as she typed her mother's suicide note. *If they investigate, she would have to have a fingerprint on every key that was used,* she thought.

The note read:

To my family,

I have never felt so alone in my life and I can't go on any longer. I have one daughter who has shown me care. Because of this, I have given Alice and my beautiful twin grandchildren what they are owed.

Emma Jean

Alice hit "print" with her mother's index finger. She went downstairs and retrieved the note from the printer, using a napkin so as not to get her prints on the paper. She put her mother's hands all over the note and stuffed it into one of the magazines lying on the bed.

Alice then wiped her own fingerprints off the medicine bottles that she kept in the baggie, but left her prints on the two bottles of pills that she always gave her mother. She would say that she had bought those bottles at her mother's request, so of course they would have her prints on them.

Finally, she took her mother's hands and placed her fingerprints all over each of the other bottles. She carefully put the bottles in the drawer of her mother's nightstand, which was on the side of the bed that her mother didn't use often. Because her mother had completed her birthday cards for the month, there would be no reason for her to get any money out of her envelope this week, so Alice took all the cash her mother had—over five thousand dollars. Just before she left her mother's bedroom for the night, she broke the plastic part of the telephone input that goes into the wall jack so that her mother had no dial tone on her phone.

Emma Jean slept the entire night. When she woke at nine o'clock Thursday morning, she told Alice that she'd had a great night's sleep.

"I think it's the first time in months I didn't waken during the night," Emma Jean said.

"That's good, you needed a good night's sleep."

Alice made her mother breakfast and poured her a large glass of orange juice. She'd had the opportunity to dissolve several Tylenol tablets in Emma Jean's juice while her mother read the paper. Emma Jean picked at the scrambled eggs that were made for her and she had one bite of toast, but drank most of her juice. It only took about ten minutes before the fierce shooting pains in her back started again.

"I have to go lie down. Thank you for breakfast."

"You ate like a bird," Alice said.

"I know and I'm sorry. It was very good, I just have no appetite."

Emma Jean leaned on her walker to steady herself for a moment and slowly went back to her bedroom. By the time she got to her toilet, she was out of breath. She had just made it before the terrible diarrhea started. Emma Jean cried as she sat there, suffering but afraid to call Alice for help. It took every ounce of energy she had to get herself back into bed. She grabbed the bottle of Tylenol that Alice had given her and took three pills for her pain.

Alice called her sister that morning. Aimee was surprised because they hadn't talked in quite a while.

"How are you? How are things at the restaurant?" Alice asked.

"Very good, we've been very busy. How is Mom doing? I need to stop by to see her soon."

"That's why I'm calling. I'm going out of town with my girls tomorrow for the weekend. I bought a house on the lake in Wilson. Would you mind stopping by the house to check on Mom while I'm gone?"

"After eight years, you finally bought a place to live?" Aimee said in a semi-joking tone.

"I bought it as a summer home, Aimee. I paid for it with the money I received from my divorce settlement—not that it's any of your business. I'm going to continue living with Mom. She needs somebody to take care of her."

"Is that right?" Aimee said sarcastically. She didn't understand how her sister, who had no job and minimal income from alimony, could afford to buy a lake house—in Wilson. During the last eight years, Alice had supposedly been splitting the house expenses with her mother. Where did she get her money? There was something fishy about that whole situation.

"I bought it a month ago," Alice said. "I got a great deal on it."

"Well, good for you … but I won't be able to stop by Mom's on Friday," Aimee told her. "However, I can be there Saturday morning."

"That will be fine. I'll let her know to expect you."

Aimee hung up the phone and immediately called Lexi.

"Did you know Alice bought a house on the lake in Wilson?" Aimee was furious.

"She did what?" Lexi replied. "When did she buy that? Is she finally moving out?"

"No, she is not moving—it's her 'summer home.' What I don't understand is where she gets her money—although I can probably guess after eight years of her living with Mom."

"You know that Mom paid for that place for her. I'm planning on coming up soon," Lexi told her. "This has gone on long enough; we will figure it all out then … together."

It was early Friday morning and the sun was just peeking through the trees. Alice was ready to leave, her car was loaded and she was anxious to get on the road.

She took three bottles of soda out of the pantry. She knew that her mother usually drank the ginger ale first because it settled her stomach. She put a massive amount of pills in the ginger ale bottle and nothing in the others.

Alice quietly went into her mother's room. She brought the soda bottles with her and put them next to her mother's bed.

"Mom, I'm getting ready to go … Mom!"

Emma Jean didn't move and a wave of fear ran through Alice. *She'd better not have died in the night*, she thought. She touched her mother's shoulder and shook her a bit. "Mom …"

Her mother finally moved and Alice breathed a sigh of relief. "Good morning. I'm getting ready to leave for the cottage."

"Have a good time. I'll see you Monday." Emma Jean could barely speak.

"Is there anything I can get you? I went grocery shopping yesterday, so there is plenty of food. I put another bottle of Tylenol on your nightstand and I brought you a few more bottles of soda. Drink the ginger ale first because it will help to settle your stomach."

"I'll be fine."

"You have my cell phone number and if you need anything right away, you can call Aimee or Blake."

Emma Jean slowly rolled over. "I wanted to give you some money so that you and the girls could go out and have a nice dinner on me," she said as she carefully reached down to get her envelope of money. "I haven't seen your girls in quite a while."

"Mom … We don't need any money!" Alice said quickly, trying to keep her mother from reaching for her envelope. "We will only be there a couple of days and we are going to cook each night, but thank you for the offer."

"Are you sure?" Alice's response surprised Emma Jean, who couldn't remember the last time that her daughter had refused money.

"I'm positive!" Alice said firmly.

"Okay." Emma Jean nestled back under her covers.

"I'll see you Monday," Alice said as she was leaving the room. She turned to look back at her mother for a brief moment. *Good-bye, Mom,* she thought to herself.

Emma Jean heard Alice close the front door and lock it. She poured herself a glass of ginger ale and reached for the Tylenol bottle to take three pills. She felt awful: her whole body ached, she felt nauseous and dizzy and the pain in her back was agonizing. The pills she took never seemed to help. Emma Jean thought about calling her friend Marla to come over and help her, but she didn't have the strength to pick up the telephone.

She dozed off and an hour later she woke up, startled. She was losing track of time and was in excruciating pain. She heard knocking on the front door. "Who could that be?" she murmured as she struggled to sit up, feeling lightheaded and faint. She heard a distant voice calling her name; it sounded like Sarah.

Sarah? It must be Friday, so she's here to clean, she thought. *She will help me.* Emma Jean began to cry. She reached for the address book that she kept in her bedside table drawer. She looked up Sarah's cell phone number, wanting to call and tell her not to leave, but when she picked up the receiver, she realized there was no dial tone. She didn't know what to do.

She put her walker in front of her and stood; it felt like each step took minutes. She got only halfway to her bedroom door before she collapsed. Emma Jean could hear Sarah calling her name; it sounded distorted. She heard the phone ring in the kitchen and wondered why her telephone wasn't ringing next to her bed. The last thing she remembered hearing was knocking on the front door.

Today Sarah had planned to confront Alice about what she had seen her doing to her mother's soda bottles. She wanted to hear an acceptable explanation or she was going to the authorities. She was also going to enlighten Emma Jean about the situation. The entire incident had bothered Sarah all week. She had a terrible feeling that she should have done something sooner.

When Sarah arrived at the house, her mind was racing and she was nervous. She rang the doorbell impatiently, but there was no answer. After what seemed like many minutes, she rang the doorbell again and knocked on the door—still no answer. She looked under the mat, where Alice sometimes left a key—nothing. She quickly tried the door handle and it was locked.

In all the years that Sarah's company had worked for Alice and Emma Jean, this would be the first time that they had missed a cleaning day. Usually, if no one was going to be home, a key was left under the mat or Emma Jean left the door unlocked. A wave of fear passed through Sarah and she felt something was badly wrong.

"Emma Jean, are you home?" she called loudly. She looked through the window and knocked on the door again. She wasn't sure what to do next, so she took her cell phone out of her pocket and called Emma Jean's house phone. The answering machine picked up and Sarah left a message.

"It's Friday morning at nine-twenty, and I'm here to clean as scheduled. Call me when you get this message; otherwise, I'll see you next Friday."

Sarah's alarm grew, but she wasn't sure what she should do. She stood by her car for a few minutes, smoking a cigarette and thinking. Alice had had a whole week to "overdose" her mother.

She thought about walking around the house to look inside a back window. *If I do, someone may see me and call the police—but maybe that's a good idea because it would get the police out here*, she thought. *But, if there was nothing going on and they'd merely forgotten what day it was, the police could be a problem for me.* She wouldn't put it past Alice to press charges against her as a "peeping Tom." She decided to call the hospital.

"Lockport Hospital, how may I direct your call?"

"I was wondering if a woman named Emma Jean Wilkinson has been admitted into the hospital at any time in the last few days," Sarah said quickly.

"I show no one by that name."

"Thank you." As Sarah hung up, she looked around and decided to go across the street to the neighbor's house because she had seen Alice talking to the woman periodically. It was about nine-forty when she knocked on the neighbor's front door and an elderly woman answered.

"May I help you?"

"Hello, my name is Sarah Stevens. I own the Clean-N-Pristine cleaning company," Sarah said as she handed the woman one of her business cards.

"I don't need a cleaning service, thank you." The woman had begun to close the door when Sarah stopped her.

"Ma'am, I'm not here soliciting. I clean for your neighbors, Emma Jean Wilkinson and her daughter Alice," she said as she pointed across the street. "I was wondering if you had seen or spoken to either of them recently."

"I spoke with Alice yesterday. I don't see her mother very often. She doesn't get out much."

"If I may be so bold … did she mention if they were planning to go out of town?"

"Is there a problem?" the woman asked. She didn't want to give out information to a stranger just because she had asked.

"Yes, I think there might be a problem. No one answers the door or the telephone, and they have never missed a scheduled cleaning day. I was wondering if Alice may have told you that she was going out of town and they forgot to tell me." Sarah was not going to explain the whole situation to this woman.

"She didn't tell me she was going away, but when I went out to get my paper this morning I saw Alice putting her suitcase into the trunk of her car along with grocery bags and bedding."

"Well, that must be what happened, then. They went out of town and forgot to let me know." Sarah still wasn't satisfied, but at this point there was nothing she could do. "My name and telephone number are on the card if you need to call me for any reason. Thank you very much for your time."

Sarah walked back across the street, got into her car and drove home. She had several hours free now that she didn't have to clean. She walked over to her mother's place to update her on her morning. Her mother suggested that they go out for a late breakfast.

Chapter Twenty-Five

ALICE'S DRIVE TO THE LAKE took her about forty-five minutes. It was a sunny day but cold; the temperature at the lake was usually ten degrees cooler. The first thing Alice did when she arrived was to turn on the heat. She unloaded the car and put all the groceries away, she put fresh sheets and blankets on all the beds, dusted and wiped down the kitchen. She wanted everything to be perfect when her twins arrived.

As she was unpacking her suitcase, it hit her: "Shit, it's *Friday*!" she said out loud. Alice had had so much on her mind the last few days that she'd forgotten all about Sarah showing up to clean. This would ruin her entire plan, especially if Sarah got there and helped Emma Jean to the hospital.

Alice tried calling Sarah, but she couldn't get through; she didn't have cell service on her phone. "God damn it!" she said angrily.

Because the girls weren't expected for at least an hour, Alice decided to drive south until she had service on her phone. She pulled into a small convenience store and called Sarah.

Sarah was in the middle of having breakfast with her mother when her phone rang. She could see from caller ID that the caller was Alice.

"It's Alice!" Sarah whispered to her mother, as if Alice could hear her.

"Hello?" she answered calmly.

"Sarah, this is Alice. I forgot all about you coming to the house today. I left early this morning to meet my daughters at the lake for the weekend and my mother had an early doctor's appointment. My sister must have picked her up before you arrived," Alice said in a pleasant voice. Sarah didn't know whether to believe her or not, but she certainly sounded convincing.

"I can be at the house in less than an hour—your mother should be home by then," Sarah said.

"With everything going on this week, next Friday will be fine."

"Honestly, I don't mind. I have all my cleaning supplies with me."

"Next Friday," Alice said firmly. Suddenly, there was quite a change in her tone.

"As you wish. How is your mother feeling?" Sarah said quickly before Alice hung up.

"Excuse me?"

"I was wondering how your mother was doing."

"My mother is fine. Why do you ask?"

"She told me last week when I cleaned her room that she wasn't feeling well."

"She is doing much better."

"Last Friday I noticed you put some tablets into your mother's soda bottles. It bothered me that you would do something like that and I should have questioned you at the time." Sarah didn't want to discuss this over the phone, but it looked like it would be her only opportunity. She wanted Alice to be aware that she knew what she was doing to Emma Jean, and waiting a week to confront her in person might be too late. She would have liked to have seen Alice's reaction in person. However, Alice's tone turned cold, which said it all.

"Yes, you should have asked. I could have set your mind at ease." Alice was obviously annoyed, and sounded shocked that Sarah would be so bold as to say something to her. "As a matter of fact, she has trouble taking pills, so I dissolve them in liquid for her—not that it's any of your business."

Sarah knew this was a lie because she had witnessed Emma Jean taking pills without a problem.

Alice continued, "If you can't show up to clean and mind your own business, I will find another company to clean for us. Is that understood?"

"Certainly," Sarah said.

"Next Friday, make sure you come alone. We have some things to discuss."

"Yes, we do," Sarah said. "I will see you then."

Sarah hung up and turned to her mother: "Mom, that woman is up to something and I don't like it."

"Exactly! I don't like you being alone with her because I don't trust her. If she can drug her own mother, just imagine what she would do to you."

"As long as Alice knows I'm on to her, she won't do anything to me or to her mother, I hope."

"I think you should drop them as a client. You don't need that job," Gloria said. "We will contact Emma Jean and tell her what we have learned about her being drugged and our being twins, okay?"

"We should do it soon. You have a twin sister, Mom. I would think you would be anxious to meet her."

"It's a scary thought after all these years—don't you think so?"

"Yes, I suppose so—from the pictures I saw in Emma Jean's bedroom, I have cousins," Sarah added with excitement.

"We will contact the family and tell them what we know and let them deal with Alice," Gloria said. "I'm afraid for you; promise me that you won't be alone with Alice … ever."

"I promise, Mom. I will have someone with me next Friday. When I see your sister," Sarah winked, "I'll tell her about you and make arrangements for all of us to meet."

"That's fine. We can 'do lunch.'"

They both laughed. Sarah and her mother decided to go shopping after their delicious breakfast. They both needed to take their minds off the stressful situation—at least for a few hours.

As Alice drove back to her lake house, she kept thinking about her conversation with Sarah. "That bitch cleans my house, who does she think she is?" she said aloud. "She is not going to ruin everything I've worked so hard to achieve for so many years, not after everything I've had to give up."

All of Alice's focus was now on Sarah and what she had to do to keep the cleaner from ruining her plan. She was so enraged about the situation that her mind was elsewhere and she didn't realize that she had passed through a small town where the speed limit dropped considerably. A New York State Trooper came up behind her with his lights flashing.

"I don't fucking believe this," Alice said, as she pulled off to the side of the road. The trooper had a stern demeanor as he walked up to her car, and Alice slowly rolled down her window.

"Is there a problem, officer?"

"May I see your driver's license and registration?" he asked without emotion. Alice got her license out of her wallet and reached into the glove compartment for her registration as he looked at her inspection sticker on the windshield. "Where are you heading in such a hurry?" he asked as he looked over her information.

"I'm traveling to my house in Wilson. I must have been lost in thought and not realized the reduction in the speed limit. I must not have seen the speed limit sign."

"What is the address in Wilson?"

"28 Apple Grove Lane."

"That's different from what's on your license."

"The house in Wilson is my summer lake house," Alice told him proudly. "The address on my license is my main residence."

He took her information and went back to his vehicle while Alice sat in her car, furious. She felt overwhelmed, as if she was losing control of everything in her life. The trooper seemed to be taking forever. It was several minutes before he walked back to her car window and gave back her information as well as a costly ticket for speeding.

"Keep an eye on your speed," he told her.

"Yeah, thanks …" she said under her breath.

She was extremely agitated when she got back to the lake house and had just enough time to gather her emotions before her girls arrived. Alice consumed several shots of chilled vodka that she'd brought with her. She then opened a bottle of red wine and poured herself a glass; she went out by the water and started a huge fire in the fire pit. She sat outside with her glass of wine, staring at the crackling flames and listening to the water crash against the shore. She finally had the house on the lake that she had always dreamed about. The thought put a smile on her face.

The twins drove up the driveway in Layla's Ford Taurus. Alice turned slowly and looked in their direction, staring as if she didn't recognize them. After several seconds, she snapped out of her trance and ran to greet them. She helped the two of them unpack and get settled in, asking them questions continuously.

"This place is really nice, Mom—very comfortable and right on the water," Layla commented.

"Thank you. I love it here. It's soothing to hear the sound of the water against the rocks and I like the fact that it is so secluded here."

Kayla looked at Layla and then back at her mom.

"I thought you didn't like to be alone," Kayla commented

"People can change," Alice said in a distant tone. "By the way, I have one request for you both. I would like the two of you to turn off your cell phones for the weekend—no calls or texting. There is very limited cell service here anyway. Promise me and I won't ask another thing from either of you while you're here." Both girls promised and turned off their phones.

For dinner that night, Alice grilled a sirloin steak and broiled three lobster tails, which she'd bought with some of the money she'd taken from her mother's envelope. *Mom said she wanted to buy them a nice dinner*, she thought to herself, *and, in a way, she has done just that.* Alice grinned. That night, the three of them ate and drank, laughed and cried and, while sitting outside wrapped in blankets in front of the fire, they enjoyed a hot mug of coffee with Bailey's.

"May I ask you a question, Mom?" Layla said as she gazed into the fire. "How were you able to buy a place like this?"

"Well, let's just call it compensation pay for all the years I had to live with your grandmother. I've taken care of her for almost nine years. I haven't had a life because of her, plus I lost your father when I wanted the two of us to move in with her to save ourselves money. Your dad and I always wanted a place on the lake," she said in an odd tone. "When you tell him about it, he will know what we could have achieved together."

Kayla and Layla looked at each other. They knew the real reason their parents had divorced. Their father had explained that he had had enough of Alice's obsession with her mother's money and couldn't take her greed and her selfish lies. He'd told the girls how their mother's personality had changed over the years. He'd seen characteristics of her behavior but thought he could bring it under control. Drew didn't know Alice as a child growing up; otherwise, he'd have known that her personality didn't change—she just got better at deceiving people and getting what she wanted. The twins understood for the first time exactly what their father had meant.

"The money you gave Layla and me to purchase our house in Rochester several years ago was a considerable amount. Was that from Grandma as well?" Kayla asked. The girls knew their grandmother had contributed, but they had been told their mother gave them most of the money. They never understood why Alice didn't want them to say anything about where the money came from.

"She didn't want me to tell you how much she contributed," Alice lied.

"The gifts and furnishings throughout the years—also from Grandma?"

Alice just raised her eyebrows and gave them a smile.

"Does Grandma have any money left?" Kayla asked sarcastically.

"I don't know." Alice did know; her mother had nothing left except the monthly Social Security checks.

Alice only slept a few hours that first night. She tossed and turned and finally decided to get up. It was completely dark outside; the sky was overcast, so there was no moonlight reflecting on the water. Alice decided that she wasn't getting any more sleep, so she made herself a strong cup of coffee. The problem she had was how to get Sarah out of the picture and make it look like an accident before she went to the authorities.

Alice knew that Sarah smoked; she had watched her many times light up a cigarette as she walked to her car. Maybe there was something she could put in one of her cigarettes to make her sick. She saw Layla's laptop sitting on the table and began to research liquid toxic poisons that would not be detected in a person's system.

She found something called nicotine sulphate; water and tobacco would make the liquid poison. All she had to do was add tobacco to boiling water, strain off the solids, scrape the sides of the container with a spoon, and then sift the liquid through a coffee filter. She could put a few drops of it into Sarah's cigarette, and the poison would take effect after Sarah left the house and was behind the wheel of her car. *That sounds easy enough,* Alice thought, *and it would look accidental.* When she was finished, she deleted all evidence of her search on Layla's computer.

Chapter Twenty-Six

THAT SATURDAY MORNING, Blake was on his way to Willowbrook Golf Course for his early tee time, and Aimee was getting ready to go run a few errands before she stopped by her mother's to check on her. She knew her mother wouldn't be awake until later in the morning.

When she arrived at her mother's, she carried a large plate of food she'd picked up at Shenanigans. Aimee pulled out the key to the house that her mother had given her; the key didn't fit, so she checked all the keys on her keychain. None of them worked and she was getting worried. "Mom, are you in there?" she yelled. "Mom, my key doesn't work."

She's got to be in there; she never goes anywhere, Aimee thought. She walked around the house to the patio door. The blinds were drawn; however, there was a spot she could see through. Her mother was lying on the carpeted floor in the middle of her bedroom.

When Aimee got inside, by breaking the decorative window pane beside the front door, she checked her mother's pulse. It was very weak, and she grabbed her cell phone and called 911.

After a wonderful, passionate night with Garret, Sarah felt relaxed and happy. It was the weekend, the two days they usually spent together after a long week, and this had been a very long, emotional week for Sarah. She cooked breakfast and she, Garret and her mother sat around the table and talked about the situation with Alice.

Garret agreed with Gloria: he didn't want Sarah to be alone with Alice. They talked about how they should approach the matter and the course of action they should take. Garret gave them the legal point of view.

"This Alice woman sounds like she has some serious problems," he said as he got up from the table. He kissed his wife and apologized because he had to go to the office for a few hours for an important meeting. "I'll make it up to you tomorrow," he promised.

"What if I make you both a nice dinner tonight?" Gloria said before Garret left.

"You don't have to do that, Mom."

"I know, but I want to. Besides, it will give me something to do this afternoon. I will get everything I need at the grocery store. Can I get you anything else while I'm there?"

"How about if I go to the grocery store for you?" Sarah didn't like her mother driving, especially when it was cold out; the roads could become icy.

"I'll be fine, honey. I'm only going a few miles to the store and back."

"If you insist, there are a few things I could use." Sarah wrote several items on a piece of paper and handed it to her mother. "Thanks, Mom, this saves me a trip to the store. If you're both going to be gone, I might as well head to the office for a while. I need to check our supplies and place an order."

"I'll have dinner ready by seven," Gloria told her.

"You know you spoil us." Sarah grinned and gave her a hug.

"I don't know what I would do if Alice hurt you," Gloria whispered in her daughter's ear.

"Don't worry, Mom," Sarah said as she turned to walk out the door.

Gloria took a moment to look around the kitchen to see if Sarah had any items she needed for her dinner so that she didn't buy duplicates.

She saw Sarah's client book sitting on the counter. She slowly walked over and opened the book to Emma Jean Wilkinson's address. She wrote down the address on the back of her grocery list. *I shouldn't be doing this,* she thought.

As she drove to the grocery store and did her shopping, all Gloria could think about was how amazing it was, after all these years, to discover that she had a twin sister living here in Lockport that she'd never met. *We must look alike—Sarah said we are almost identical. Was she also given away as a baby?*

When she left the store, she decided to drive by the address she'd written down. If she had her nerve up, she just might stop. As Gloria pulled into the cul-de-sac, she saw a lot of commotion at one of the houses. There were quite a few police cars and several people were standing around talking to one another.

Gloria put a hand to her mouth and gasped when she saw that the police were parked in front of the house she was looking for—Emma Jean's house! Her heart started beating extremely fast. She pulled over and rolled down her window to get some air. Then she parked and walked over to talk to a woman standing across the street from the house.

"What happened?" she asked. She was afraid to hear the truth.

"The older woman who lives there was taken by ambulance a little while ago. Her daughter found her," the neighbor said.

"She was taken by ambulance? Was it her daughter Alice that found her?" Gloria asked. Her voice was shaking and her knees felt weak.

"No, a different daughter. I understand she had to break in to get to her."

"Was she—alive?" Gloria asked, holding her breath.

"I honestly don't know."

Gloria felt sick. She thanked the woman for the information and walked back to her car and sat there a moment. "I waited too long to try to get a hold of my sister," she whispered to herself.

"Are you okay?" The woman she had been talking to tapped on the window.

"I'm fine, thank you." Gloria rolled up her window and quickly drove away. She wasn't okay, however; she couldn't think straight. She had to hurry home to tell Sarah what had happened to Emma Jean.

Gloria had so many questions running through her head that she could barely see straight. She certainly wasn't aware of how fast she was driving. As she turned right from Davidson Road onto East Avenue she took the turn too fast and too wide. Trying to recover, Gloria looked up and saw a large semi truck coming toward her.

She turned the steering wheel sharply to the left and hit a patch of ice on the side of the road. Her car slid and went down the embankment of the Town and Country Club. The car rolled several times until it landed upside down in the middle of the golf course's first fairway.

The first people to arrive were two men working at the golf course, who had seen the accident. They knew not to move her. Car after car stopped along East Avenue in both directions to see if there was anything they could do to help or to glance at the wrecked car. Many people called 911 from their cell phones.

Once rescue arrived, it took them almost an hour to get Gloria out of her car and it was going to take more time to carefully get her up the steep hill to the ambulance. She was unconscious and barely alive. The traffic was backed up for miles in each direction.

Sarah heard about the bad accident on the radio and the back-up on East Avenue. She took the long way home from her office, going around town and driving down Day Road, which crossed over East Avenue. When she arrived at the house, her mother wasn't home yet, even though it was six o'clock. *She should have been back from the grocery store by now,* she thought.

Garret was listening to his satellite radio in his car, so he had no idea about the accident and got stuck right in the middle of the traffic along East Avenue. He called Sarah and told her he was going to be late. She told him about the bad accident.

"Mom must be stuck in that same traffic because she's not home yet. I'm a little worried about her, Garret. She should have been back by now, and there would be no reason for her to be coming from that direction because the grocery store where she shops is in the other direction."

"I'm sure she's fine. Maybe she made a few more stops other than the grocery store."

"I hope you're right."

"I'm coming up on the accident now. Once I get by, it shouldn't take much longer to get home," Garret said. "Tomorrow I have special plans for us."

"Tomorrow we force my mother to get a cell phone for this reason." They both laughed.

"I'll see you soon," he said and hung up.

As he slowly neared the scene of the accident, the police were detouring the traffic through Carlyle Gardens. Following the detour, he looked over and saw the car from the accident being hauled up to the top of the hill by a large tow truck.

Garret stared, appalled when he saw the destroyed white Lexus. He pulled over into someone's driveway and got out of his car to get a closer look. A policeman told him to get back into his car and keep moving, but he didn't listen. He ran over to get a closer look as the policeman stopped him.

"Let me go!" he yelled, trying to pull away. "It's my mother-in-law's car!"

As soon as he said this, a man in a sports coat brought him near one of the police cars to calm him down and ask him a few questions. The man confirmed that it was Gloria's car and Garret started to cry.

Chapter Twenty-Seven

In his many years in law enforcement, Detective Randal had learned that everyone lies and everybody is a suspect. He began each investigation with that in mind. On Saturday he was given a case file and started working on it immediately.

An elderly woman had tried to commit suicide, but she hadn't died. By the looks of the information he'd received, there could have been foul play involved. The detective quickly set out for the hospital to talk to the woman and her family. He wasn't able to talk to Emma Jean; however, he did talk to her daughter and son-in-law.

Detective Randal asked to talk to the doctor privately because he learned more about a case when the family wasn't present.

Doctor Christie insisted that he could only discuss it with the family present. When he asked, the family agreed.

"It appears that your mother may have tried to attempt suicide," the doctor said to the family. "She ingested a massive dose of acetaminophen. When her blood work came back, however, it showed she has fulminate hepatitis. The medical records we received from her general practitioner show that he diagnosed her condition as viral hepatitis many months ago. Because of the condition, your mother developed a severe inflammation, and her liver was slowly failing.

Even though there was a massive amount of acetaminophen taken at once, she must have been taking the medication continuously before now, so that her liver failed at a faster rate."

Doctor Christie continued his diagnosis as everyone listened intently. "She is in a coma and is extremely ill with the symptoms of acute hepatitis and permanent liver failure. The effects of the disease would have dramatically curbed her appetite, which is why she was severely dehydrated. Other symptoms such as nausea, diarrhea, fatigue and abdominal pain would have been very noticeable. We have her on life support and she will need a liver transplant to survive."

"But I don't understand," Aimee exclaimed. "Wouldn't my sister Alice have noticed these symptoms, while living with our mother?"

"It would be hard *not* to notice," the doctor replied.

"Thank you, Doctor—this information helps considerably," Randal said. The question that he couldn't answer was why, if she'd truly wanted to commit suicide, Mrs. Wilkinson needed to overdose on Tylenol. Why not use the prescribed medicine she had in her possession? The medication her daughter turned over to him would certainly have been more effective.

Aimee and Blake were stunned by what the doctor had just told them. They had had no idea of any of this. Before the detective left, he told them that he would send an officer to their residence in a day or two to get their official statement and he would keep them updated on what he learned from the investigation at her mother's house.

Aimee looked at Blake and then back at the detective. "Are we suspects?" she asked in surprise.

"Everybody is suspected at the beginning of every investigation," he told them. He didn't think they were involved, but he wasn't going to let them know that. He handed Aimee a piece of paper from his notepad that had his name and his personal telephone number at the police station, along with the case file number.

"Call me if you think of anything and use this case number. If you get a hold of your sister Alice before we do, tell her I will need to talk with her." He turned to walk away.

"Of course," Aimee said in a distant tone. How could he even think she might be involved in her mother's terrible condition?

"It sounds like he doesn't believe it was suicide," she said to Blake. "Do you think he actually believes we had anything to do with this?"

"He's just doing his job and investigating," Blake told her. "I'll call Lexi and the kids and update them on what the doctor told us." He stepped outside while Aimee stayed with her mother.

"Why didn't you tell us about your condition, Mom?" Aimee asked, looking sadly at the unconscious figure on the bed. "We would have helped you."

Blake called Lexi and broke the news to her gently.

"I don't believe this! Mom has hepatitis? She never said a word about it," Lexi said, crying. "As a matter of fact, Alice never said anything. Don't you think Alice would have known?"

"We asked the same question," Blake said. "The doctor said it would have been obvious. There is a Detective Randal asking us all sorts of questions, and he said they have an investigation going on at your mother's house."

"How is Aimee doing after finding Mom like that?"

"Your sister isn't taking this well, but she'll be better when you get here. We haven't been able to get a hold of Alice and no one knows what the address is to the place she bought in Wilson. I'll call you if we have any more information on your mother," Blake told her.

"You can fill me in on everything when I get there. I'll get a flight tomorrow morning, and I'll rent a car, so I won't need a ride from the airport. I will call you when I get to Lockport. I'll see you all tomorrow."

Blake called Skye next and told her what was going on. He asked her if she could handle things at the restaurant for a few days. "I'll try to stop by if I can get away," he told her.

"Don't worry, Dad, I've got it under control. You stay with Mom; it sounds like she needs you there." Blake then called Nathan and Brooke and told them about their grandmother.

After Blake made his phone calls, he got Aimee a cup of hot coffee from the cafeteria while she sat with her mother. Although Emma Jean had spent most of her life depressed and sick in bed, today's crisis seemed incredible. Aimee thought, *My God, Mom, why would you try now at the age of eighty to end your life?* There had to be more to this situation, she believed.

While Aimee and Blake were in Emma Jean's room, they noticed that a woman had been brought into one of the other intensive care rooms. There was a lot of commotion, with many doctors and nurses going in and out of the room as they had for Emma Jean.

Aimee said a prayer for her mother—then one for the woman they had just brought in. There wasn't much she could do for her mom at this point. She was in a coma and wasn't going to wake any time soon. Aimee and Blake had been there for hours. It was late and she decided to go home to get some rest; she would come back early Sunday morning. "Lexi will be here tomorrow," she said with a sense of relief.

After Lexi had talked with Blake, she had immediately called her husband to update him on what had happened. Chase could hear how upset Lexi was.

"I'll make arrangements to stay home with the kids while you're gone. Did you get your ticket yet?"

"Yes, I already booked it. My flight leaves at seven tomorrow morning, and I'll arrive in Buffalo at eleven."

"I'll take you to the airport in the morning. Everything will be all right," he said, trying to calm her. "I'll see you tonight."

Lexi then called her friend Jessie. She knew she would want to know about her mother. She told her friend she wasn't sure how long she would be gone.

"Don't worry," Jessie said, "Just let me know if there is anything I can do to help while you're gone."

When Lexi tried calling her sister Alice, the call went straight to voicemail.

As Lexi finished packing, she thought of a way she might be able to contact Alice. Lexi and Kayla were "friends" on Facebook and she was also "friends" with Kayla's boyfriend, James. If Alice didn't have cell service, then Kayla probably didn't either. Lexi sent James a message via Facebook, not having his telephone number: "I know Kayla is with her mother this weekend. If you talk to her, would you have her call me ASAP? It's important."

She didn't want to elaborate on what was going on with her mother; she didn't have all the details anyway.

CHAPTER TWENTY-EIGHT

DETECTIVE RANDAL LEFT THE HOSPITAL and went straight to Emma Jean's house to check on the investigation of her apparent suicide. He stopped at the front door to take a look at the window that Aimee had broken to get in. As he walked into the house and looked around, he could tell immediately that the cleaning girl hadn't been there to clean on Friday.

Randal was updated by the policeman in charge, who said they'd found twelve empty Tylenol bottles inside the right bedside table and two bottles of the same brand on top of the left table. One was empty and the other was almost full.

"We didn't find any other medications."

"I have them," Randal said. "Her daughter brought them with her to the hospital." The policeman told him about the soda bottles next to her bed; one was empty and the other two were full.

"Did you bag them?" Randal asked quickly.

"Yes, we did."

A printed suicide note had been found sticking out of a *Redbook* magazine, and the officer handed the note to Randal.

"The laptop computer she typed the note from was sitting on her bed. We have two sets of prints on the laptop and just one on the note."

"Where is the printer located?" Randal asked.

"Downstairs in a nicely renovated basement. The printer is in an office down there."

"I want to see where this printer is," Randal said and headed down to the basement looking around as he went. He noticed a bedroom, bathroom and living area. He went through a closed door and into the office.

"Wow! This *is* nice, wall-to-wall office equipment—they have everything an office needs."

An officer in the basement told the detective, "This is the printer she printed the note from. This one over here is a fax machine and copier."

"Any prints on the printer?" Randal wondered.

"Just one set," the officer told him. "We looked around in the office and all the bills are in Mrs. Wilkinson's name and the daughter pays them from her mother's checkbook as far as we can tell. We also found in one of the drawers a few prescriptions written for Mrs. Wilkinson dated several months ago."

"This poor woman never knew her liver was failing. Her daughter never told her or filled her meds. Did you bag them?" Randal asked.

"We will," the officer told him.

"What was on Mrs. Wilkinson's bed?" he asked as they all went back upstairs.

"The laptop computer I told you about and a large tray. On the tray were two handheld games and several magazines, one of which had the suicide note inside. She had a small pad of paper with a list of grocery items on the top page and a pencil inside the pad. There were two remotes, one for the television and one for her DVD player, and a box of tissues."

"Was there anything near her on the floor when she was found?"

"Her walker was by her side, tipped over," the policeman said. "Her cat was lying next it."

"Let me ask you something," Randal said. "We have this eighty-year-old woman obviously depressed and apparently very sick from what the doctor told me. She decides to kill herself. She is barely eighty pounds, very weak, dehydrated and in a lot of pain, plus she uses a walker to get around. Do you believe she typed a suicide note on the laptop computer, printed it, went down to the basement into the office, retrieved the note from the printer, brought it back upstairs and stuck it in one of her magazines?"

Randal continued, "When she had a pencil and a pad of paper right next to her? It doesn't make sense."

"I agree it doesn't make sense," the officer said.

"We need to locate the daughter who lives here, Alice Dickson. She has some explaining to do."

He issued directions. "Track her credit cards and see where and when she has used them recently. Get a couple of your men and head to Wilson, ask around at stores, gas stations, restaurants and find out if anyone recognizes her. I'll get you a picture." A policeman stationed in front of the house came up to Randal and interrupted him.

"There is a woman outside who wants to talk to the person in charge. She says it's important."

"I'll be right out." Randal finished what he was doing and went outside to where the woman was standing.

"Hello, I'm Detective Randal."

"I live across the street," the woman said. "I don't have all the details of what went on here earlier, but I thought it was coincidental that a woman who owns the Clean-N-Pristine Cleaning Company was at my house yesterday morning asking questions about Alice and her mother." The woman continued, "She wanted to know if they went out of town; she couldn't get into the house to clean."

The woman handed the detective Sarah's business card. "This is the card she gave me."

"Let me ask you a question, ma'am. Is this a picture of the daughter that lives with Mrs. Wilkinson?" He showed the woman a picture that he'd removed from the top of the piano.

"Yes, that's Alice. She has lived with her mother for quite a few years."

"Thank you, your information was helpful."

"Excuse me, detective. I wasn't finished!" the woman snapped.

"I'm sorry. What else did you want to say?"

"Today there was an older woman here not long ago asking questions about Emma Jean. I gathered she must have known her, but not well. It seems to me if she knew her well she would have gone up to a policeman and asked questions, but she didn't. The woman parked her car, came to me and asked me what had happened.

"She got very upset and started crying when I told her Emma Jean had been transported by ambulance to the hospital. I asked if I could help her, but she shook her head and got into her car and drove away. The woman was driving a white Lexus with dark gray interior. She had New York plates but I didn't get the plate number."

Randal hesitated a moment. "Is there anything else?"

"No, that's it. I just thought it was out of the ordinary."

"I agree," he told her. "Give this police officer your statement and thank you." Randal went back into the house and handed the picture of Alice to the officer he was sending to Wilson.

"This is the daughter, Alice. Use this photo; I want her found."

"I'll get right on it," the officer replied.

Randal had Sarah's company card in his hand and decided to call before it got too late. One of the cleaning teams had just arrived back at the office and the women were unloading their supplies when the phone rang.

"Clean-N-Pristine Cleaning. May I help you?"

"Yes, this is Detective Randal from the Lockport Police Department. May I speak to Sarah Stevens?"

"She's not here right now," the girl said.

"Do you have another number where I may reach her?"

"I can give you her cell number." She quickly rattled off Sarah's number.

"Have you seen or talked to Mrs. Stevens today?"

"Yes, I saw her early this afternoon, when she stopped by the office to take inventory. What happened? Is everything okay?"

"Nothing to be concerned about. I just need to ask her a few questions about one of her clients."

"If I talk to her, I'll tell her to call you."

"Do you have caller ID?"

"Yes, we do. Should I have her call you at that number?" the girl asked.

"Yes, thank you."

Randal hung up and called Sarah's cell number, which went to her voicemail, so he left a message: "This is Detective Randal from the Lockport Police Department. Please call me at this number when you get this message." He gave his personal number. "I have a few questions to ask you about one of your clients."

Randal thought for a moment about what the neighbor had told him: an older woman in a white Lexus asking questions. He had been at the hospital emergency room when they'd brought in an older woman who had been in an accident on West Avenue. The woman was critically injured—driving a Lexus. Could this all be related somehow?

Chapter Twenty-Nine

Garret was in shock; he didn't know what to do. This was going to devastate Sarah; how was he going to tell her? He had no idea of Gloria's condition, only that she was alive when they had transported her. It couldn't be good from the looks of her car.

"I have to get home ... I have to be the one to tell my wife about her mother before she hears about it from someone else," Garret said, feeling disoriented.

"We'll use one of our cars to take you home," the policeman said. "One of my officers will follow in your car. We will pick up your wife and bring you both to the hospital." They used an unmarked SUV to take Garret to his house; when they arrived and Sarah saw the lights, she came running out of the house.

"Garret, my mother isn't home yet!" she said as she looked around. Garret was getting out of the SUV when she said, "Who brought you home? Who's driving your car? What's going on, Garret?" She walked up to him, frightened and confused; she could see that her husband was upset.

"Sarah, I need to talk to you."

"What is it? You're scaring me!"

He held her arms tightly as he told her. "The car accident this afternoon was your mother."

"*NO*! Dear God, no!" Sarah screamed and almost fell to her knees. "What happened? Are you sure?"

"I don't have any details, Sarah. I went by the accident right after I hung up with you; I had a bad feeling when I saw the car and I went closer to check it out. It was her car. I came right home to tell you." Garret had tears in his eyes as he told her, "This gentleman is going to take us to the hospital so that you can be with her."

"Is she still alive?" Sarah asked softly, with a glimmer of hope.

"She was when they transported her. I haven't received any updates on her condition. Let's get you into the car, and we'll go be with her." Garret helped her into the vehicle, and then he ran into the house to get her purse. He looked around before he left and he saw Sarah's cell phone sitting on the counter next to her client address book. He grabbed them both and locked the door as he left.

Garret climbed into the back seat next to Sarah, who put her face on his chest and cried. The officer driving them to the hospital took a route they would not have normally taken because he wanted to avoid the scene of the accident.

Sarah and Garret were escorted directly into the intensive care unit. A distinguished-looking doctor came out of the room as soon as they arrived. Sarah tried to gather her emotions as he spoke to them.

"How is she?"

"I'm Doctor Graham," he started out saying. He hated this part of his job. "Your mother has been seriously injured. There was a massive blow to her head and upon my physical examination there is no clinical evidence of brain function. She has no response to pain and no cranial nerve reflexes."

The doctor continued to give the details carefully and give the couple time to understand. "I am having examinations done by two independent neurologists. The exams must show complete absence of brain function to confirm the condition is irreversible. We will do two flat-line EEGs on her, but due to the dysfunction being physical trauma to the head, we don't expect there will be any change."

"What are you saying?" Sarah asked in confusion.

"There is no clinical evidence of brain function," the doctor explained. "We have your mother on life support equipment, which can maintain body functions indefinitely. I will discuss this more with you after we perform the necessary tests."

"When will she wake up?" Sarah asked, like a little girl would ask. The doctor looked at Garret and didn't say anything for a moment.

"The tests will confirm our findings of no brain activity. In other words, she would not function on her own if we took her off the life support," he told them in layman's terms.

"My mother is being kept alive right now?" Sarah could not comprehend what the doctor was telling her.

"Yes," he said sympathetically.

"Is there nothing that can be done?" Sarah asked out of desperation and the doctor just shook his head. Sarah turned to Garret and fell onto his chest crying.

"How long do we have?" Sarah cried.

"We have more tests to perform. We can discuss that after our findings."

"May I see her?" she whispered.

"Of course, give me a few minutes." The doctor hesitated a moment and then said, "When you see her, I want you both to be aware that, because of the accident, there is massive swelling and bruising to her head and face." He went back into Gloria's room.

Sarah cried uncontrollably. Garret picked her up and carried her to a chair. A nurse came over to check on her, as Garret sat holding Sarah. He was overwhelmed himself about what had happened. Not knowing what to say, he just held her as she cried. Finally, she looked up at him.

"What am I going to do? I can't lose her, Garret ... she is my life. I don't know what I will do without her."

"You will take one day at a time and I will be right here to help you through this. I think you should go in and spend some time with her."

After several moments, Sarah stood slowly; she had been crying so much she was lightheaded. Garret helped her slip on the protective cover, mask and gloves before entering the room and, when she saw her mother, she gasped. She didn't recognize her. Along with many cuts and bruising, there were tubes and machines all around her.

"She isn't in any pain, is she?" Sarah asked the nurse who was assisting her mother.

"No, she's not in any pain."

Garret pulled up a chair for Sarah. "Spend some time with her, talk to her and tell her how much you love her. I'm going out for just a minute to call my girls. They would want to be here because they love your mother very much."

Sarah seemed to be a little better when Garret got back into the room.

"Can I get you anything?" he asked her.

"No, I'm fine," Sarah said in a whisper of a voice.

It didn't take long for the girls to arrive. Garret saw them as they walked up and he went out to meet them. He told them everything he knew about Gloria's condition and they both began to cry.

"How is Sarah? She has to be devastated!" Ella said.

"I think she's in shock. I don't think she truly understands the seriousness of the situation," Garret told them.

"Is there nothing they can do for Gloria?" Nicole asked.

Garret just shook his head.

"I'm so sorry, Dad. May we see Sarah?"

"I will tell her you're here. She could use a break because she has been in there a while." Garret hugged both his girls and walked in to tell Sarah that they were there.

It took her a few minutes to leave her mother's side and, when she walked out, both girls hugged her for several minutes and cried. They sat and talked for a while, and then Garret tried to get Sarah to go home for a few hours. It was past midnight, but Sarah refused; she was not leaving her mother.

"Ella and Nicole are going to take me home so that I can let the dog out, get a few things done on the computer so that I can have the next several days off and get my car. Will you be okay for a few hours? What do you want me to bring you?"

"I'll be fine. I don't need anything," Sarah said with no emotion.

"I grabbed your phone and client book off the counter and put them in your purse, which is right here. Call me if you need me." Garret had turned Sarah's phone off when they were on the way to the hospital so that she wouldn't get any calls. "I'll be back soon." He bent down and gave her a kiss. "I love you," he whispered in her ear.

When Garret got in the car with his girls, he told them the details of the accident. He hadn't wanted to tell them in front of Sarah.

"Oh my God, Dad! I heard about it on the news earlier and never put it together. It's just awful. I feel so sorry for Sarah because I know how close they are," Ella said.

"I know, I feel helpless. I don't know what I can do for her," he replied.

Garret's daughters dropped him off at the house. When he walked in, the dog came running to the door and he let her out. He looked around the house; it felt so cold and empty and there was an eerie silence. Garret let the dog back in and got on the computer to reschedule a few appointments he had coming up. He lay on the couch and dozed off for a few hours.

Chapter Thirty

It was very late, but Kayla had promised she would call her boyfriend before she went to bed. Her mother finally fell asleep and Kayla was able to sneak out of the house to call.

"Don't let Mom catch you using your phone," Layla told her.

It was very cold outside, and Kayla had on her pajamas, a pair of slippers and a blanket wrapped around her. She and Layla had found a few places around the outside of the house where they could get service, so Kayla went to a fairly sheltered spot.

"Hi, baby, I miss you so much," she told James. "I have to sneak out because my mother asked us to turn off our phones for the weekend. There's not much cell service up here anyway, but if I stay in this one spot I should be okay."

"Are you all having a nice time and getting along?" James asked jokingly.

"We're actually getting along fine. My mother is very doting; she always has been. But, James, she seems different somehow—I can't explain it."

"How's the cottage?"

"It's very nice, right on the water. Layla asked my mom how she purchased such a nice cottage, and she told us my grandma pays for everything. My mother was a little drunk and said more than I think she wanted to. She told us Grandma was the one that gave Layla and me the money to buy our house, and even bought the furniture and all the gifts we've received over the years. I had no idea, James. My mother lied and said she bought them for us." Kayla felt her voice starting to rise and tremble. "Now I know exactly how my father felt!"

"What's done is done, Kayla. There isn't anything you can do about it now. Maybe you can talk to your mother or your grandmother to let them know you feel uncomfortable about getting the money and tell them to stop."

"That's a great idea, I'll do that," Kayla said, feeling some relief.

"Hey, honey, have you received any messages or missed calls?" James asked.

"A few from my friends, and I had a missed call from my Uncle Blake, which I thought was odd, but he didn't leave a message."

"I'm asking because I received a Facebook instant message from your Aunt Lexi. It said she knew you were with your mother this weekend and if I talk to you, to tell you to give her a call ASAP. She said it was important."

"I wonder what's going on. If I call my aunt and there is a problem, my mother is going to want to know how I found out. I'm not supposed to be using my phone—I promised her," Kayla said, but James didn't respond—she'd lost her cell service. "Damn! Not now." Kayla decided she would call her Aunt Lexi in the morning.

While Garret was gone, Sarah sat by her mother's bedside wondering what she was going to do without her. Her mother had struggled through difficult times as a child growing up and worked hard to better her life. She gave up a lot to raise Sarah as a single parent and Sarah knew she was blessed with having such a wonderful mother. Her mother had given her everything she ever needed as a child—most importantly, love, affection and understanding.

Sarah noticed that her mother's belongings were in a large plastic bag next to her purse. She slowly looked through the bag. Her mother's clothes were torn and dirty, and a piece of paper was sticking out of her coat pocket. Sarah saw that it was her shopping list and that each item had been crossed off.

As she folded the paper to put it back into the pocket, she saw writing on the other side; it was an address … a familiar address. *This is Emma Jean Wilkinson's address*, Sarah thought. *That's where my mother went! It makes sense now.* Her mother had known that Alice was out of town for the weekend. Emma Jean would have been home by herself and her mom knew that as well. *I bet she went to meet her*, Sarah thought.

"What did you do, Mom? I hope you met your sister," she said softly.

Sarah didn't get much sleep that night due to her trepidation over her mother's injuries and wondering how this all had happened. Also, the chair was not very comfortable and Garret wasn't with her. Her mind was racing but after a few hours she finally dozed off.

Garret woke concerned, quickly looking at his watch. He took a quick shower, got a small bag from the closet to put a few things in for Sarah and also grabbed a few bottles of water from the refrigerator. As he walked out to his car, he stopped for a moment and looked over at Gloria's house. *What a wonderful relationship Sarah and Gloria had*, he thought. He didn't remember them ever fighting. Garret headed back to the hospital.

When Sarah woke, Garret was next to her.

"Good morning, I've missed you," Sarah told him.

Garret leaned over and gave her a kiss. "How are you holding up?"

"I was actually having a good dream," she said, thinking about it. She looked at her mother and said, "Back to reality." Sarah sat up in her chair energized, remembering what she'd wanted to call Garret about.

"I know where my mother was coming from when she was in her accident. She had her sister Emma Jean's address on the back of her grocery list. I found a paper in her coat pocket—she'd written the address on her grocery list. She knew Alice was out of town, so she went to the house to meet Emma Jean."

"How did you figure that out?" Garret asked, amazed.

"It makes sense. The accident happened close to Emma Jean's house. Mom would have been coming home from that direction."

"It does make sense," Garret said. "She was driving fast, Sarah. She drives like that when she is upset and she overcompensated the turn onto East Avenue."

"I know. I took a walk during the night and I pulled up the Internet on my phone. I Googled the news of her crash." Sarah had tears in her eyes. "I'm going to call Emma Jean later and ask her if Mom came by, then I'm going to tell her everything I know."

"There were witnesses who saw the accident. The police will figure out what exactly happened," Garret reassured her.

"That reminds me: I got a call from a Detective Randal. He wanted to ask me questions about a client of mine. That's all he said; he must think my mother must be a client or something. It was an odd message."

Lexi boarded her flight in Jacksonville at six-forty in the morning; she had a connection in Charlotte, North Carolina, and was on her way to the Buffalo airport. She arrived right on time at eleven-ten, picked up her rental car and drove north to Lockport. She hadn't been back to her hometown since the previous summer when her kids were with her. This time, it wasn't going to be an enjoyable trip.

When she pulled out her phone and turned it on, she saw that she had two missed calls, one from Chase and the other from Kayla. *It worked; James got a message to her,* she thought. Lexi called her sister Aimee's cell, but there was no answer. She then called Blake, who picked up on the first ring.

"I'm on my way to Lockport—I'm heading directly to the hospital," she told him.

"Aimee is already there, and I'll be there in a few minutes. I understand there's no change in your mother's condition since the last time I talked to you. Your mother is on the second floor, room 202."

"Blake, I figured out a way to get a hold of Alice. I'll tell you how when I see you. In any case, I have a missed call from Kayla, so I'll call her back and have her tell her mother she needs to get home!"

"Perfect! Thanks, Lexi. See you in a little while."

Lexi had to be careful talking on her cell phone; she was used to being able to talk when driving in Florida, but in New York it was against the law. She was just about to call Kayla when her phone rang; it was Kayla.

"Hello, Aunt Lexi, this is Kayla. I don't have much time to talk, what's up?"

"I'm on my way to Lockport; we have been trying to get a hold of your mother. Mom is in intensive care on life support with liver failure."

"Oh my God, what happened?"

"Aimee went to check on her while your mother was away. When she got there Saturday, she found her unconscious on her bedroom floor barely breathing. We don't know how long she had been lying there."

"That's awful—I'll tell my mom right away. Is Grandma in the Lockport hospital?"

"Yes, room 202. They think she tried to commit suicide, Kayla, and the police want to talk to your mom."

"I can't believe it! Why would Grandma do that at her age?" There was no response, "Aunt Lexi, can you hear me?" Kayla had lost service, which was fine because she heard her mother calling.

Lexi arrived at the hospital and went to the second floor, which was the intensive care unit. A nurse kindly escorted Lexi to her mother's room and helped her put on the protective cover, gloves and mask, which everyone who entered the room had to wear. Lexi stood at the door and began to cry when she saw her mother hooked up to all the tubes. Aimee, Blake and Nathan were already in the room; Nathan had arrived that morning with his father. Aimee went right over to her sister and hugged her.

"She looks terrible," Lexi said. "She is so skinny."

"She was very dehydrated as well as her liver failing. She's in a coma."

Kayla walked into the cabin to tell her mother what was going on.

"Where have you been? You need to get ready so we can go to lunch. There are also a couple of charming boutiques I want to stop at as well," Alice said excitedly.

"Mom, I have to talk to you." Layla came out of her bedroom because she could tell by the sound of Kayla's voice that something was wrong.

"What's the matter? You look upset," Layla asked.

"Grandma is in the hospital on life support."

"What? What are you talking about? How do you know this?" Alice asked.

"I know you asked us not to use our phones, but I wanted to talk to James. I called him late last night and he told me he received a message from Aunt Lexi to have me call her, so I did. I was just outside talking to her and she told me about Grandma."

"What happened to her?" Layla asked.

"She's on life support for liver failure. I didn't get many details because I lost service," Kayla gasped.

"You promised me you would *not* use your cell phones!" Alice said angrily. "I asked one thing of you this whole weekend and you couldn't abide by my wishes." Both girls looked at their mother in confusion and disbelief.

"Your mother is in the hospital dying and you're upset with *me* because I used my phone?" Kayla snapped back.

"People react to situations in different ways, so don't mistake my response for not being concerned," Alice said. "I'm very disturbed about what happened to my mother. How dare you question my worry for her?"

Alice turned and went to her bedroom, shutting the door behind her. She took a moment and then let out a sigh of relief. *My plan worked and I have an alibi for the weekend.* She picked up her cell phone from the dresser, turned it on for the first time in days; she saw there were several missed calls from Blake and Lexi and one from a number she didn't recognize. She dreaded making the call to Blake. *I would have liked one more day before we had to leave*, she thought. Alice emerged from her bedroom with her cell phone and car keys in her hand.

"Are you leaving already?" Kayla asked.

"I'm going to drive south a bit so that I can get service on my phone; I need to call Blake and find out about your grandmother."

"You don't have to drive anywhere," Kayla said. "I'll show you a spot where you can get service." The two of them walked out the door to the back of the house. "Your reaction about Grandma surprised me, Mom," Kayla said.

"What do you mean? I'm devastated, Kayla!"

"You didn't seem devastated or very surprised when I told you."

Alice didn't respond. She looked at her phone.

"Well, what do you know … ? I have service," Alice said. Kayla just looked at her mother, shook her head and went back into the cottage.

"Blake, this is Alice. I just found out about my mother! What happened to her?" she asked him in her concerned voice.

"The doctor thinks she may have taken an overdose of pills and tried to commit suicide." Blake wasn't going to tell Alice they knew about her hepatitis, not yet anyway.

"When did she do this?" Alice asked, pretending to be surprised.

"Saturday, Aimee found her unconscious on her bedroom floor. They don't know how long she had been there. Your mother is on a life support system. She took a large amount of aceta … something—a bunch of Tylenol pills—and her liver failed. Lexi just arrived from Florida and they want you to come back to Lockport for questioning."

"Me? They want to question me? What did I do? I've been here all weekend!"

"I don't know, Alice. You've lived with the woman for nine years, and they want to ask you some questions." Blake was plainly annoyed.

"Okay, I'll be home in a few hours," Alice told him. She hung up from her conversation, thinking, *Good! It looked like suicide, and that's how it was supposed to look.* She felt some relief as she walked back into the house and told her girls what she'd found out. "We had better get packed and head to Lockport."

Just as she spoke, there was a knock on the door and the three women jumped. "Who could that be?" Layla asked.

Alice went to the door and could see two police officers through the glass. A wave of fear surged through her body. She opened the door and, before the officers could say anything, she spoke up.

"Is this about my mother?" she asked in concern.

"It is, ma'am. We are here to inform you about your mother and escort you back to Lockport, where Detective Randal would like to question you."

"I just talked to my brother-in-law on the phone and he told me what happened to her. My daughters and I were just packing to go home." Alice pretended to wipe a tear from her eye.

"We will wait for you in the squad car to escort you to Lockport."

"There's no need for that," Alice told them.

"We'll be waiting." The two officers walked back to their squad car and waited for them to leave.

One of the officers called Detective Randal. "I'm at the cottage. Ms. Dickson had just talked to her brother-in-law on the phone and he informed her of the mother's condition. We'll wait for her and her daughters to leave and escort them back to Lockport."

"Very good," was all the detective said.

Before Randal went back to the hospital, he made a call to Emma Jean's primary care physician's office and talked to the answering service. He told them it was a police matter and it was imperative the doctor call him. It had to do with Emma Jean Wilkinson's fulminate hepatitis condition.

The doctor called back within five minutes. He couldn't reveal any medical information about Emma Jean's condition but he did tell Randal that her test results had indicated that it wasn't that severe.

"When you called Mrs. Wilkinson to give her the test results, did you speak to her personally?"

"No, actually, I talked to her daughter, Alice. She was with her mother when Mrs. Wilkinson came for her appointment. Alice then stopped by the office about twenty minutes later and picked up the prescriptions I wrote for her mother."

"Have there been any follow-up appointments or prescription refills since her last appointment?" Randal asked.

"As a matter of fact, no, I haven't seen her."

"Thank you for your time." Randal was right: Emma Jean had never known of her condition.

Chapter Thirty-One

DETECTIVE RANDAL GOT TO THE HOSPITAL, hoping to time it just before Alice was due to arrive. He gave himself enough time to check on Emma Jean.

"How is your mother doing?" Randal asked Aimee.

"Not well. She's still in a coma." Aimee introduced the detective to Lexi and Nathan and told him that they'd been able to reach Alice, who was on her way back to Lockport.

"Good! She should be arriving soon and then we can discuss your mother's condition and get this whole 'suicide' thing taken care of."

"Are you saying that you don't think it was suicide?" Lexi asked.

"I will talk to everyone when your sister arrives," he said as he left the room and began walking down the hall.

The neurosurgeon did the final EEG test on Gloria that morning; it confirmed that there was no clinical evidence of brain function. Doctor Graham had the test results and escorted Sarah and Garret to a secluded waiting room down the hall from her mother's room so that he could talk to them privately.

"We have finished all the tests on your mother and I regret to inform you that it's not good news. The tests confirm there is no brain activity. They corroborate my findings that if we took your mother off the life support she wouldn't survive. I'm very sorry." Sarah began to cry, the small flicker of hope that her mother would be okay gone. Garret held her while the doctor continued, "Do you have any questions you want to ask me?"

"Is there any chance at all she could get better?" Sarah asked, although she already knew the answer.

"No, I'm sorry,"

"What do we do now?" Garret asked.

"I know this is a tough time for you both. I bring this up now because it's a time factor. Your mother would be a good candidate for organ donation." Doctor Graham waited a moment for a reaction but there wasn't one. "She filled out an organ donor card with her driver's license. When she did this, she agreed to donate her organs when she died."

"Believe it or not, my mother and I have discussed this," Sarah told them softly. "She always said the greatest benefit of organ donation is being able to save the life of a very grateful stranger."

"That's a very profound statement," the doctor told her.

"Who do her organs go to and when?" Garret asked.

"They go to patients who have been placed on the national waiting list for organ transplantation. We will do a medical assessment to determine what organs can be donated. If there is any actively spreading cancer or severe infection, that would be a reason to exclude an organ donation."

"My mother was very healthy," Sarah said quietly.

"We will get you the paperwork that needs to be signed." Doctor Graham thanked Sarah and left the room. That moment, Sarah's cell phone rang from inside her purse; she and Garret were both surprised.

"Do you want me to get that?" Garret asked.

"No, I've got it, thanks." She quickly reached into her purse and pulled out the phone before it stopped ringing. It was a number that she didn't recognize. "Hello, this is Sarah Stevens."

"Ms. Stevens, this is Detective Randal from the Lockport Police Department. May I have a few minutes of your time?"

"Oh yes, Detective. I listened to your message this morning and I think you were confused about the woman in the accident being a client—she was my mother."

There was silence on the other end for a moment.

"Excuse me, ma'am, what accident?"

"Isn't this about my mother's accident?"

"Do you own the Clean-N-Pristine Cleaning Company?"

"Yes."

"And Emma Jean Wilkinson is a client of yours, correct?"

"Yes." Sarah was the one confused now.

"You were at her house on Friday, March 16, to clean?"

"Yes … I mean no; I was there, but I couldn't get into the house to clean. What is this about? I thought you were calling to update me on my mother's accident investigation."

"I'm sorry. Your mother was in an accident?" Randal knew exactly what she was going to say the minute he asked. This was much more than a coincidence. Sarah's mother was the woman in the white Lexus that went to Emma Jean Wilkinson's house.

"Yes, Detective—yesterday, she was in a very bad car accident." Tears filled Sarah's eyes.

"Ms. Stevens, I need to speak to you in person. Where would you like to meet?"

"I'm a little busy, detective. I'm at the hospital with my mother spending my last few days with her if you must know." Sarah didn't mean to be so rude but she didn't understand any of this.

Detective Randal shook his head in disbelief; it was all falling into place.

"May we meet in thirty minutes at the intensive care waiting room?"

"Is this about my mother or Emma Jean Wilkinson?"

"Both. I'll see you in thirty minutes," he told her as he hung up.

Chapter Thirty-Two

Garret was very annoyed with whoever was on the other end of Sarah's phone conversation. The caller had upset her terribly and she didn't need that right now.

"I'm okay, Garret," she said after she hung up, sounding surprisingly calm. "It was a very confusing conversation. I'm not sure what the detective was asking me. He wants us to meet him right here, in this room, thirty minutes from now."

"Let's not wait here the whole time," Garret said. "We'll go back to your mother's room for a while; he can wait a few minutes for us if we're late."

"It's not like we have far to go," Sarah told him. The two of them walked back to her mother's room hand in hand. Sarah sat with her mother and told her they were abiding by her wishes.

"We're doing as you planned, Mom; we're donating your organs." Sarah held her mother's hand as she talked to her. "This is what you wanted. You're going to save lives just as you wished," she said with tears in her eyes.

Detective Randal stood in the distance in an inconspicuous spot where he could observe everything going on in the two intensive care rooms. He watched as Sarah and her husband went into her mother's room. He understood it now, he knew who Sarah was ... she was the daughter of Gloria Michaels—the older woman who had driven her Lexus to Emma Jean's house and ended up in a car accident after she left. Sarah cleaned for Emma Jean Wilkinson, who was also in intensive care with liver failure.

Sarah was associated with both women but had only been in and out of her mother's room. Both families were cordial when seeing one another, but they didn't seem to know each other. He understood Sarah's association to the two women; now he had to figure out how Gloria Michaels and Emma Jean Wilkinson were connected.

As Randal thought about this, he watched as two young girls in their early twenties walked down the hall and went to Gloria's room; Garret came out to meet them. Randal assumed that they were Garret's daughters, as he helped them with their masks and gowns and all went in to visit.

Not long after Garret's daughters arrived, two other young women came down the hall together and went to Emma Jean's room. Nathan met them at the door ... grandchildren of Emma Jean, Randal presumed. He got on his phone and called the officers escorting Alice and her daughters back to Lockport.

"What's your ETA?" he asked.

"About thirty minutes."

"I want the two of you to 'escort' Ms. Dickson and her girls to the second floor. I intend to have the whole family here," Randal told them. "I would like for you both to stay as well."

Randal took a few minutes and updated the officers on the investigation. He hadn't questioned Alice yet, but, based on the evidence he'd gathered so far and the information the doctor had conveyed to him, there was no doubt in his mind that Alice was the one who had put her mother in the hospital. Now that Randal knew what time Alice was due to arrive, he went to Emma Jean's room and asked the family to meet him in the waiting room.

"I'm sorry to interrupt. May I have a moment of your time?" he said. Aimee, Lexi and the rest of the family in Emma Jean's room turned their attention to Detective Randal, who was standing in the doorway. "In twenty minutes I would like all of you to meet me in the intensive care waiting room located just down the hall. I want to update you on the investigation of your mother's so-called suicide attempt."

"Didn't you want my sister Alice to be here when you talked to us?" Aimee asked.

"She will be here by then." Randal was matter of fact. He was eager to gather both families together in the same room and figure out the correlation between them. He had a feeling that Alice was responsible for both families' heartaches.

"Did you hear what the detective said? Grandma's 'so-called' suicide attempt?" Nathan commented.

"He doesn't think Grandma tried to kill herself!" Brooke replied.

"I think it has to do with Alice and that's why he wants her here when he talks to us," Aimee told them.

Twenty-five minutes later, Emma Jean's family walked down the hall to the waiting room. As they entered the room, Alice exited the elevator located at the opposite end of the hall, hurrying because the two police officers shadowing made her very nervous. She and her daughters walked down the hall, donned their isolation gowns and entered Emma Jean's room. There was a nurse tending to Emma Jean and Detective Randal stood just outside the room. Even though there was a nurse and Kayla and Layla were in the room, he didn't want Alice left alone with Emma Jean.

"How is she … ?" Alice asked the nurse. There was very little emotion in her voice.

"Your mother is in a coma due to liver failure," the nurse said. Kayla and Layla were crying. "The doctor will be here later to update you."

"I'm Detective Randal," the detective said from the doorway.

"I understand you want to ask me some questions," Alice said in a peculiar tone.

"Yes, I do, about the investigation of your mother's 'suicide attempt.' If I could have the three of you follow me to the waiting room down the hall, we can get this all taken care of."

"My daughters don't have to be there, do they?" Alice asked.

"Yes, I would like them there as well."

"I don't understand why. They have nothing to do with this situation."

"It's okay, Mom," Layla said. "We'll go with you for support."

Alice and the twins took off their gowns and walked with Randal down the hall to the room where both families were waiting; the two uniformed police officers followed.

Sarah, Garret and his girls were already in the waiting room when Lexi, Aimee, Blake and their children entered.

"Hello," Aimee said, surprised when she saw Sarah's family sitting there. "I understand your mother was in a bad car accident. We're very sorry and we apologize for interrupting."

"You're not interrupting," Sarah said. She looked at Aimee and Lexi as if she recognized them from somewhere other than the hospital, but she couldn't put her finger on it. "We're supposed to be meeting a detective here. He wanted to talk to us about our mother's situation," Sarah said. "We can move our meeting elsewhere."

Aimee looked at Sarah curiously. "The detective that you're meeting—would that be a Detective Randal by any chance?"

"Yes, it is," Sarah said immediately.

"What the hell's going on?" Garret asked as they all looked puzzled.

"Detective Randal requested us to be here as well," Blake told them.

"This is crazy," Nathan commented.

"I wonder what this is all about?" Brooke's eyes looked startled at the strange situation.

Just as the question was asked, Detective Randal entered the room with Alice, Kayla, Layla and the two police officers.

"What the hell are you doing here?" Sarah shouted as they walked in. Everyone thought she was talking to the detective until Alice spoke up.

"I was summoned here by this detective," Alice said furiously. "For Christ's sake, I just got back into town and only had five minutes with my ailing mother in intensive care and now I have to be yelled at by my cleaning girl?"

"You two know each other?" Lexi asked in surprise. "You clean for them?" Lexi pointed toward Alice.

"Emma Jean is in intensive care?" Sarah asked, horrified. "Dear God! She's the woman in the room next to my mother? I didn't know … I'm so sorry … I didn't know. I should have done something right away!" Sarah cried hysterically.

"What is she talking about?" Aimee asked. "What should she have done right away?"

"What the hell is going on here, detective?" Garret said as he tried to calm Sarah. "You're tormenting everyone in this room."

"We all deserve an explanation *immediately*!" Blake spoke up.

"I want everybody to take a seat and listen," Randal said firmly. "I've gathered you all here today because of the two women lying in intensive care on life support. Sarah Stevens and Alice Dickson know each other. Sarah's cleaning company works for Ms. Dickson and her mother."

"She *used* to work for us," Alice said under her breath.

Randal gave her an unpleasant look and then continued. "Mrs. Wilkinson was found unconscious by her daughter Aimee on Saturday. It appears she took an overdose. We found a suicide note on her bed and many empty bottles of extra-strength Tylenol in her nightstand." Randal paused a moment to look around the room.

"Through my experience, I've found that most people committing suicide don't type out their suicide note. There is no earthly way your mother could have typed a note from her laptop, gone down to the basement, retrieved the paper from the printer and then gone back to her room. She would have been incapable and, in any case, she had a pad of paper next to her on the bed that she could have used."

"I don't think she has ever been in her basement," Aimee commented.

"The suicide note was your first mistake, Alice."

"What is that supposed to mean?" Alice snapped, as she started to panic.

Detective Randal continued, "I have also learned through my investigation that Mrs. Wilkinson was diagnosed with viral hepatitis several months ago and the illness was never taken care of. My guess is that she wasn't told about her illness when the doctor called with her test results." Randal turned toward Alice. "On that day you took the call for your mother—correct?"

"That was months ago! How am I supposed to remember that?" Alice lied.

"I talked to the doctor and he recalls telling you."

"Oh, yes … I did tell Mom about that! I went right away to pick up her prescriptions."

"The doctor told me the same thing. He said you were there within twenty minutes," Randal said.

"It's not my fault she didn't take her medicine—she told me she took her pills."

"Are you sure about that?" Randal asked shrewdly.

"Of course I'm sure! How dare you insult me in front of all these people!"

"In a drawer in your office, we found the prescriptions. You never filled them because your mother didn't know she was sick."

"Mom …" Layla said softly.

"It's not true, Layla. Don't listen to him!" Alice's heart was racing; she couldn't think what to do or say as Randal continued.

"Over the next several months Mrs. Wilkinson was given large doses of acetaminophen, which is the main ingredient in Tylenol."

"She took those pills on her own," Alice said sharply, snapping at the detective. "She told me to buy her a bottle every time I went to the store."

Randal ignored her comment. "Because of her condition, the Tylenol rapidly destroyed her already failing liver."

"That was my mother's decision. She knew of her condition and told me not to fill the prescriptions and she took the Tylenol for her pain."

"We have your laptop, Ms. Dickson. Our computer expert discovered your research on acetaminophen right around the time you found out about your mother's test results. You can never totally get rid of evidence of inquiries on a computer," Randal said.

"You can't take my computer without a warrant. You can't take anything out of my house," Alice said desperately.

"That would be our house, Alice … remember we all own equal shares," Aimee commented.

"Actually, we had a warrant," Randal said. "We had the right to take whatever we deemed suspicious in the house as evidence."

"I may have bought the pills for her, but you can't prove I gave them to her!"

"Do you hear yourself?" Lexi said to her.

Everybody in the room was in complete shock. The twins were devastated, just staring at their mother. Sarah had never imagined that Alice could be so calculating; she'd planned this whole elaborate scheme for months.

Sarah stood up and addressed the detective. "I'm a witness," she said boldly. "I watched Alice put the Tylenol pills in her mother's soda bottles last Friday when I was there cleaning."

"You're a liar!" Alice yelled.

Sarah ignored her. "I didn't know what to do. I thought about telling Emma Jean but I didn't," she said regretfully. "I decided to confront Alice about what I had seen and she told me her mother had trouble taking her pills. I knew this wasn't true because I'd watched Emma Jean take medication." Sarah looked straight at Alice. "She put the empty pill bottles in a large baggie she kept on the top shelf of her kitchen cabinet."

"This is all a lie! I didn't do any of that!"

"Sarah told her mother and me about all of it that day when she got home from work," Garret said.

"I didn't do what everyone is saying. Please believe me! Everybody is against me: Sarah and her family … my family has been resentful of me for years and my own mother treated me terribly."

"We have the soda bottles that were next to your mother's bed—two were full and the third one was empty, but there was plenty of sediment to test. I have a feeling the test results will confirm what Ms. Stevens has just told us. This cruel plan of yours was set in motion months ago, even though you planned an alibi for this weekend," Randal told her.

"That's why you insisted on meeting us this weekend?" Layla snapped. "So you had an alibi? You used us … your own daughters?"

"What did you do, Mom?" Kayla was crying. "How could you do that to your own mother? She has given you everything. For God's sake, she bought you that house on the lake!"

"She did what?" Aimee said, surprised.

"Oh, yeah, Aunt Aimee. Make sure you check all Grandma's finances," Kayla told her.

"Kayla, Layla, please listen to me. I didn't do what everyone is saying!" Alice said in desperation.

"You make me sick!" Kayla told her mother.

"Please, Kayla, I'm innocent until proven guilty, please remember that." Kayla grabbed Layla's hand and the two of them ran out of the room. Layla took her phone out of her purse and called their father Drew.

"Her envelope with thousands of dollars was empty. Did you take that as well?" Blake asked.

"My mother gave me that money before I left for the weekend. I wondered why, but I didn't think she was going to try to kill herself."

Detective Randal nodded at one of the uniformed police officers, who took out his handcuffs and put them on Alice.

"I didn't do anything! You have to believe me! I wasn't even in town when all this happened!" she screamed, fighting for her life. The two families just looked at each other.

"Motive, means and opportunity," Randal said to Alice. "The presence of these three essentials is not, in or of itself, sufficient evidence to convict beyond a reasonable doubt, but having a witness is."

"I want a lawyer! I'm being railroaded!"

"Get her out of here and don't forget to read her her rights," Randal told the policeman. As the officer took her away in handcuffs, Alice couldn't comprehend what was happening to her. She thought she had had everything worked out so that it would look as if her mother had done this to herself. The way Alice saw it, she had helped her mother along to what was inevitable—Emma Jean wasn't going to live very much longer anyway.

Chapter Thirty-Three

Those left in the waiting room sat as though stunned, most of the women crying.

"How can one person destroy so many lives?" Brooke said softly.

"I'm very sorry I had to do this here and now. There was more to this case and I had to figure it out while everyone was together. I was relieved you could come forward as a witness, Mrs. Stevens," Detective Randal said.

"I just can't believe our own sister could be so cold and callous," Lexi said, crying. "What happened to her?"

"Her husband, Drew, left her years ago because of her greed and lies, and it took over her heart and soul," Aimee said.

"One thing I do know," Randal said as he addressed everyone in the room. "Gloria Michaels went to Mrs. Wilkinson's house and discovered that an ambulance had taken her to the hospital. She got terribly upset and when she left to drive home she lost control of her car."

"How do you know that's where Gloria went?" Garret asked.

"She talked to one of Mrs. Wilkinson's neighbors, who told her what had happened. What I don't know is how Mrs. Michaels and Mrs. Wilkinson know one another."

Sarah looked at Garrett and then back at the detective. "My mother went to Emma Jean's house on Saturday afternoon to meet her for the first time. I had just found out the week before that my mother and Emma Jean were born on the same day and were probably twins. I was going to talk to Emma Jean more about it on Friday, but as we all know I didn't get the chance."

Sarah said sadly, "Now the two of them lie next to each other on life support, never having met."

"I have proof they were twins," Lexi said as she looked at Nathan.

"Why are you looking at Nathan? You both knew about this?" Aimee said to them.

"I just found out myself," Lexi said. "I found an old poem hidden in my antique clock. It was about giving up a baby and it was dated and signed 'Rose.' I called Nathan because I wanted him to help me investigate before I said anything. He had a friend who was able to get the information we needed."

"So they really were twins," Sarah said in relief, glad that this question wasn't left unanswered.

"Yes, in 1932 our Grandma Rose gave birth to two baby girls five minutes apart. They were both premature and remained in the hospital for eight days as baby 'A' and baby 'B.' Grandma and Grandpa took baby A home with them and called her Emma Jean. Hospital birth records were changed and baby B went home with Joan and Earl Michaels, who named her Gloria. I have the poem and a copy of the file documents in the car. That's all the information I have about Gloria."

"I can tell you what I know about my mother's childhood growing up," Sarah said, taking a deep breath. "She was raised by Joan and Earl Michaels for twelve years. The father who adopted her when she was a newborn got drunk and physically abused her and her mother. The state came and took my mom from the only life she knew, away from her mother because the woman chose to stay with her husband.

Joan told my mom that she had been adopted. She was placed in a foster home and was then sent to Wyman Land Home for Children."

"You're kidding—that's awful!" Skye said.

"Her paperwork from the state was filed incorrectly and that's why she was sent there. It took the state over a year to correct the paperwork because of all the red tape involved. My mom was then placed with another foster family that only wanted her for slave labor in their fields," Sarah continued with tears in her eyes. "At the age of sixteen she ran away to live on the streets of Lockport." Brooke and Skye were both crying and Detective Randal had to take a seat.

"She used to tell me how cold the winters were. She said she would climb under the main street bridge by the locks and try to get away from the cold blowing snow. She was afraid to sleep because she might never wake up." Sarah wiped a tear and continued as everyone listened intently.

"An older couple saw my mom begging on the street and took her home. This couple took her in, saved my mother's life and helped turn her life around. She obtained her GED and went to college," Sarah said proudly. "My mom dated a young man and became pregnant. My father died of an illness before they could marry." Sarah was describing only what she herself was aware of, as her mother had never revealed the horror of rape that she'd endured.

"My mother managed a grocery store for years and provided me with a wonderful life. She is also a terrific artist and one of her drawings hangs in Garlock's restaurant." When Sarah said this, Lexi's family all turned and looked at her. "Something I said?" Sarah asked.

"It's funny you say that—I'm an artist," Lexi said. "I sell my artwork at a place in Jacksonville called The Art Montage. It must run in the family. I would love to see your mom's work."

"I think we could arrange that sometime," Sarah smiled.

Garret helped Sarah to her feet. "I think we could all use a break. Let's go be with your mother for a while," he told Sarah gently.

"I agree," Aimee said. "Would you mind if we kept in touch?" she asked Sarah.

"I would like that." Sarah, Aimee and Lexi exchanged information.

Garret escorted his wife and daughters out of the waiting room. The doctor had told them earlier that day that Gloria's tests had come back negative for any infections and they could do her organ donation as soon as Tuesday.

Chapter Thirty-Four

"I'm very sorry I kept you all in the dark," Randal said to Aimee, Blake and Lexi. "I couldn't reveal my investigation to you because I wasn't sure what your sister was capable of. If you knew something and confronted her, she could have felt trapped and gone after any of you."

He told them, "You have my permission to go to your mother's house and go through her finances. If you find that your sister has done anything illegal regarding that, which I'm sure you'll find, give me a call and I'll help you out."

"Thank you, detective, for getting this ended in a timely manner," Blake told him.

"If I can find a way to stick that woman with theft as well, I will," Randal said seriously. "It's time for me to get to the station and process your sister. Attempted pre-meditated murder, she won't get out on bail—I'll make sure of that."

"What do we do?" Lexi asked.

"Take care of your mother, focus on her and get her the help she needs," Randal told them as he exited the room.

"Our sister is being arrested for attempting to murder our mother," Aimee said. "It makes me sick. Why didn't we see what was going on?"

"Your sister has gone off the deep end. There's nothing you can do for her now," Blake said.

"I feel sorry for Kayla and Layla," Nathan said.

"We all do," Aimee said softly.

"Let's get out of here. I think we could all use some fresh air. We'll go check on your mom, stop by her house and pick up her financial information, then get a bite to eat at the restaurant," Blake told them.

Aimee, Lexi and Blake returned to the house after eating dinner at Shenanigans, and their kids went their separate ways for a few hours. The three adults were sitting in the family room, and Lexi was talking to Chase on the phone, updating him on everything that had gone on that day, when there was a knock at the door. They all looked at each other curiously because it was late. Blake got up from his chair and went to the door; he looked through the window before he opened the door.

"It's Detective Randal," he told them as he opened the door.

"I'm sorry to disturb you so late. May I come in?"

"Of course, come in," Blake said. "Have a seat."

"I'm fine, I won't be long." Randal took a deep breath. "I thought I should be the one to tell you about your sister." He hesitated a moment. "She committed suicide in her cell tonight."

"No … she didn't!" Lexi cried out.

"How … what happened?" Aimee asked, stunned.

"She must have had a bobby pin in her hair, and she scraped the tip of it on the metal part of the bed until it became very sharp. She slit her wrists with it. We didn't get to her in time. She was transported to the hospital where she died." Randal didn't know what else to say except, "I'm sorry." He knew they had had a very difficult day and, now, receiving this news had to be overwhelming.

"I can't take anymore!" Lexi fell to her knees. Randal helped her to a chair as Blake helped Aimee to a seat.

"When did this happen?" Blake asked.

"About eleven o'clock tonight."

"Did she leave a note and explain why she did all of this?" Blake wondered.

"There was a note … she apologized to her daughters," Randal told them. The note had been written by an angry, disturbed woman who needed help. He didn't think they needed to know what else it said.

Chapter Thirty-Five

Garret's daughters told Sarah they had to go but would be back in the morning.

"I'm so glad you both were here to support me through this difficult time. I love you both more than you will ever know," Sarah told them. Garret walked Ella and Nicole out to their car while Sarah stayed by her mother's side. When he got back to the room, he persuaded Sarah to go home to get some rest.

"You can come back in the morning and spend all day with her before she is taken off life support." It took a while to convince her, but Sarah finally agreed.

As Garret drove Sarah home, there was very little conversation. Garret would wait until she was ready to talk, and he would be there to listen. When they pulled into the driveway, Sarah felt as if it had been ages since the last time she was home. Her eyes filled with tears as she looked over at her mother's home. She'd bought this property specifically for that home and fixed it up especially for her mother.

How could Alice have treated Emma Jean the way she did … her own mother! It made Sarah angry and sick when she thought about it; she couldn't comprehend the cruelty. All Sarah wanted to do was take care of her mom and make life easier for her in her later years.

She realized that she would never be able to talk to her again, and she had so much to say to her.

"What am I going to do, Garret? I feel so empty without her."

"Each day will get easier, I promise." Garret held her as they walked into the house; it was dark and cold. Their golden retriever came running up, excited to see them; Sarah petted her and kissed her nose. Then Garret let the dog out the back door and fed her as Sarah headed straight to the bedroom—she was exhausted.

"I'm going to draw you a hot bath. Give me five minutes." Garret ran the water in the bathtub and added extra bubbles; he turned on some soothing music and went to the kitchen to get her a glass of red wine. Sarah was sitting on the side of the bed staring at nothing. He got her up and escorted her to her bath.

"I want you to try to relax. I'll order us a pizza from Pontillo's—your favorite—and have it delivered."

"Thank you, love, this will help me unwind." She undressed and stepped into the bubbles. Garret made her bath just the way she liked it … very hot; however, Sarah didn't feel a thing. He came to check on her and refilled her wine glass. After a while Sarah heard the doorbell and knew the pizza had arrived. She got out of the bathtub and put on a comfortable pair of sweats. She emerged from the bedroom tranquil and relaxed; she didn't realize how hungry she was until she smelled the pizza. She bent down and gave Garret a kiss and then took a seat at the kitchen table next to him.

"Thank you, I needed that." They ate, drank wine and talked for an hour. "When I was in the bath, I had an idea and I want your opinion," Sarah said at last.

"Of course. What do you want to ask me?"

"Tuesday is the day we …" Sarah could barely say it, but she took a deep breath and continued, "turn off my mom's life support. When they do the transplantation, what if we request that Emma Jean receive my mother's liver? We know they will be a perfect match."

"I think that's a wonderful idea, Sarah. You are your mother's daughter … thoughtful and caring. We should talk to the doctors about it to make sure before we say anything to Emma Jean's family."

"I think my mom would be pleased."

"I think your mom would be proud of you—as she always was."

The next morning Sarah was up before the sun. She was having a cup of coffee, staring out the window into the dark when Garret walked into the kitchen with the dog right behind him. He let her out the back door, got himself some coffee and then sat at the table and leaned in to give Sarah a kiss. "Good morning."

"Do you have to go into work today?" Sarah asked.

"Nope, I've cleared my schedule." He fixed Sarah some eggs and toast; he wanted her to eat something before they left for the hospital.

The first thing Sarah did when they arrived was go to her mother's room, sit beside her and hold her hand, while telling her in a loving voice what they were planning. Then she went to the nurses' station and requested to see the doctor as soon as he arrived.

"I will send him a message right away on his voicemail, Mrs. Stevens," the nurse told her.

Sarah sat with her mother waiting for the doctor and feeling anxious as Garret walked up and down the hall and made phone calls. He called friends and family and he talked to his clients and the people at work to inform them of Gloria's condition. It was at least two hours before the doctor arrived. Sarah had dozed off in the chair.

"Sarah, the doctor is here," Garret said softly as he lightly touched her arm, waking her.

"Good morning, Doctor," she said. "I have a request on behalf of my mother. She would like to donate her liver to her twin sister, Emma Jean Wilkinson, in the next room. Can she do that?"

The doctor smiled, "I don't see why not. I will speak to her doctors and the transplant surgeon right away."

Lexi and Aimee had a difficult night trying to come to terms with and understand what their sister had done. The entire family had mixed emotions: they were angry, disappointed and confused. They would never be able to confront Alice concerning what she had done or be able to get her the psychological help she needed.

That night, Nathan went through his grandmother's finances. It took him several hours and he concluded that she had no money left. All the company stocks her husband had left her when he died were gone. They had been cashed in after Alice moved in with her, as was her IRA account. He discovered that his grandmother had paid all the household bills every month, and she paid all the property and school taxes at the end of the year.

Her credit card had considerable monthly purchases, many to online websites. In December her credit card charges had been in the thousands. He found the ridiculous amount of money given to Kayla and Layla to buy their house in Rochester—over fifteen thousand dollars. Emma Jean's checkbook showed that she had been writing a check to Alice for several hundred dollars at the end of every month for years. She had barely any money in her savings account—only enough to keep it open—and she had a few thousand dollars in her checking account.

"The last six months of Grandma's bank ledger had been handled by Alice—it's in her handwriting," Nathan told them.

"How could Mom have become so vulnerable and allowed this to happen? Why didn't she say anything to anyone!" Lexi and Aimee were heartbroken as well as appalled at their sister's greed.

None of them got any sleep, so they decided to get some breakfast. Then Blake headed to their restaurant, while Lexi and Aimee went to the hospital. When they got there, the doctor told them that Emma Jean had made a dramatic improvement.

"During the night, your mother came out of her comatose state. She woke up and responded normally to painful stimuli, light and sound.

She has a normal sleep-wake cycle and initiated voluntary actions. It's rather amazing," he told them. "I've contacted Doctor Andrews, a hepatologist specializing in liver transplantation and liver diseases."

"When did this happen?" Lexi asked.

"Around eleven o'clock last night," the doctor responded.

Aimee and Lexi looked at each other. They were both thinking the same thing: what a coincidence! That was the time Alice had taken her own life.

"So she will recover?" Aimee asked.

"She urgently needs a liver transplant. If she had continued in her comatose state, we would have had to pass her up for transplantation, but now she is eligible."

"How long does she have to wait?" Lexi asked.

"There are criteria for liver transplantation. The donor should be approximately the same weight and body size as the recipient, free from disease, infection or injury to the liver and usually of the same or a compatible blood type. Doctor Andrews and I have started the process for your mother because we have a donor."

"You're kidding … already?" Aimee said excitedly.

"Does it usually happen this fast?" Lexi asked.

"Not usually," the doctor said honestly. "She has a donor that is a perfect match. It's her twin sister in the next room. Gloria Michaels' family is taking her off life support and donating her organs. Her daughter Sarah requested that Emma Jean receive her liver."

Both Lexi and Aimee were speechless. They were grief-stricken for Sarah and her family and could hardly fathom what they must be going through, yet they were touched by their decision to help Emma Jean in her time of need.

"Does my mother know?"

"Yes, Doctor Andrews and I discussed her surgery with her early this morning."

"Does she know where the liver is coming from?" Aimee asked.

"We didn't tell her from whom. I'm leaving that to you to tell her when she gets through the challenging stage of this procedure. I didn't know how she would react and she doesn't need that stress right now."

"I agree. I don't know how she'd take it because she didn't even know she had a twin," Lexi said sympathetically.

"The surgery will begin at seven o'clock tomorrow morning," the doctor told them. "The surgeon will have your mother prepared for her new liver; the donor will be in a room next to your mother. Once it's removed, the liver will be delivered to her immediately. The operation can take anywhere from six to twelve hours," the doctor explained. "Do you have any questions for me?"

"Are there any complications?"

"Two of the most common complications following liver transplant are rejection and infection. Your mother will be given anti-rejection medications to fight off the immune attack. These drugs overpower the immune system, so there is an increased risk for infection." The doctor continued, "This problem diminishes in time, but there are drugs she will have to take for the rest of her life."

"You explained all this to our mother?"

"We did."

"Thank you, Doctor Christie. We'll be here tomorrow morning."

Sarah and Garret, along with Ella and Nicole, spent the day sitting with Gloria, reliving all their wonderful memories. Gloria's doctor came into the room and sat with them. He explained the procedure and how they conducted the transplantation. He told them it could take anywhere from six to twelve hours.

It had been a long, emotional day. Garret again persuaded Sarah to go home and get some rest so that she could be back early the next morning. When they arrived home, Sarah drank a glass of wine to calm herself. She didn't say much to Garret or his daughters, who were spending the night. She headed to her bedroom, climbed into bed and cried herself to sleep.

At six o'clock in the morning, the moon was bright and the weatherman on the radio had predicted a beautiful, sunny spring day, as Garret drove Sarah to the hospital.

Sarah was having a tough time signing the papers that turned off her mother's life support. Just as she took the pen in her hand, there was a light knock on the door. They all turned and saw Lexi and Aimee standing in the doorway.

"We want to thank you for your incredible gesture," Aimee said. "We weren't blessed to know your mother ... our Aunt Gloria, but if you approve, we would like to stay and support you while you go through this difficult time."

"I would like that," Sarah said with a smile. Aimee and Lexi entered the room and hugged Sarah.

"This is the hardest thing I've ever had to do," Sarah said, crying. She went to the table and signed the papers. Garret gave her a hug and then took the papers to the nurse waiting just outside the door.

Everyone in the room stood quietly; no one moved as the doctor came in and turned off all machines except the heart monitor. Sarah was holding her breath, but her last flicker of hope ended as the heart monitor went to a flat line with a solid buzzing sound.

Doctor Andrews entered the waiting room after seven hours of surgery and told Emma Jean's family that the operation had been a success. He said she'd be in recovery all night, and they should go home and get some rest because she had a long road of recovery ahead of her.

Sarah had a small, intimate service for her mother. Gloria was buried in Cold Springs Cemetery, not far from Walter and Conrad, relatives she had never known she had. Lexi's family flew up for the ceremony out of respect for Gloria's family. Sarah, Garret and his daughters planned a special dinner at her mother's favorite restaurant ... Garlock's.

They invited Aimee, Lexi and their husbands and children, as well as Kayla and Layla. Emma Jean was still recovering. They spent the evening getting to know one another and staying away from the subject of Alice. On their way out Sarah showed them all the picture her mother had sketched over sixty years before. Lexi examined it most closely, admiring the work.

Aimee checked on her mother often during her recovery and Lexi flew up several times to help. A few weeks after Emma Jean was home from the hospital, her daughters told her about Gloria being her twin sister and what Gloria's family had done for her. It was hard for her to comprehend how all of this could have happened, and she was saddened that she had never had the chance to know Gloria.

Lexi showed her the poem her mother, Rose, had written. Emma Jean stared at it and tears came into her eyes. She couldn't believe that it was the poem she had hidden in the clock all those years ago; she had forgotten all about it.

Several months passed. Lexi flew up with her family for their two-week summer vacation in Lockport. They stayed at her mother's house and helped her out as much as she needed. However, her mother was doing quite well on her own.

Emma Jean had a difficult time with the facts of what Alice had done. She couldn't understand why her daughter would try to kill her and make it look like suicide. After everything she'd given Alice and the twins, how could she be so cruel? She realized now how much she had been scared of Alice.

Kayla and Layla, who also suffered tremendously about the whole situation with their mother, were able to get Alice's money out of her bank account and they gave it to their grandmother. The twins also obtained the deed to the house on Lake Ontario and had it transferred into Emma Jean's name. That became where the family spent most of their summers.

Sarah and Garret spent a lot time with her new family, as she enjoyed the experience of having relatives. One afternoon Sarah sat down with Emma Jean and the two of them talked for hours. Emma Jean told her about Rose and Albert and her three older siblings, who had passed away many years ago, as well as about her life in the boarding house growing up.

Sarah told her more about Gloria's childhood and her mother's striving to make a better life for herself. They both agreed the twins should never have been separated and they would never understand why Rose and Albert made the decision to give one of them up for adoption. Life would have been very different if the two of them had grown up together. At eighty years old, Emma Jean had a new liver and a new outlook on life. Sarah told her it was never too late.

As Emma Jean lay in bed resting after a long day of therapy, she thought about her family and how much they truly cared—and now she had Sarah and her husband also involved in their lives. She dozed off; she dreamt she was a child again, playing in the yard where she grew up. She was running through the snow laughing and having fun with Gloria.